BILLIONAIRE
Bachelor
IN
VEGAS

BILLIONAIRE Bachelor IN VEGAS

Sabrina Wagner

The following story contains mature themes, strong language, and sexual situations. It is intended for adult readers 18+.

Stay Connected!

Want to be the first to learn book news, updates and more?
Sign up for my Newsletter.

https://www.subscribepage.com/sabrinawagnernewsletter

Want to know about my new releases and upcoming sales?
Stay connected on:

Facebook~Instagram~Twitter~TikTok
Goodreads~BookBub~Amazon

I'd love to hear from you.
Visit my website to connect with me.

www.sabrinawagnerauthor.com

Books by Sabrina Wagner

Hearts Trilogy
Hearts on Fire
Shattered Hearts
Reviving my Heart

Wild Hearts Trilogy
Wild Hearts
Secrets of the Heart
Eternal Hearts

Forever Inked Novels
Tattooed Hearts: Tattooed Duet #1
Tattooed Souls: Tattooed Duet #2
Smoke and Mirrors
Regret and Redemption
Sin and Salvation

Vegas Love Series
What Happens in Vegas
Billionaire Bachelor in Vegas

Spotify Playlist

omg~ Gloria Kim
I'm not Pretty~ JESSIA
Love You Like A Love Song~ Selena Gomez & The Scene
Gorgeous~ X Ambassadors
Boys Like You~ Anna Clendening
Better~ Arc North, Rival, Cadmium
Feels Like Love~ Syn Cole, MIYA MIYA
STAY~ The Kid LAROI, Justin Bieber
1000 Times~ Sara Bareilles
Can't Live Without You~ Owl City

Listen and Enjoy!

Prologue

I saw the redhead sitting at the bar of The Rabbit Hole at the same time Trent did. It was supposed to be a night for us to relax, but I quickly saw it was going to turn into something else.

Trent and I had an anonymous threesome with Gia a week ago. That was before Trent found out she was his new employee. We'd been seducing women together for years and we never had it backfire until now. Despite his attraction to her, he was determined to make her quit. She was determined to stay. At this point, it was a test of wills.

"Whatever you're thinking, do not do it!" I warned him. He popped to his feet anyway, so I grabbed his arm. "What's your plan?"

"I'm not sure yet," he said with a snarl.

"You're not sure? You always have a plan." With the lasers shooting from his eyes, the poor girl was already toast.

He brushed my hand off his arm. "Relax. I'm not going to do anything impulsive."

That was a lie. "You were a dick to her at work today. Try starting with an apology." I owed her an apology too, but not for being a dick. My apology was more for breathing. When I showed up at Trent's office, Gia

1

took it as an ambush. It wasn't. It was bad fucking timing. Once I walked out of that hotel room last Friday, she was already forgotten. It was just sex.

"Fine. I'll apologize." He placed a hand on my shoulder. "I'm a big boy. I don't need an escort."

"Oh, but you do. Your self-control is nonexistent where she's concerned."

Trent rolled his eyes. "Pleeease. Give me more credit than that. I know how to conduct myself around gorgeous women."

"Women you're never going to see again? Absolutely. One who works with you and seems to push all your buttons? I'm not so sure."

Gia spotted us walking her way and tapped her red nails on the bar. "Well, well, well… look what the cat dragged in. And I see you've brought your sidekick."

I chuckled because I'd been called a lot of things but never a sidekick.

"Ms. Romano," he said curtly.

She rolled her eyes so hard they were liable to fall out of her head. "Cut the shit, Trent. We're not in the office, so you don't have to pretend you respect me. Gia will be fine." Her assistant covered a giggle behind her hand.

I'd seen the assistant around Trent's office before, but I'd honestly never paid attention. She blended into the background like a piece of furniture, but sitting here at the bar with a martini in her hand, I noticed her bright smile and marvelous tits.

"Then Gia it is." He turned his attention to the dark-haired assistant. "Hello, Penny."

Penny? Yep, that rang a bell.

Her eyes went wide, and I was sure if she could scurry under the bar, she would have. Trent wasn't known for his hospitality. "Mr. Dorsey."

Trent turned on his charm, or what he thought was charming. He was definitely off his game. "As Gia already pointed out, we're not in the office. You can call me Trent."

I nudged him to the side and took Gia's hand. "We haven't officially met. I'm Brett, and despite what you may think, our meeting this morning wasn't planned. I'm sorry if you felt ambushed."

Her lips twisted to the side as she contemplated the awkward situation. "Apology accepted. For some reason, I believe you." She jerked her head in Trent's direction. "Him, not so much. To what do I owe the pleasure of your company?"

"Well, Trent wanted to buy you ladies a drink for acting like a total douchebag this week."

His head snapped in my direction. "I never said that."

"But it's what you meant." I elbowed him in the gut.

"Is that so?" Gia asked suspiciously.

"Absolutely. Trent, why don't you pay their tab while I escort the ladies to our table?"

I left Trent at the bar and led the women to our booth. They both scooted in, and I sat next to Gia to ruffle my friend's feathers.

I leaned my head on my hand. "So, tell me about your fundraiser proposal." This seemed to be the bone of contention. Gia and Penny put together a comprehensive proposal Trent refused to read.

As Trent approached the table, Gia hiked a thumb over her shoulder. "What did he tell you?"

"Nothing. He hasn't read it yet."

She narrowed her eyes at him. "Of course he hasn't."

"It's on my planner. I'm going to read it," he defended.

Penny sipped her martini, seductively licking the sugar off the rim. "Sure you are," she murmured.

I kept my amusement to myself. She was quite cute, with big green eyes and freckles sprinkled across her slightly upturned nose. Penny wasn't someone I'd normally notice in a bar, but in this weird foursome situation, it was difficult not to notice her.

"Give me the CliffsNotes version," I prodded.

Gia straightened her back. "It's a New Orleans-themed masquerade ball to benefit domestic abuse. A thousand dollars a plate, a Dixieland jazz band, and a silent auction."

"Don't forget the surf and turf," Penny added, holding a finger in the air. "We haven't got the entire menu figured out yet, but steak and seafood definitely. Oh, and a dessert bar to die for."

3

"You need crawfish and shrimp. My mouth is watering just thinking about it," I said.

Penny clapped her hands together excitedly. "You know what else we need? A tarot card reader and a fortune-teller. Totally New Orleans." Her enthusiasm was completely adorable.

"Yes, and yes! It all goes together." Gia leaned across Penny and glared at Trent. "Mystique. Mystery. Masquerade. Masks. It'll be fun and profitable."

"It's a costume party. We don't do costume parties."

Gia waved her hand at him. "That again? You're hopeless. You wouldn't know fun if it bit you in the ass."

"I know what fun is," he pouted.

"Sign me up." I slapped the table to pull the girls' attention away from the sad sap who was, in fact, being a funsucker. "But you're underselling it. You can easily charge five grand a plate."

"Five grand?" Gia fanned a hand in front of her face. "No one's going to pay that much."

"This is Vegas." I spread my arms wide. "People have money and it's for a worthy cause. I can hook you up with names of the A-listers."

"Can you send them to me?" Penny asked, pushing her dark hair behind her ear. "I've already got a spreadsheet started. With your help, it'll be the who's who event of the year." She finished off her martini in one gulp. "And on that note, I need to use the ladies' room. Can someone let me out?"

Trent slid out of the booth, so Penny could leave, then slipped back in closer to Gia.

She looked between the both of us, sipping the last of her drink. "Now that Penny's gone, let me be frank. What happened between the three of us was a first for me. It was fun, but it's not happening again, and no one can know about it."

I chuckled. "Believe it or not, this is a first for us too. Not the ménage à trois, but this." I motioned between the three of us. "We've never met up with one of our... how shall I say it?"

"Conquests?" she provided.

Trent cringed. "That sounds so tawdry."

4

"Let's not pussyfoot around it. We had an anonymous... now, not so anonymous... threesome. I don't regret it, but it does complicate things. I'm not a cheap whore to be played with. I came to Vegas to start a career. I don't want to be the butt of some joke between you two. I want to be taken seriously."

Not a problem. I had no desire to ever fuck Gia again. It was a one and done. "To new friends." I lifted my glass and they clinked theirs against it.

Penny returned while we were midtoast. "What'd I miss?"

I tapped the seat next to me. "We're celebrating new friends. And to Trent and Gia not killing each other."

She slid in and picked up her fresh drink, clinking it with ours. "I'll drink to that. They've been at each other's throats all week."

The lights dimmed and the DJ came over the loudspeaker announcing the next performer. I'd seen Laney do her striptease before, so instead of watching the stage, I watched Penny. Every time Laney shimmied her shoulders, Penny did too. She knew all the words, and her full lips mesmerized me as she quietly sang along. Her body swayed side to side, gently brushing into me.

When the performance was over, the lights came on and dance music blasted through the speakers. Gia leaned toward Penny. "That was amazing!" she yelled over the music.

Penny clapped her hands excitedly. "I knew you would like it. I'm so glad we came."

"Unfortunately, I need to call it a night or I'm going to turn into a pumpkin." Gia finished her drink and set the glass in the middle of the table.

"I should get home too," Penny said. "Fred will be wondering where the hell I've been all night. He gets hangry when his dinner is late." She slid out of the booth and grabbed her purse.

She had someone waiting at home for her, and I wondered why it bothered me. It shouldn't have. It *absolutely* shouldn't have, yet it did. "Sounds like you need a better boyfriend," I grumped.

Penny blushed. "Oh, I don't have a boyfriend. Fred is my cat."

5

My lips turned up. "Good to know." That information made my heart thump. Again, it shouldn't have, but it did. Penny was so far outside my usual type that they were in different stratospheres.

Penny was a petite, curvy woman with a sharp wit and the ability to hold an intelligent conversation. She intrigued me.

"Do you ladies need a ride home?" Trent asked as he let a tipsy Gia out of the booth.

"That would be—" Penny started.

Gia grabbed her arm. "We'll take an Uber home. Thank you for the drinks. It was nice to officially meet you, Brett."

Penny stumbled and gave us a wave over her shoulder. "Thank you!"

"You're welcome!" I yelled.

Trent scowled at me.

"What?"

"You're not fucking her, that's what. Penny isn't even your type."

I leaned back in the booth and swirled the ice in my almost empty glass. "Says who?"

"Every woman you've ever dated before."

I shrugged. "Maybe I'm ready for something different. She's smart and witty. I like a woman with a brain."

Trent laughed. "Since when?"

That was a good question.

Chapter 1
Penny

I had the uncanny ability to fall in love with men who were out of my league. Case in point, my trek down the Strip in three-inch heels that were already making my feet scream. Two questions blared in my head. One, why the hell did I let Gia, my well-intentioned boss, talk me into these stupid shoes? And two, what kind of bird brain would actually think Brett could be interested in a lowly office assistant?

Me! I was the bird brain.

There was a term for it. Emophilia... the tendency to fall in love quickly and often. I'd suffered from the condition my entire life.

That's what happened when I met Brett. Bam! I instantly fell in love. I loved his soul-searching eyes. I loved the deep timbre of his voice. I loved his confident swagger. And I especially loved the way he listened to me ramble on about the fundraiser I was helping to plan as if it were the most interesting thing he'd ever heard. He leaned on the table with his chin in his hand and took in every word I said while staring at my lips.

My fingers pressed against said lips as I fantasized about him leaning forward and pressing his to mine. *Come home with me tonight, Penny. You're the sexiest woman I've ever met. I want to rip your clothes off and ravage you until dawn. Do you think you can take all ten inches of me?*

"Watch it, lady!"

I was thrown off balance and nearly fell on my ass from the shoulder that crashed into mine. Teetering in my heels, I righted myself and glared at the guy who'd selfishly knocked me out of my daydream. "Excuse you, asshole!"

Dressed in shorts with suspenders—minus the shirt—and a sport coat, he did a quick shuffle of his feet, a Michael Jackson hip thrust, and tipped his hat at me. "You're excused!" Then he literally danced away from me. I squinted to read the back of his jacket. Did that say *Linguini Man*? It sure as hell did.

Vegas was full of freaks, weirdos, and the bizarre, yet it never quit surprising me. You couldn't make this shit up.

I looked at my watch. "Crap." I had five minutes to get to the Mexican restaurant and it was at least a seven-minute walk. I double-timed it down the sidewalk, weaving in and out of tourists. They might have had all day, but I was a woman on a mission. Nothing was going to keep me from love.

With a minute to spare, I slipped into the restroom to inspect myself before my meeting with Brett to get those names he had promised me.

I shrieked. The sophisticated woman who left the office fifteen minutes ago was nowhere to be found, and in her place stood a sweaty mess with frizzed-out curls.

Fuck, fuck, fuck! Think fast, Penny!

I hit the button on the hand dryer and squatted down under it, drying one armpit, then the other. It wasn't ideal, but it'd have to do. As I bent over and lifted my blouse to shoot air on my damp back, a barely twentysomething twit walked into the bathroom and scrunched her nose at me. "Ewww!"

There wasn't time to deal with embarrassment. "It's hot outside and I have overactive sweat glands. Mind your business."

She tossed her perfect locks over her shoulder. "Whatever, loser."

I growled. Why did everyone have to be so damn judgmental? I hastily tucked my blouse back in and headed for the mirror. Wetting my hands, I ran them over my curls in an attempt to wrangle them back in place, then wiped at the smudges of mascara under my eyes. Still wasn't perfect, but at least I looked presentable. *You're a beautiful woman. Own it.* Gia's words rang in my head. Why the hell not? I undid another button on my blouse, showing more than a bit of cleavage. God blessed me with curves, and I rarely used them to my advantage. If there was ever a time to do it, it was now. Maybe Brett wouldn't notice my still slightly frizzy hair if he was looking at my boobs. It was worth a shot.

Checking my watch again, I cringed. I was officially five minutes late for our lunch meeting. I spritzed myself in a fruity spray, popped two mints in my mouth, and slashed pale-pink gloss across my lips. There was no more stalling. It was showtime.

I stepped outside the restroom and squared my shoulders, then made my way to the main dining room. "I'm meeting with Brett Kingston," I said to the hostess.

She scanned her list and gave me a tenuous smile. "He hasn't arrived yet, but I can seat you while you wait."

I was half-disappointed and half-relieved. I wanted to think he would be waiting on pins and needles for my arrival. That he couldn't wait to see me as much as I wanted to see him. But this was better. I followed the hostess to a table in the corner and sat facing the door. Taking a deep breath, I took a moment to collect myself.

"Would you like some water while you wait? I can bring some chips and salsa too."

"Actually, can you bring me a margarita? Light on the sauce. I have to go back to work."

She winked at me and zipped her fingers across her lips. "Mum's the word."

One thing about Vegas was no one really cared what you did. Drinking at lunch was almost expected. It was a first for me, but *when in Vegas...* Within minutes, a waitress, who looked like she'd been doing this longer

9

than I'd been alive, delivered my margarita and a basket of chips with salsa.

"Are you ready to order, hun?"

I pointed at the empty seat. "I'm waiting for someone. It won't be too long."

She tucked her pad and pen into her apron. "Let me know when you're ready."

"Sure thing," I said to her retreating back. That was another thing about Vegas. Everyone was in a goddamn hurry.

Except Brett, apparently.

I licked some of the salt from the rim of my glass and took a small sip. *Damn, that was good. And dangerous.* My toe tapped as I checked the door every thirty seconds. He was only ten minutes late. Well, five if you subtract my own five-minute tardiness. I resisted pulling out my phone to check my Instagram feed and homed in on the chips and salsa instead.

About three chips in, an awful thought popped into my head. *What if I got the place wrong? Maybe he said twelve thirty, not twelve o'clock?* Pulling the sticky note from my purse with the date, time, and place written on it, I squinted at my own writing. Even without my glasses, I could see I was in the right place at the right time.

Huh?

On the other side of the restaurant, the twit from the bathroom giggled as the staff sang "Happy Birthday" to her in Spanish. She held a gaudy sombrero on her head with one hand as she lifted a margarita twice the size of mine with the other. Twenty-first birthday, I guessed. She was the epitome of Vegas women. Tall with legs for miles. A tight waist and a bursting bosom. Long, blond hair that reached her waist and a smile that probably cost ten grand in dental work. She was gorgeous, and I immediately hated her.

That was the problem with Vegas; most of the people migrated here from other parts of the country. It attracted the wealthy, beautiful people like Kardashians and Hiltons, leaving those of us born and raised here to look like the outsiders. There was no way to compete with so much perfection.

I unconsciously patted my dark, frizzy curls. I would die for hair like that twit's. And I could probably have it if I was willing to shell out cash every month at the salon. It wasn't in my budget or my nature. Salons were for people who didn't use coupons at the grocery store.

"You want more chips?"

I hadn't even realized I'd worked through the whole basket. Even more shocking was my empty glass. I hadn't wanted to look preoccupied with my phone when Brett came in, so instead I made a meal out of what was supposed to be an appetizer. I cringed. "No, thank you. I should wait until my date shows up." I cringed again. This wasn't a date. It was a business meeting.

The waitress looked at me with pity. "If you change your mind, let me know."

I glanced at my watch again. Brett was officially twenty minutes late. How long was it appropriate to sit here before I looked pathetic? All the other tables were full. No one was sitting alone except for me.

Five more minutes.

That's all I would give him before I slunk out of this cantina with my tail between my legs. It was embarrassing enough to be sitting alone, but it was worse knowing I wasn't worth showing up for.

Was I shocked? Not at all, but it still stung. There were only two men in my life I could depend on, my father and Fred. The latter barely counted because he peed in my shoe yesterday when I worked late. The finicky feline was particular about dinnertime.

Deciding Brett wasn't showing up, I flagged down the waitress for my bill. Five minutes was late. Ten was a mismanagement of time. Twenty-five was a blow off. I pulled out my credit card and handed it to the waitress. "I got stood up."

There. I'd said it. The words were out in the universe, and I couldn't take them back. The admission felt like glass on my tongue. I was hurt, but more than that, I was mad at myself for thinking I even had a chance with him.

Her gaze darted to the door and then back at me, her wrinkled face quirking up on one side. "You sure about that?"

Chapter 2
Brett

I rushed through the door, looking less composed than I preferred. My client meeting ran long, and traffic was a bitch. I hated being late and I was just that. Late. And not a little late, but way fucking late.

Scanning the restaurant, I found Penny sitting in the back corner, pulling her credit card out of her wallet, an empty margarita glass on the table.

Damn it!

I buttoned my jacket and strode to her table like I was right on time. I swiped the credit card from the waitress and handed it back to Penny. "We're going to be a little longer."

Penny's eyebrows shot up to her hairline. "We're? I've been sitting here for almost a half hour." She pushed her card back across the table.

"A moment, please," I begged the waitress.

She shrugged her shoulders and mumbled, "You better be worth it," as she walked away.

"I'm sorry…"

Penny held up her hand. "Save it. I may not have a fancy job like you, but my time is just as valuable. You could have simply emailed me the files or sent them to Trent. Either would have been better than me sitting here like a lost puppy."

She was pissed and I deserved every bit of the anger radiating off her in waves. The waitress brought another basket of chips, and I popped one in my mouth. "You think I have a fancy job?"

Penny sat back and crossed her arms. "Honestly, I have no idea what you do, but you dress like that," she said, waving a hand in my direction. "I assume it must be pretty important."

"What? Because I wear a suit to work? So do half the guys in this town."

She rolled her eyes. "They might wear suits, but they're not Tom Ford suits. Don't act diffident with me."

Two points for her. She knew designer clothes and had a phenomenal vocabulary. "Diffident?"

"Coy. Modest. Demure. It isn't becoming on a man wearing a six-thousand-dollar suit."

I chuckled. The suit actually cost more than that, but who was counting? "I know what it means. Can we start over? I'm really sorry I'm late. I got stuck on the phone with a client who had a hard time coming to terms with the fact that I bought his business out from underneath him. Plus, traffic was a nightmare. I would have called, but I didn't get your number the other night."

Her face softened.

"Also, I don't take your time for granted. I know your job is as important as mine."

"You're a liar, but I appreciate your efforts. We both know I'm just the assistant." Penny picked up her glass and brought it to her lips before realizing it was empty. Blowing out a frustrated breath, she set it back down and leaned her elbows on the table.

And that's when I saw it… the red spot, presumably from the salsa, on her left breast. But it wasn't the stain that stole all my attention. It was the cleavage bursting from her opened blouse. Her tits were like two soft, overfilled pillows I wanted to stick my head between and live in. Preferably forever.

"You're staring at my boobs."

Caught in the act of being a perve, I deflected. "You've got a little… something…" I pointed to my own chest.

She stared at me blankly and scrunched her nose in the most adorable way.

"Maybe salsa?"

Her eyes widened and she looked down at her chest. "Well, crap on a cracker," she mumbled. Penny dipped her napkin in her glass of water and started rubbing at the spot furiously. As she did, her pink blouse became transparent, and the lace of her bra showed through.

I bit my lip. She was sexy and she didn't even know it. "I think you got it," I said, trying to stop her before the entire blouse was see-through.

"Actually, I think it's worse." She tried to move her arm to cover the wet spot.

I shrugged out of my jacket and placed it over her shoulders. "Better?"

She pulled the lapels together. "Thank you."

"You're welcome." I resumed our conversation from before she decided to take a bath at the table. "Saying you're *just the assistant* underestimates your worth. A good assistant is almost impossible to find and is a valuable asset. I would be lost without mine." I raised a finger in the air to flag down our waitress. "Shall we order now?"

"You don't have to stay for lunch. I know this was a formality, a favor to Trent to make sure the fundraiser goes well."

"I'd like to have lunch with you, Penny. My treat since I kept you waiting."

"Okay." Her cheeks reddened.

Our waitress came back, and we placed our orders. Before she walked away, I added, "Would you please bring the lady another drink and one for me too?" Penny started to protest, but I cut her off. "Gia's not going to care, and neither is Trent."

Trent was technically her boss's boss. Yes, I wanted his event to be successful for him, and I *could* have emailed the files, but that wasn't what this was about.

Vegas was full of beautiful women. Real stunners. And I'd dated my fair share of them. I usually took them on a date, maybe two, before I got bored. Beautiful faces and hourglass figures with nothing in the brains department.

However, when I talked to Penny last Friday night, I realized she had qualities that were severely lacking in the women I'd been dating. She had smarts, opinions, and wit. Not to mention stunning green eyes and a smile that showed off her slightly crooked bottom teeth. By the end of the night, she had me wanting a second look.

Hence, this impromptu lunch meeting. I called her office this morning and offered her a list of the major players in Vegas to invite to the fundraiser. I knew she wouldn't say no. It was the perfect catnip to lure her into a casual meetup. A chance for me to give her a proper inspection.

"Check the inside pocket," I said with a wink.

She reached inside the suit coat, pulled out a flash drive, and held it up. "Is this what I think it is?"

"It's a list of the top hitters in Vegas. Add them to your invite list and I can guarantee the fundraiser will be the event of the season."

Penny held the drive to her chest like it was a treasured heirloom. "Oh my god! This is better than M&M's dipped in peanut butter."

"You mean peanut butter M&M's," I corrected.

She shook her head, her dark curls bouncing. "Nuh-uh. They got it wrong. Everyone thinks the peanut butter should be on the inside, but it's definitely better on the outside. That way, you get the perfect chocolate and peanut butter blend."

I chuckled as I pictured her dipping the candies, popping them in her mouth, and licking her fingers clean. The image made my dick twitch, a most inconvenient reaction to the woman sitting across from me. "I'll take your word for it."

"You really shouldn't, nothing beats the real thing."

And there was that twitch again. "Hmmm. I'll keep that in mind." Steering the conversation back to safer territory, I focused on the flash drive still clutched in her hand. "I had my assistant add bios and contact information to everyone on the list."

She set the drive on the table and gave it a little pat. "Of course, the list. You don't know how much I appreciate this. Trent approved the fundraiser, but he's still not sold on it being a masquerade ball. If Gia can guarantee a top-tier guest list, it could be the factor that wins him over."

"You're going to let Gia take all the credit?" I raised an eyebrow at her. "How much of the event was your idea?"

"I'm not worried about taking credit. I assisted. That's what I do. I'm perfectly content standing in the background," she said dismissively.

"You shouldn't be. Don't let anyone take advantage of you."

Our food came and the plates were set before us. She picked up a fork and dug into her meal. "I don't see it as being taken advantage of. I see it as doing my job. If I wanted to have the fancy title and recognition, I should have gone to college." She took a bite and moaned around the cheesy enchilada.

I started on my burrito. "Out of curiosity, why didn't you go to college?"

She took another bite and held her hand in front of her mouth as she chewed. She had small hands, tiny even, and I wondered what they would look like wrapped around my— "I have two sisters. We didn't grow up rich, but we had enough to get by. College was never really part of my future. Since Mr. Dorsey and my dad have been friends forever, he got me the job at Mystique right out of high school. Ever since then, I've been Penny, personal assistant extraordinaire. It pays decent, so it's all good." She took a sip of her margarita. My eyes zeroed in on her tongue as it licked the salt from the rim of the glass.

"I see." Actually, I didn't at all. College was never a question for me. It was expected. Since I was ten, my father instilled in me the value of an education.

She pointed her fork at me. "You're judging."

I was, but I'd never admit it. "Everyone has their own path. What really matters is if you're happy."

16

She laughed. "That's such a rich-person thing to say. I'm happy for now. I've got a new boss who's letting me have a voice and that's nice for a change. Gia's only been at Mystique for a week, but I like her."

"She'll give Trent a run for his money, for sure." I chuckled, thinking about the redhead who was ruffling my friend's feathers. "Oh, I almost forgot!" I reached into my pocket and pulled out the blue-and-green plastic ball. "This is for Fred." I jingled the bell inside as I handed it across the table.

She smiled. "That's very sweet, but why?"

"You said he gets mad when you get home late, so I thought if he had something to play with, he wouldn't be so angry." I saw the toy at the register when I stopped to buy condoms Saturday night and immediately thought of Penny. The smile on her face was well worth the weird look I got from the cashier.

"He'll love it. Thank you for remembering." She slipped the ball, along with the flash drive, into her purse and finished the rest of her margarita. "I don't want to be rude, but I need to get back to work."

"It's technically a business meeting, so you have some flexibility." I pulled out my credit card and laid it on the table.

"Right." She smiled again, but it didn't reach her eyes. "Even so, I have a ton of work to get caught up on. Thank you for lunch. It was nice."

Nice? Nice was the kind of word you used when your grandma gave you an ugly sweater at Christmas and you didn't want to hurt her feelings. Nice wasn't what I was going for. *Shit! What was I going for?* I wanted casual, and that's what I got. Not many women had the ability to make me feel like a schmuck, but that's exactly what I felt like.

The waitress came and took my card as Penny stood from the table. "Thank you again."

That was the second thank you for greasy Mexican food. "Wait. Let me escort you to your car."

"Oh, I walked."

I looked down at her feet to the sky-high heels she was wearing. "From Mystique to here?"

"It's not that far." She teetered in the heels and caught herself on the table.

"It's not that close either. Let me drive you back." I was a fan of the shoes, but they weren't made for walking five blocks on the Strip.

Relief washed across her face. "That would be really awesome. Are you sure it's not too much trouble?"

"It's no trouble at all. As a matter of fact, it would be my pleasure." I stood and placed my hand on her lower back, leading her out of the restaurant. Even in the heels, she barely came up to my shoulder. I hadn't realized she was that short. Five foot two at the tallest and that was being generous.

The lights of my car lit up as I clicked the fob. Penny stopped dead at the curb. "This is your car?"

I opened the door for her. "It's one of them."

"It's a Ferrari," she said with wide eyes.

"Very good. Now are you going to get in it?" I smirked.

"I don't feel worthy."

I rolled my eyes. "Don't be ridiculous. Get in the car, Penny."

She lowered herself onto the seat. I closed her door and ran around to the other side, slipping in before some idiot ran me over.

"This is the softest thing I've ever had under my butt," she said to herself, rubbing the leather.

I chuckled. "You realize you said that aloud?"

"Actually, I didn't… but yeah… my butt is in love with your car." She wiggled her ass back and forth on the seat. "Who am I to stand in the way of love?"

I shook my head in amusement as I pulled away from the curb. "You're quirky, you know that?"

Penny shrugged her shoulders. "I've been called worse. I have a bad habit of saying whatever's on my mind, even if it's totally inappropriate. My mom says they forgot to give me a filter between my brain and my mouth. My dad says it's because there's too much running through my head that sometimes I have to purge. Unfortunately, that usually ends up as word vomit. I used to get in trouble a lot as a kid. Teachers had my parents on

18

speed dial. I've gotten better as I've gotten older, but sometimes it still slips out. Like right now. I have no idea why I told you all that." She pressed her fingers to her lips. "So... tell me about you."

My lips curled up on one side at her cuteness. "What do you want to know?"

"I want to know about your fancy job. What exactly do you do to afford this car my butt's in love with?"

"I'm in mergers and acquisitions."

"See. Fancy," she huffed. "No offense, but it sounds boring."

"None taken." I chuckled. "It's not boring. I like the adrenaline of sealing deals and making money." I pulled up in front of the hotel, frustratingly disappointed that our time together was over. "If you have any questions about those files, don't hesitate to call. Give me your phone." She handed it over and I texted myself. "Now I have your number and you have mine. Don't be shy about using it."

"Okay. Thanks for everything." She got out, removed my suit coat from her shoulders, and laid it across the seat. Shutting the door, she leaned through the window, giving me a fantastic view of her cleavage. "I have one more question. Are *you* happy?"

Touché.

Nobody ever asked me that before. I had a dream job, a penthouse to die for, and beautiful women at my beck and call. "I'm happy enough."

Her lips scrunched to the side. "Happy enough isn't really happy though, is it? You should do something about that." Then she waved her fingers at me. "Toodles."

All I could do was stare at her retreating ass that filled out her skirt quite nicely. She was a puzzle I couldn't figure out. My fingers tapped against the steering wheel.

What do you do with a girl like Penny? And why did my car smell like strawberries on a summer day?

19

Chapter 3
Penny

Was I delusional to think that Brett could see me as more than a business meeting?

Yep.

Lunch certainly wasn't the romantic encounter I envisioned in my head. Sitting on the closed toilet seat, I wrapped bandages around my mangled toes. I should have never borrowed Gia's shoes for my lunch *date*. I couldn't deny the extra height they provided gave me more confidence, but maybe I'd be better off with open-toe shoes. When the blisters healed.

Fred flicked his tail in irritation as he waited for his dinner. I adopted the ginger-haired furball from the local rescue two years ago. He was too mean for anyone else to take, and I figured all he needed was love. For the most part, it worked, but he still had a bad attitude.

I reached into my purse and tossed Fred the blue-and-green ball Brett had bought him. "Be patient. I'll get you food in a few minutes." He sniffed it and gave it a hard whack with his paw that sent it sailing through the bathroom door and into the pile of other unused toys. "You're ungrateful, you know that?"

He let out a huge yawn, showing me all his teeth. I reached down and snagged him into my arms, carrying him to the kitchen and trying to get some snuggles. As soon as I opened the cupboard door, he wiggled and twisted until I let him go. He landed on my bruised toes with no care for my poor feet and meowed like crazy. I held up two cans. "Salmon pâté or chicken with extra gravy?" He placed his paws on my knees and proceeded to run his claws down my shins. "Fuck!" I kicked out, trying to push him away, but he circled me like I was the meal. Before I incurred any more injuries, I opened the chicken and plopped it into his bowl. "There you go, you little crapper."

With Fred fed, I stripped out of my work clothes and stood sideways in front of the mirror. The Spanx bodysuit created an illusion. It made me feel slim when I was anything but. I pulled down the straps and peeled the contraption from my body. My belly was too round and my thighs too thick. My lack of height didn't help either. I poked at my legs and tried to smooth out the obvious cellulite that rippled across my skin. It was useless. I wished I'd been blessed with long legs and a tiny waist, but it wasn't in my genetics.

Sucking in my gut, I straightened my spine and pushed my boobs out. Women paid big bucks to have breasts like mine. At least I had one good asset. It was the rest of the package that was severely lacking. How could Brett ever find me attractive when twits like that twentysomething from the restaurant crowded Vegas with their perfection?

He won't.

It should have been obvious when he showed up late today. There was nothing alluring about me. No need to get there early or even show up on time. Girls like me waited for men like him. I didn't have stunning facial features or a size-zero waist, or a killer job.

I was average. Rich men who looked like Greek gods didn't date average women.

My ability to choose clothes that masked my flaws allowed me to become complacent. At twenty-five, complacent might as well have been synonymous with cat lady. If I wasn't careful, before I knew it, I'd be thirty without a love life on the horizon.

Most women my age already had a résumé of boyfriends. My résumé had exactly one name on it, my twelfth-grade physics partner. It lasted two weeks. We went to prom, and I gave him my virginity because it seemed like a rite of passage. It was lights off and neither of us knew what we were doing. To say it was underwhelming would be generous.

Since then, I'd been everyone's *friend* but nobody's *girlfriend*. I had a couple of hookups, but that was it. I was a hopeless romantic with no outlet besides my Kindle and a vibrator. Pathetic but true. Everything I'd learned about sex was through the pages of a book.

I pinched the extra skin around my waist and promised myself, "Starting tomorrow, I'm starting on a new path. Goodbye, enchiladas. Goodbye, peanut butter and M&M's. Hello, salads. Hello, exercise. Hello, love."

Fred let out a meow from his post outside my bedroom. "What you got, handsome?"

He picked up the small blue-and-green ball with his teeth and shook it, making the bell inside jingle. Of all the toys to choose from, he'd selected the one Brett gave him. I took it as a sign to not give up.

I swiped the ball from Fred and shook it. "You want to play?" He danced at my feet, and I tossed it into the hallway. Taking off like a rocket, he scampered back with it clenched in his mouth. We played the game a few times before he got bored and abandoned the ball completely, prancing into my room and parking himself in the middle of the bed.

As I changed into my pajamas, I thought about Brett. *Why did I say my butt was in love with his car?* Even *I* thought it was weird and I was the one who said it. Yet, despite my word vomit, he programmed his number into my phone. He knew how to reach me at Mystique. A quick call to the office was professional. A call to my cell phone was personal. If he didn't plan on using it, he wouldn't have done it. A man like Brett was intentional, he didn't do things out of obligation. It meant something.

I picked up my phone and stared at the number, then clicked into my contacts and saved it as *Mr. McHottie Pants*. Fred stared at me as if he knew what I'd done. "Stop looking at me like that. A girl can dream."

Chapter 4
Brett

I lifted the tanned, slender fingers from my thigh and set them on the mattress, then did the same for the other hand, which was identical except for the dark-red nail polish. Scooting out from between the two sleeping bodies, I shook my head. *What a fucking night!*

Twins.

It was a first for me. I'd slept with two women before, but never twins. They approached me and proceeded to tell me, "We share everything." Who was I to deny such lovely ladies their biggest fantasy?

Carina and Sarina. I wasn't even sure which one was which, but honestly, it didn't matter. All I cared about was having enough tits and ass in my face to occupy both my body and my mind.

When I stopped in the bar after work, I wasn't looking for a hookup, I was looking for an escape. It came in the form of two blond bombshells from Georgia who were seeking an escape of their own. Although my body was exhausted, my mind still raced.

Quietly pulling my pants and shirt on, I left the ladies sleeping in the hotel room and drove across town to my penthouse. Usually, a good romp in the sheets made me less wired, but there was something niggling at the back of my mind. Or someone, I should say. And there was a part of me that felt… guilty?

The feeling was ridiculous. There was no logical reason for it. I barely knew her, yet I wanted to. I was sure there was more to Penny than met the eye.

True… Penny wasn't the typical type of woman to attract my attention, as Trent so blatantly pointed out to me the other night at The Rabbit Hole, but she stole my attention, nonetheless. She was witty and funny and didn't have a problem speaking her mind.

Even at our lunch, she had no issues letting me know that my tardiness wasn't appreciated. I didn't disagree, but because of my status, wealth, and looks, I rarely got called out on my bullshit. I was willing to admit I got away with more than I should.

As I rode the elevator up to my penthouse, even though I still reeked of perfume from my unexpected romp with the twins, I couldn't get Penny out of my head. I held a hand to my mouth and breathed into it. Yep. Still smelled like pussy too. I needed a shower. Badly. And a good gargle of mouthwash.

The elevator opened into the entryway that led to the two apartments on the top floor. I pulled my key out and shoved it into the lock. The soft click of the other door opening echoed in the hall.

"Late night?" Amanda leaned against the doorjamb in her black satin robe, arms crossed and blond hair falling over her shoulders. We had a thing, the two of us. Nothing serious. Nothing complicated. Simply an occasional fuck when the need struck.

"Later than I intended," I mumbled, opening the door.

"You're grumpy for a man who just got lucky."

I leaned against my own doorway. "What makes you think I got lucky? I could have been working or hanging out with the guys."

"Hmmm." She pressed a finger against her lips. "Let's see. It's one a.m. You're a workaholic, but even you have limits. As for hanging out with the

24

guys, I highly doubt it since it's a Wednesday. Plus, you have a little..." Amanda pointed to the collar of her robe.

I pulled at my shirt and inspected the collar. Sure enough, red lipstick stained the fabric.

"Also, here." She tapped her stomach.

Of course, she was right. "Fuck." I was a mess.

"I'm not judging, but I hope she was worth it. Good night, Brett." Amanda turned and disappeared through her open door.

I hope she was worth it. They definitely weren't. The one-night hookups. The short-term companionships. It all left me hollow inside.

Even my relationship with Amanda didn't fulfill me and she was the constant in my life. She said she wasn't judging, but the look on her face told me otherwise. When your fuck buddy judges you, there's definitely something wrong. The train was off the track, out of control.

I gave Trent a lot of shit about his sexual habits, but the truth was, I wasn't much better. Shrugging out of my suit coat, I poured at least three fingers of bourbon and headed to the bathroom. I stripped down and stepped into the shower, taking my drink with me. The hot water soothed my aching muscles, and the stress of the day swirled down the drain along with my pride. The lipstick wasn't only on my shirt, it was smeared across my abs and covered my nutsack.

As I scrubbed myself clean, my thoughts reverted back to Penny's question. *Was I happy?* I should have been after just getting laid. Meaningless sex had always been enough. Made me happy enough. Yet the question bothered me.

I'd laughed with Penny more in an hour than I'd done in the last month. Time with her was effortless.

Finding something that made me whole?

Maybe it didn't come in the form of long legs and bubbleheaded blonds. Maybe it came in the form of a tiny brunette with a big attitude.

Chapter 5
Penny

"Suck it in. I almost got it." My sister, Beatrice, tugged on the zipper.

I swatted her hand away. "I'm sucked in as much as I can. It's not going to fit."

"Here, let me." My mother stood from where she sat primly on the ornate bench in the bridal boutique. Bless her for being an optimist, but the dress wasn't going to magically fit because she deemed it would.

The last thing I wanted was someone else trying to squeeze me into a dress that was obviously two sizes too small. "Stop, Mom." I gulped. "I'm going to lose the weight."

Loretta, my oldest sister and the bride-to-be looked down on me from her place on the raised platform where she inspected herself in her wedding gown. "Reeeally? My wedding is in less than three months."

The doubt in her voice was a hit to my self-esteem. "I can do it. I already started on a diet, and I spent an hour on the treadmill this morning."

My mom wrapped her arm around my shoulders. "Oh, honey, you're putting too much stress on yourself. You don't need to change. You're perfect the way you are." She kissed me on the side of the head.

"I want to do it."

"Get the bigger size, Penny," Loretta insisted.

"She's right," Bea said. "You're perfect the way you are."

It was a full-blown pity party, and I couldn't take it anymore. "That's easy for you guys to say. Look at you." I motioned to my sisters, who were both over five foot six. "You were both blessed with Mom's genes. You're tall and lean. I got Grandma Martha's genes. I'm sick of being the chubby sister. Hell, most of the time, people don't even think we're related." I stripped out of the dress and tossed it to the side. "I want to stop wearing these stupid Spanx for once in my life. I'm tired of being this." My hands ran over my generous curves and rounded belly.

"Honey," my mom sniffed with tears in her eyes, "you're not chubby."

"Well, I'm not skinny either. I'm doing this. You can either criticize my choice, or you can help and support me."

"We'll support you," Bea said. "You want to come to my yoga class with me?"

I bit my lip and nodded. "Yeah, I'd like that."

"I can help meal prep," my mom offered.

"If you're not making progress in a month, promise me you'll order the bigger dress," Loretta said. "All my bridesmaids need to match."

"She's such a bridezilla," Bea whispered in my ear.

"I heard that!"

"I won't let you down. I'm determined to do this." It was the extra motivation I needed to succeed at something that really had nothing to do with the dress.

27

"Good morning, Penny."

"Oh, hey, Tom." I fixed Gia's coffee with a bit of cream and sugar and prepared one for myself as well. There was a busy day ahead, preparing the list of guests for the New Orleans-themed fundraiser. Trent finally gave Gia the green light, and all systems were go.

Tom was Trent Dorsey's personal assistant. The guy was a saint for putting up with all Trent's shit. Trent was notoriously gruff and demanding, which made me wonder how long Gia was going to last working for him. She was a no-nonsense kind of woman who, so far, held her own with the tyrant. I crossed my fingers and my toes that she wouldn't quit because, honestly, she was the first boss that didn't make me feel like a subordinate put on this earth to do her bidding. Gia asked for my ideas and actually listened to me. I already loved her.

Tom, on the other hand, wasn't much more than a lapdog. Trent barked orders and Tom scurried to comply. He wore dark-rimmed glasses, sweater-vests, and the occasional bow tie. We connected because we were both misfits. "Mr. Dorsey asked me to help you compile the guest list for the fundraiser," he said as he prepared his boss's coffee.

My eyebrows shot up. "He did?" I appreciated the help, but Trent offering his assistant to assist me? That was new.

"Uh-huh. He said, and I quote, 'We don't have time to fuck around. Get it done.'"

I laughed. "Sounds about right. The invitations are supposed to arrive tomorrow, so I appreciate the help."

"No problem. Your place or mine?" He pushed up his glasses and gave me a crooked smile. Tom was cute in a boyish sort of way. I guessed he was about my age, maybe a bit younger.

"I'll come to you. I don't think Trent would appreciate you being too far away. See you in ten."

I headed back to Gia's office with her mug of coffee and entered her open door. "Hell has frozen over."

Gia looked up from her computer. "How so?"

"Apparently, Trent has commandeered Tom to help me with the invite list. What did you do to sell him on the masquerade ball?" I set her mug on the corner of her desk.

She picked it up and took a small sip, giving it a taste before indulging in a longer swallow. "I'm not sure I can take all the credit. I simply laid out the plan we created, which was phenomenal, by the way, and explained all the high points. I think having domestic abuse as our charity sold it."

"Well, whatever it was, he seems on board," I said, sitting across from her with my own cup of coffee. I liked how she said *we* and *our,* not *I* and *my.* Gia wasn't about ego; she was about getting the job done. "I'm glad he finally pulled his head out of his proverbial butt and saw how great the plan is, especially the dessert bar." Something I wouldn't be able to indulge in… if I even got to attend. At five grand a plate, it was way out of my price range, but I was still hoping that, somehow, the gods would drop a ticket in my lap. If it was sprinkled with fairy dust and changed me from the chubby sister to Cinderella, that would be nice, just for one night. I didn't think it was too much to ask for.

"Don't get too excited. He's already proposing *modifications,*" she finger quoted. "I'm not sure what those entail, but I'm going to fight for our original vision."

"Modifications? Pfft!" I crossed one leg over the other and bounced it.

"I know, right?" Gia glanced at my Converse-clad feet and cringed. "How are your toes?"

"Getting better. I don't know how you wear those shoes."

She laughed. "Years of practice. I'm pretty sure my feet gave up the battle years ago and have accepted that I'm going to torture them on a daily basis. You need to try something more open."

That was my thought exactly. But until I needed fancy shoes, I'd stick with my flats. "I'm going to be working at Tom's desk if you need me."

"Okay. Let me know if I can help."

"My job is to help you, not the other way around."

She leaned over the desk and held out her fist for me to bump. "Teamwork. We help each other."

I stood and brought my knuckles to hers. "Teamwork."

After collecting my laptop and the flash drive, I made my way over to Tom's desk. He'd cleared a large space for me so we could work side by side and even brought over a cushy office chair. "Well, this is cozy."

Tom blushed. "Do you want to work somewhere else? We can move." I waved a hand at him and sat. "Don't be silly. This is perfect."

"Great. I have a spreadsheet from the last fundraiser, so I thought we could start there. We'll eliminate the no-shows and the cheapskates."

I quirked my lips to the side. "You didn't even work here for the last fundraiser."

"True, but I have the files. I've actually already sifted through the guest lists from the last three and compiled them in one document."

"So have I," I interjected. My organization and file management skills were second to none.

"Okay, but I've also run background checks on everyone to make sure they haven't been involved in anything scandalous." He waggled his eyebrows, and the shaggy hair that fell over his forehead moved with the motion. "You should see what I found."

That piqued my curiosity. "Care to share? You can't drop a bomb like that and leave a girl hanging."

He turned his computer toward me and did some clicking. "Politicians are the worst. A senator was found in a hotel room, literally tied to the bed for the maid to find. He was left with no wallet and no keys. His wife filed for divorce a week later."

I gawked at the pictures on the screen. There was no way this showed up in the local newspaper. "How did you get these?"

Tom cracked his neck and knuckles. "I have my ways."

"Are you a hacker?" I whispered.

He held a finger to his lips. "Hacker has such a negative connotation. I prefer data detective."

"So, that's a yes."

He nodded. "If it's been stored electronically, it can be found. You just have to know where to look. I'm also a mad programmer."

I motioned to his computer. "If you can do all this, why are you working here getting Trent coffee and picking up his dry cleaning?"

He leaned back in his chair. "Can I tell you a secret?"

I leaned in closer. Like Fred, curiosity always got the best of me.

"I got a little somethin' somethin' on the side. When I finish, it's going to be huge, but working on a computer day in, day out, alone in my apartment, wasn't paying the bills. This is a temporary stop on the way to something bigger."

"I'm intrigued. Tell me more."

Tom held up his hands. "Sorry, it's top secret. I could tell you, but then I'd have to kill you and I kind of like you Penelope Anne Quinn."

I gasped. "How did you know my middle name?"

Tom laughed. "That didn't take much hacking. It's in your personnel file."

"True, but I don't like the idea of you using your data detective skills on me. Friends don't snoop on each other."

"I haven't snooped on you… yet. However, even if I did, I doubt I'd find anything too scandalous."

I didn't know if I should feel reassured or offended. "My life is totally snoopworthy," I lied, sitting taller. "I could have a whole secret identity like Catwoman, sneaking off in the middle of the night doing Lord knows what."

He cocked his head to the side. "Do you?"

My body slumped into the chair. "No, but I do have a cat. My life is agonizingly predictable."

Tom patted my shoulder. "That's not a bad thing."

"Ugh! Even you have a secret life. I'm utterly boring."

"Boring would be the last word I'd use to describe you."

My phone buzzed on the desk, and I scooped it up before Tom could see *Mr. McHottie Pants* slashed across the screen. I hurried away with the device held to my chest. "I'll be back in a minute."

"See… you do have a secret life!"

31

Chapter 6
Brett

"Hello?"

I chuckled because I was damn sure she knew who it was. "Hello, Penny. This is Brett."

"Oh, hi. Hello. What's up?" I could practically feel her blush through the phone.

"I wanted to apologize again for my tardiness the other day. It was rude and I'd hate for you to think that's the type of man I am." I paced my office, looking out over the city of Vegas.

"That's sweet of you but unnecessary. By the way, thank you for the contacts. I'm working on assembling our list today."

I would have given the list to Trent regardless… if he'd asked. Trent never would. Although we were best friends, we kept our business separate from our friendship. It was more about ego and pride than selfishness. We shared plenty of other things.

"I'm glad I could help, but I still feel bad about our lunch. I'd like to make it up to you."

"I'm listening." Most women would be giddy, but not Penny. She was cool, calm, and collected.

"I'm thinking about dinner tomorrow night. French cuisine and fine wine."

"Dinner?"

"Yes, a meal shared between two friends. Call it getting to know each other."

"I see. Let me check my schedule. Is it okay if I get back with you?" There was a distinct echo in the background.

My fingers tapped in irritation on my desk at her noncommittal answer. "Of course. Where are you? You sound like you're in a tin can."

"I'm in the bathroom."

"What?"

"I'm not using the bathroom," she clarified. "It's the only place around here where I can get any privacy. There are a lot of snoopers in this place, and I don't need everyone knowing my business."

I laughed. "Okay. I suppose the bathroom is a good place for privacy."

"Yeah. I don't have a fancy office like some people. There's no door on my cubicle, so I had to improvise."

"Quick thinking. I like that."

"That's me, Penny the quick thinker, but now that I'm thinking about it, talking to you next to a public toilet is awkward. And it's even more awkward that I'm telling you about it."

I shook my head in amusement. "The cat's out of the bag, you can't stuff it back in. And speaking of cats, how did Fred like his new toy?"

She sighed. "He's an ungrateful little bastard. I found it in the litter box this morning. Sorry to say, I had to throw it out."

"Sounds like a challenge."

"That it is. He's got dozens of toys, but none of them hold his attention." I heard a door open and someone talking in the background. "Listen, someone just came in. I gotta let you go. Is it okay if I text you later?"

"Of course. I'll look forward to hearing from you."

"Okay. Thank you. Bye."

The phone went dead in my hand, and I stared at it. I didn't even get a chance to say goodbye before she hung up. The call didn't go exactly as anticipated. I expected her to say, *"Yes, Brett, I'd love to have dinner with you."* Not, *"Let me check my schedule."*

Why did that bother me so much? Unexpected aggravation crawled up my back and tensed my shoulders. I tossed the phone on my desk, then remembered her words at lunch, *"My time is just as valuable as yours."* *Bravo, Penny. Bravo.*

I assumed she'd have nothing going on and jump at the chance for dinner with me, but she put me in my place without a single derogatory comment. Making me wait on her. *Tricky. Very tricky.*

There was one thing I knew about myself. If Brett Kingston wanted something, then he got it. Nothing stood in my way. And right now, what I wanted was to take Penny to dinner.

I buzzed my assistant. "Make me a reservation at Le Coucou for eight o'clock tomorrow night. Party of two."

By the time the sun set, I was about to crawl out of my skin. I worked out again after I left the office in an attempt to keep myself occupied. After a hot shower and two drinks, I'd given up. Penny was not going to text or call, and for some strange reason I hadn't yet figured out, that disappointed me. It's not like she owed me jack shit, but Penny didn't strike me as the kind of person not to follow through. She specifically said she'd text me back and yet my phone had been irritatingly silent.

I wasn't used to being ignored or put off. I wasn't the kind of man to sit around waiting for his phone to ring. Women waited on me, not the other way around. What was worse was knowing I could go sit in any bar across the city and have my pick of lovely ladies. However, I had no inclination to do so. I was waiting on one particular quirky woman. What she lacked in stature, she made up for in personality. I couldn't stop thinking about her.

34

It was an obsession without reason.

My thumb hovered over her name on my phone as I resisted the urge to call her. My patience and determination had served me well in business. I was never the first to cave. It drove my associates crazy.

Make them wait.

Make them sweat.

Make them wonder what my next move would be.

And with one simple action, Penny turned the tables on me.

I was waiting.

I was sweating.

I was wondering what her next move would be.

For God's sake, I'd offered her French food and fine wine, not a Happy Meal with a cheap toy inside. It should have been a no-brainer. It should have been, *"Yes, Brett, I'd love to."* It should have been...

The ringing of my phone pulled me out of my pondering. My lips curved up when I saw her name on the screen. I let it ring twice before answering. "You've been keeping me waiting."

"Sorry about that. I worked late, went to the grocery store, and my mother was here. It's been a long day."

So mundane, but I wanted to know more. "Did you get the guest list done?"

She sighed. "Yes, but I had help. We nixed some of the people you recommended."

That list I gave her was top-notch. She'd be foolish to eliminate any of them. "Can I ask why?"

"I'd rather not say."

Now I was curious. "Come on. If there's a problem, I need to know about it."

"Not a problem, per se, but from a PR standpoint, it made sense," she said cryptically.

My feathers ruffled. I'd never suggest someone who would make Trent or Mystique look bad. "Trent vetoed my list?"

"Oh...no. Not Trent. Tom was helping me and found some scandalous info on a senator and a major company holder. I really shouldn't say anything else. Actually, I shouldn't have said anything at all. I promised to keep my lips zipped. As a matter of fact, I'm doing that right now. Zip." I imagined Penny running her fingers over her lips in a zipping motion. She was cute. "Fine. I won't press for details except one. Who's Tom?" The mention of another man acquiring her time while I was waiting for her phone call made my jaw clench.

"Tom? You don't know who Tom is?"

"If I knew, I wouldn't be asking."

"Right. Of course, you wouldn't. Tom is Trent's PA. You know, dark, shaggy hair and glasses. Surely, you've met him before." When I didn't respond, she whispered, "He's a tech genius, but I'm not supposed to tell anyone. A real Snoopy Snooperton."

I remembered now. Nerdy kid who had an affinity for bow ties. My spiking blood pressure dropped back to normal. The guy was straight as an arrow and hardly a threat. "I remember him, just didn't know his name."

"So... how was your day?" Penny asked in a singsong voice.

"It would be better if a certain woman had accepted my invitation to dinner tomorrow night, but she's making me wait and it's driving me crazy."

"Me?" she squeaked.

"Yes, you. Have you decided whether you can fit me into your busy schedule?"

"Well... I do have to eat. I suppose I can squeeze you in," she said with a laugh.

This girl. "Way to kill a guy's ego."

"Oh, I highly doubt there's anything wrong with your ego." Something crashed in the background. "Fred, no! Come back here right this minute." She must have dropped the phone because her voice faded as she went after him. I laughed as she scolded the cat. "You give that to me. If I have to come under there and get you, you're going to be in big trouble, mister. That's right. Give it to me. Let go. Good boy." She came back and tried to catch her breath. "Sorry about that."

"Everything okay?"

"He stole a piece of chicken off the counter. It was going to be my dinner."

I laughed. "You might as well give it to him."

"I will, but not tonight. It'll only reinforce his bad behavior. It's not his fault. Fred was feral when I got him and used to scavenging for food. He's come a long way, but he's a work in progress."

"Aren't we all? I can't wait to meet him tomorrow." I'd never been a cat person, or a dog person for that matter, but Penny seemed to love him, so I could at least try to tolerate the furball.

"Ummm. I can just meet you at the restaurant. That's what I usually do when I go out."

"Then you've been dating the wrong type of men. A proper date requires me to pick you up at the door and make sure you return home safely." My declaration was met with silence. "Are you still there?"

"Yes. I… uh… wasn't sure this was a date. I thought it was an apology."

My forehead creased. "Consider it both. If I haven't made myself clear, let me do it now. Penny, would you like to be my date for dinner at Le Coucou tomorrow evening?"

"I'd love to."

Chapter 7
Penny

Le Coucou?

It was the height of French cuisine, and I was utterly unprepared. I'd only ever had french fries and French toast. Sadly, neither was allowed on my new diet and probably wouldn't be on the menu anyway. I pulled up their website and browsed the entrées. Most I couldn't pronounce, and none had prices. I may not have grown up wealthy, but even I knew that meant it was expensive. If you needed to know the price, you had no business eating there.

Let the record show I was one of those people. All I needed to know was which dish was chicken. I googled the menu items. Tout le lapin turned out to be rabbit. Imagining the furry little creature on a plate made my stomach turn.

Next.

Bar noir à la sétoise was black sea bass with… sea creatures.

No, no, and no. If it swam, it wouldn't be going in my mouth.

Finally, halfway down the list, I came across coq au vin, better known as chicken, cooked in wine with mushrooms.

Winner, winner, chicken dinner.

Brett was picking me up. At my home. Therein lay the second problem. My condo was what most would call shabby chic. The furniture was secondhand, with mismatched pillows in bright colors, the flooring desperately needed to be replaced, and Fred's claws had taken their toll on just about everything. I'd never been embarrassed about where I lived, but then again, I'd never had a visitor who drove a Ferrari.

I tidied the best I could, fluffing the pillows and stuffing all Fred's toys in the closet. My home wasn't dirty, just lived in. I was so proud when I bought it on my own, but now as I looked at it with fresh eyes, it seemed… lame. If nothing else highlighted how different Brett and I were, I was sure this would have him running for the hills.

And if tonight was the one and only date I ever had with Brett, then I was going to enjoy the hell out of it. It might be the only chance I ever got to eat at Le Coucou. It wasn't the fancy food that enticed me, but the opportunity to see how the other half lived. To see what it felt like to order off a menu that didn't even have friggin' prices on it.

Regardless of my financial situation, I did have something fabulous to wear. Thanks to Gia's help, I had a dress that didn't scream *thrift store* and a pair of strappy black heels that let my toes breathe. After wrangling my hair with a curling iron, my frizzy locks looked sleek with big waves that hung halfway down my back. My makeup was subtle, with eyeliner that made my green eyes pop. Covered in half a dozen coats of mascara, my lashes almost looked fake but without the big butterfly effect that was all the rage. After forty-five minutes of primping, I remembered why I didn't do it on a regular basis. The process exhausted me.

With ten minutes to spare, I pulled on my Spanx and slipped my dress from its hanger. Fred stared at me with curiosity. "Don't even think about rubbing up against me. I'd like to have one outfit not covered in cat hair." He yawned as if my words meant nothing and hopped up on my bed, curling into a fluff ball. "Good boy." I swear he smiled as he rested his head on my pillow. With Fred out of the way, I stepped into the dress, reaching my arm behind my back to get the zipper up.

Turning toward the mirror, I inspected the woman staring back at me. She looked… pretty. The black dress was high-waisted with a flouncy skirt that hit above the knee. The scoop neck showed off the girls without being overly scandalous and the bell sleeves hid my flabby arms. The entire dress was trimmed in black ostrich feathers that added softness and understated elegance.

I slipped into my new shoes and fastened the straps around my ankles. My painted toes felt free as I wiggled them in the heels that made me three inches taller, and my legs appeared a bit longer. My height was one thing I couldn't fix, but I accepted I'd never be mistaken for a runway model years ago.

The doorbell rang and a little shiver of anticipation ran down my back. This date was so out of my league, I hoped I didn't embarrass myself. Or worse yet, embarrass him.

Fred lumbered out of my bedroom and planted himself in the hallway. "Please be good, Fred. I really like this guy." His ears twitched and I wanted to believe he understood the importance of this evening.

Grabbing my purse, I went to the door. When I opened it, I was speechless. In his black suit with a cobalt-blue tie and his dark hair slightly tousled, he looked like every fantasy I ever had come true. "Hi."

His eyes ran the length of my body, making me self-conscious and wondering if I'd overestimated the appeal of the dress. "You look… lovely."

Lovely? My mind went into hyperdrive as I analyzed his word choice. Not pretty or beautiful. Gorgeous might have been too much to hope for, but lovely was good. Right? "Thank you. You don't look so bad yourself." I held my purse up. "I'm all set."

"Aren't you going to invite me in?"

"Now? We don't want to be late."

His lips quirked up. "They'll hold the reservation. You promised I could meet Fred."

A bit of panic shot through me. My frisky feline was unpredictable at best and could ruin the night before it even started. "I did, didn't I?"

"Yes, you did." Before I could stop him, Brett pushed through the door and into my underwhelming condo.

I expected him to cringe, but his eyes weren't looking at my old furniture or worn floors. They were locked on my long-haired ginger cat, who'd taken up sentry in the middle of the rug. Brett squatted down to Fred's level.

"That's not a good idea. He's not much for strangers."

Not heeding my warning, Brett reached to pet Fred. All I could imagine was my date's hand slashed to ribbons and blood dripping onto the rug. We'd end up in the ER instead of the restaurant. When Brett touched the soft fur of Fred's head, I winced and covered my eyes.

"He's not so bad." Brett chuckled.

I peeked through my fingers to find Fred rolling on his back while Brett rubbed his belly. My arms fell to my sides. "Well, I'll be damned. It took three months for him to let me do that. You must be a cat whisperer."

"He's a good judge of character and likes me."

Was it stupid I felt jealous of a cat? Yes. Yes, it was, but the affection he showed Fred was what I longed for. I tapped Brett on the shoulder. "We should go before he changes his mind."

"We have time." He stood and looked around my home. "I like it. It's very… you," he said, picking up a turquoise pillow with sequins and tassels.

I took the pillow from his hand and placed it back on the couch. "It's not much, but I own it, so there's that."

"Impressive. Not many people own their own home in Vegas at…" His forehead scrunched. "How old are you?"

"Twenty-five."

His eyebrows went up. "Very impressive. I didn't realize you were so *young*."

It felt like a slap in the face. One more reason the two of us would never work. I crossed my arms. "And how old are you?"

"Thirty-two."

"Wow! I didn't realize you were so *old*. Are we getting the senior discount tonight?" I should have reined in my tongue, but I couldn't let the slight go.

He chuckled. "Point taken. I apologize if I seemed rude. I assumed, with your job and the way you present yourself, that you were a bit older."

"I got my job right out of high school, so I've had time to grow into it. Also, I was raised to be self-sufficient and not depend on a man to take care of me. I'm good with finances, even if they're not much."

Brett shoved his hands in his pockets. "We're not getting off to a very good start, are we?"

I shrugged. Yeah, this date was going downhill fast.

"Let's start over. Penny, you have a home that perfectly fits your personality, which I adore, by the way. I admire your independence and quick wit. Would you do me the honor of accompanying me to dinner?" He held his hand out to me.

His hand dwarfed mine as I placed it in his. I glanced down at his feet. Yep. They were big too, and you know what they say about men with big feet. *Inappropriate! Focus, Penny!* "I suppose I don't mind being seen with an older man. Especially one who's able to charm my grumpy cat. Shall we hit the road?" *Hit the road? Jeez, get it together!*

"Yes. They'll hold our reservation, but not forever."

I grabbed my purse again and headed to the door, signaling for him to go before me so I could lock it up. We walked out to the curb and a blacked-out limo waited for us. "Where's your Ferrari?"

"I wanted to enjoy the night and have a couple glasses of wine with you." He opened the back door, and I scooted across the soft leather. This was luxury on a whole different level. Someone driving us to dinner, and I got to sit next to Brett the entire way without the distraction of him navigating the busy city streets. His cologne infiltrated my senses. Something woodsy and manly and entirely intoxicating. I took a deep whiff and settled back into the soft seat. "I've never been to Le Coucou," I said stupidly. It should have been obvious I'd never eaten at such an extravagant restaurant.

"Then you're in for a treat." He took my hand in his and stretched his other arm along the seat so that it wrapped around my shoulders. His fingers danced along the fabric, and I wished I'd worn a strapless dress so I could feel the pads of his fingers on my bare skin.

When we pulled up in front of the resort that housed Le Coucou, I reached for the door handle and his hand settled on my arm. "Wait."

Within seconds the driver opened his door, and Brett stepped out, extending his hand to me. I took it and stepped out of the limo. I'd never felt such opulence or luxury in my life. Rich people didn't open their own doors. I was starting to realize the privileges that existed for the rich. I wasn't wealthy, but tonight I got to live like I was.

Brett thanked the driver and settled his hand on my lower back. He led me through the lobby and to the bank of elevators. Pressing the call button, we waited in silence for the car to arrive. Once it did, we stepped inside, and his hands circled my waist as the car ascended to the top floor. My mind left me.

Brett's hand skimmed up my thigh and under my skirt. When his fingers reached the top of my hip, his hand splayed across my naked butt cheek. "Perfect," he whispered. His fingers trailed down my flesh to the juncture of my thighs. He pushed the fabric of my panties aside and rubbed one finger along my seam. It pushed inside, and my body contracted at the feeling of him inside me. It was so naughty. His long, thick finger slid in and out, and then he added another. I was in heaven as he stroked me from the inside out. "Do you like that?"

"Yes," I moaned breathlessly. It felt so good that I never wanted to come down from the euphoria he was providing. I could feel my orgasm creeping up on me and I couldn't stop it.

"What was that?"

My eyes snapped open, and I realized I'd been fantasizing. Brett's hands were planted firmly on my hips and his chin rested on my head. "Nothing," I said, trying to deflect the awkwardness of my delusion. He couldn't know I was imagining him fingering my pussy in the elevator on the way to dinner.

"Hmmm," he mused as his hands ran up my arms. "You're so tiny I think I could put you in my pocket."

He was the one who was delusional. "Only if it was an extra-large pocket."

"Stop it," he scolded. "You're perfect."

43

My mind spun in a million different directions. *Did he have a vision problem? A fat-girl kink? Or maybe he was mentally unstable.* The last seemed most probable. On the outside, he was damn near flawless. There had to be some kind of mental condition that would make him consider taking me on a date.

The elevator opened and he led me to the hostess stand. "Table for Kingston."

She looked him up and down, devouring Brett with her eyes like I didn't even exist. "Right this way, sir."

The hostess led us to a table next to the floor-to-ceiling windows that overlooked the Strip. It was phenomenal. Magical. Everything I'd ever imagined but never experienced. The lights glittered like stars in the darkness. Brett pulled out a chair for me, then settled into his own.

"Your waiter will be with you shortly. Enjoy," she said as she placed two menus on the table, running her fingertips over Brett's shoulder as she strode away.

"So, what do you think?" Brett asked, ignoring the hostess's flirty display.

Annoying was my first thought. Was I invisible? "It's fantastic." What else could I say? The table was elegantly set with silverware I wasn't sure how to use and we had a view that rivaled what I imagined France would be like on a starry night. A replica of the Eiffel Tower shone brightly outside the window.

"I was hoping you'd like it," he said as he spread the cloth napkin across his lap.

I followed suit, hoping that my lack of culture didn't stick out like a sore thumb. "I do."

Our waiter arrived prim and proper, and I was secretly relieved it wasn't a woman. I didn't know if I'd be able to watch *another* woman fawning all over my date. "Welcome to Le Coucou. My name is Pierre and I'll be your server for the evening. Can I start you off with a glass of wine or an appetizer?"

Brett answered without hesitation. "We'll take a bottle of the Pierre Péters Les Chétillons Cuvée Spéciale." I had no idea what it was, but it sounded exquisite. "Also, an order of the Escargots à la Bourguignonne." The words slipped off his lips effortlessly.

I held my hand up. "Wait." It all sounded very fancy, but the word *escargot* caught my attention. "Did you know they starve the snails for a week and then drop them into boiling water? I'm going to have to pass. It's inhumane."

The waiter fidgeted with his notepad, clearly not knowing how to respond. "Of course. Is there something else I can get you?"

Brett raised an eyebrow at me. "Your choice."

This was awkward, but I wasn't willing to compromise my morals. "Something that doesn't require torturing an innocent animal for our pleasure."

Pierre shuffled from foot to foot, trying to navigate the bullet I'd sent his way. "May I suggest the crispy bruschetta, a lightly toasted French bread topped with our fabulous parmesan and mozzarella cheeses, plum tomatoes, red onion, and fresh basil?"

"That would be perfect." I set my unused menu aside and smiled at him.

The waiter looked to Brett for approval.

"As the lady requested," he said without missing a beat.

"I'll put your order in and bring your wine immediately." Pierre nodded as he walked away. I would have felt bad, but I could hardly feel remorse for saving the poor snails.

"I'm sorry. Did I embarrass you?" I asked.

"On the contrary. I'm impressed. You're a woman who knows what she wants."

I wasn't sure if that was true. Just because I didn't promote animal torture didn't mean I was refined. To be honest, it was an excuse not to eat the slimy things. I'd seen *Pretty Woman,* and it didn't bode well for women like me. The last thing I needed was a debacle where the snail went sailing across the dining room while I held a petite fork in my hand, trying to look sophisticated. I was relieved bread with cheese was the suggested alternative. "I have a selective palate." *Code for no slimy snails, please.*

"You surprise me, Penny, but I can't say I'm disappointed."

Pierre was back in a heartbeat with our wine and filled our glasses with the sparkling liquid. I took a sip and the flavors exploded on my tongue. "This is delicious." I took another sip and set the glass on the table.

"I'm glad you approve," Brett said with a smirk. "Le Coucou is known for its fine wine."

"And it delivers beautifully." I held my glass up and clinked it with his. The gesture was cliché, but it seemed appropriate.

We chatted effortlessly. I told him about my parents' bookstore and he told me about his mother. I learned his father passed away two years ago and left him the controlling shares in the family business. Mergers and acquisitions. Boring but obviously profitable.

When Pierre returned, I ordered coq au vin without looking at the menu and Brett ordered what I thought might have been eel. I wasn't sure. I studied Spanish in high school, not French, but it seemed vaguely familiar from my research earlier in the day.

Our entrées arrived, and I dug in tentatively. Starving myself to lose weight had its benefits, but so did eating food that tantalized my tongue. It was the best meal I'd eaten all week. Even so, I took it slow and savored each bite so I wouldn't overeat. By the time Brett finished his dinner, my plate was still half-full. Asking for a take-out container didn't seem socially acceptable at a Micheline star restaurant, so I pushed my plate aside and wiped my mouth with the napkin that sat primly on my lap. "That was delicious."

Brett frowned. "You barely touched your meal. Was there something wrong with it?"

"Not at all. I thoroughly enjoyed it." It was the truth, and I considered sliding the leftovers into my purse.

He nodded. "Another glass of wine?"

I'd already had two and was on my way to drunky town but acquiesced anyway.

Brett motioned to Pierre, who quickly filled our empty glasses. "Dessert?"

"Oh, I couldn't," I said, holding up my hand.

"We'll have the tarte au chocolat," Brett said, twisting the words on his tongue. It was sexy as hell and my mouth watered, not for the dessert but for the man who ordered it.

When Pierre returned with the pastry, it looked divine. Chocolate was definitely not on my diet, but I couldn't resist dipping my spoon into the gooey goodness. "OMG! This has to be the best thing I've ever had in my mouth!"

"Yet."

My spoon froze halfway to taking another bite and my eyes locked with his.

"I can think of another thing that might be more appealing."

Surely, he wasn't suggesting what I thought he was. My mind spun with the implications of his words. He scooped out a healthy portion of the delicious chocolate and let his tongue slide over the silver spoon.

I was transfixed.

On his mouth.

On his tongue.

And all the things it could do to me.

I watched as his throat bobbed when he swallowed.

I was stunned stupid.

He dipped his spoon into the dessert again and held it up to my mouth. "You can't tell me you don't like it."

I was tipsy, but my lips opened, and he pushed the spoon between them. I greedily took what he offered. It was sexual. Not the chocolate, but the words he was feeding me. There was no denying it. "Decadent."

"Yes, you are."

Heat pooled between my legs and crept up my body until my cheeks felt aflame. My body burned for this man. He continued to feed me, and I grieved when the last bite hit my lips. It was well after eleven and the restaurant was all but empty. I was wet and needy. I wanted nothing more than for him to swipe the dishes from the table, lift me on top of it, and take me with the lights of Vegas shining in the background.

My fantasy ended abruptly when Pierre appeared with the bill. I had no idea how much it was, but I would have paid a week's worth of wages for this night.

Brett handed over a black credit card as if it were nothing. Reality set in. "If you'll excuse me, I need to use the restroom."

I pushed my chair back and headed to the bathroom. Slipping inside, I pressed my back against the door. What the fuck was wrong with me? Not only was I wet, but I was horny as hell. The man was too tempting for his own good. I was setting myself up for disappointment. We'd finished an entire bottle of wine. This night could end with earth-shattering sex, but it wouldn't mean shit. It was an apology. Barely a date. If I gave in to him tonight, I'd never see him again. Men like him took what they wanted. He might want me in the moment, but tomorrow I'd be nothing but an insignificant memory. Another notch on his bedpost.

I wasn't ready for that kind of heartbreak.

I took my time in the bathroom and regrouped. As enticing as Brett was, I wanted more. Just because he gave me the attention I sought, didn't mean we had to have sex. I wanted love. A commitment, not a one-night stand. I was going to punch myself in the face for this tomorrow, but I resolved to be strong. "Don't be a needy bitch. You're worth more than one night," I told myself.

I returned to the table to find Brett waiting for me. He escorted me out of the restaurant with his hand on my lower back, grazing the top of my butt. It sent a fresh wave of need through me, but I refrained from fantasizing on the ride in the elevator. An achievement I deemed award-worthy.

The limo waited for us in front of the hotel, and I slid inside, mourning the sex I wasn't going to get. Brett wrapped an arm around my shoulder on the way back to my condo and ran his other hand up my thigh. He didn't seem turned off by my less-than-slender legs. I stopped his wandering hand with mine and gave it a squeeze, afraid he'd realize I wasn't the modelesque type of woman he was accustomed to.

I self-sabotaged the entire ride home. I convinced myself that he was tipsy and slightly delusional. When he woke up in the morning, he'd be thankful I put the brakes on. I was saving both of us from an embarrassing morning after.

The car pulled up in front of my place and Brett walked me to the door. His eyes glassed over as they took in my cleavage while we stood on my porch. Yep. It was the right call. "Thank you for a wonderful night."

"It was my pleasure." His fingers skimmed along the side of my face and clasped my chin. "The night doesn't have to be over."

"Sadly, it does." I pecked him on the cheek and unlocked my door, leaving him to watch me walk away. It was one of the most painful moments of my life.

I was definitely going to punch myself in the face tomorrow.

Chapter 8
Brett

My feet hit the pavement and my mind continued to reel. I barely noticed the squirrel running across the path or the dog pulling at its leash to chase it, dragging his owner behind him. It was all a blur as I replayed last night over in my head.

I woke with the feeling I'd fucked up, and running in the park was the only way I could think without getting interrupted by work emails and text messages. Running and sex, those were my only two escapes. I tried to do both at least four times a week. Five, if I was really stressed.

And for some reason, my stress meter was maxed out and it had nothing to do with work. I wined and dined Penny last night. We talked like two people that had known each other for years and not merely a week. She was funny and witty. I couldn't remember the last time I'd laughed so freely or talked so openly.

She looked beautiful and I couldn't keep my eyes off her breasts. And the feel of her soft, round ass under my palm? Mmmm. The thoughts sent blood to my dick and woke him up, which was very inconvenient. I stopped and rested my hands on my knees, trying to catch my breath and begging my dick to behave.

I thought the night was going in one direction, but when we got to her porch, it took a sharp left turn. A thank-you and a kiss on the cheek were hardly what I expected. A. Kiss. On. The. CHEEK. The last time a date ended that way, I was fifteen. I might have been a bit buzzed when we got back to her place, but I definitely recognized a brush-off when I saw it.

What had I done wrong? Admittedly, the date started off rough. Seemed I couldn't say anything right. She thought I was judging her. I could see it in her eyes. And if I was being honest, I did judge her, even if I didn't mean to. I judged her at lunch for not going to college. I judged her home. And worst, I made a stupid comment about her age.

None of that mattered to me though. I had a great time with her last night. Right up until the moment she turned me down.

Me.

I had more charm and charisma in my pinkie finger than most people had in their entire being.

Most women would have dropped to their knees for a chance to eat at Le Coucou.

But not Penny. She would have rather kissed one of those slimy snails she refused to eat than put her lips on mine.

Fuck that shit!

I straightened up and continued down the trail, pushing myself harder. My lungs burned and sweat dripped into my eyes.

Penny wasn't my type anyway. We were a total mismatch. Beyond the obvious income difference, she lacked the traits that usually attracted me. I liked my women tall, with long legs, a tiny waist, and big boobs. I didn't care if they were airheaded or couldn't hold a conversation. I wasn't with them for their intellect. If something stupid came out of their mouth, I found another way for them to use it. As long as they looked good on my arm and had a willing pussy, I was all in.

I wined them, dined them, took them to exclusive events, and gave them the best sex of their lives. It was a win-win for everyone involved.

For a date or two anyway, until I got bored out of my mind and moved on to the next bimbo.

"Are you happy?" Penny's question niggled at the back of my mind. Was I?

I had more money than God, a business I thrived in, and beautiful women falling at my feet. Men wanted to be me, and women wanted to fuck me. What was there not to be happy about?

"Do I seem happy to you?"

"Well, hello to you too." My mom looked up at me from where she was digging in a flower bed. We hired landscapers, but she said she liked getting her hands dirty. Made her feel less bougie. Kept her grounded in the real world. My mom wasn't born into wealth and after thirty years of living in the Spanish Hills, she still hadn't accepted she could spend her days at the club or the spa.

I leaned down and kissed her on the cheek. "Hi."

She stared at my sweat-soaked shirt and shorts. "I'm not used to seeing you so casual." She patted the grass next to her. "Come help me. It'll be good for you."

I kneeled, and she shoved a garden rake into my hand. We used to do this together a lot when I was younger, but then I went to college. When I graduated, I was so driven to impress my father that I threw myself into work and didn't bother with the little things anymore. I scraped at the dirt around the bougainvillea, removing the weeds that were threatening to choke out the flowers. We worked side by side for the better part of an hour. She didn't hound me to expand on my initial question, letting me take out my frustrations on the earth and the weeds. The rhythm of scraping and pulling lulled me into a peacefulness I hadn't felt in a while.

"There are some bags of mulch in the garage. Do your mom a favor and bring them over, will you?"

"Of course." I went to the garage and shook my head at the large stacks of bags. Our landscaper would have had this done already if she would let him. Ignoring the garden cart, I hoisted one over each shoulder and carried them around the front of the house. After several trips back and forth, we started spreading the dark-brown mulch around the greenery, making sure it was evenly applied throughout the flower bed.

When we finished, my mom stood back and inspected our handiwork. "That looks better. Fresh and clean, which is more than I can say for you." She wiped a streak of dirt from my face. "How do you feel?"

"Better," I admitted. The physical labor was what I needed to quiet my brain.

"Come on. Let's eat and you can tell me about whatever it is that has you so tense." I followed my mom to the house, where she pulled out the fixings for sandwiches. We carried our lunch out to the veranda overlooking the pool. "So, what's bothering you?"

"Do I seem happy to you?"

She shrugged. "I think you work too much. You haven't really seemed happy since Katy."

I frowned. Katy and I had been inseparable. We grew up together and she'd been the love of my life. I planned on proposing to her right after high school.

My mom reached over and patted my hand. "It wouldn't make her happy to know all these years later you still haven't moved forward."

We never talked about Katy. Bringing up her memory seemed cruel. We were two peas in a pod with our whole life laid out before us and it ended without any warning. "I've moved on."

She took a sip of her iced tea and smirked at me over the rim of the glass. "If you call sleeping your way through the women of Vegas moving on."

I pulled back in surprise. I mean, she wasn't wrong, but it's not like I flaunted it.

"Don't look so shocked, Brett. I may be your mother and I try to afford you your privacy, but we run in the same social circles. You always have a new Bambi or Barbie on your arm."

53

"Just to be clear, I've never dated anyone named Bambi or Barbie."

She waved her hand at me dismissively. "Whatever. The point is there's no substance to them, and I think you're using the word *dating* a little loosely. Don't you want more than a roll in the hay?"

Sex was not a topic we discussed, and I was surprised she was bringing it up so casually. "A roll in the hay? Really?"

"I'm not naive, Brett. Call it what you want, but I know what you're doing. Hooking Up. Would that be better?" She laughed.

I cringed. "Absolutely not." I was glad she didn't say *fucking*. Because if I heard her say that word when referring to me, I'd probably throw up in my mouth. "And just so you know, I went on a date last night without *rolling in the hay*," I said to prove her wrong. "She was actually a nice girl. I think you would like her."

"Now I'm intrigued. Why do you think I'd like her?"

I rolled my eyes. "Because at the end of the date, she thanked me and kissed me on the cheek."

My mom held a hand to her mouth and giggled behind it. "And?"

I threw my hands in the air. "And what?"

She leaned on her elbows and rested her head on her hands, clearly invested. "Are you going to see her again?"

"I don't know." I raked a hand through my hair. "We're so different, we shouldn't work, but she makes me laugh."

"Laughing is good. What's so different?"

"She's not my type."

"You mean she's not a blond bimbo?" she asked with a raised brow.

"She's the exact opposite of a blond bimbo. She's independent, smart, and says exactly what's on her mind."

"That doesn't sound different from you at all. It sounds like you might actually have something in common with this girl," she said with a smile.

"She's only twenty-five."

"Your dad and I were nine years apart. Try again."

I didn't even know why I was entertaining this game she was playing with me. "She's short."

"Like a midget?"

I laughed. "No, but compared to me, she might as well be. She comes up to here." I hit myself in the chest with the side of my hand. "And that's with heels on."

"Now you're reaching. I haven't heard a single reason why you two wouldn't work. You've got to have something better."

I tried to think of a way to say it without sounding like a total douchebag. "She's... uncultured. I took her to Le Coucou, and she struggled with which silverware to use."

"Oh, Lord! You should never see her again," she said with an eye roll. "You sound like a snob, and I didn't raise you that way. Who cares if she didn't grow up with money? Neither did I. Sometimes I don't think you realize how fortunate you are."

"I realize I grew up with more than most, but I also work damn hard."

"I'm not saying that you don't. In fact, you work too hard. Do you know what I think? I think you're making a million excuses why you can't go out with this girl again when the biggest reason is smacking you right in the face. And it has nothing to do with her."

I tried to keep my irritation at bay as I leaned back in the chair. "And what is that, oh wise one?"

"Commitment. You haven't had a single meaningful relationship since Katy and you're afraid of getting hurt."

"Can you blame me? Losing Katy destroyed me."

"I'm aware, however, that was almost fifteen years ago. Do you plan on living the rest of your life alone?"

"I'm not alone. I have plenty of company." I smirked at her.

"I'm being serious, Brett. You can joke about it all you want, but if you want my opinion, the answer is no. You're not happy. As your mother, I want more for you than meaningless flings. I want you to find someone who'll be your anchor through good times and bad."

"Like Dad was for you?"

"Exactly."

"But you were a mess after Dad died. What good is an anchor if it pulls you down in the end? Be honest, if you had to do it all over again, knowing you would lose him, would you do it?"

55

"Oh, Brett," she said sadly. "In a heartbeat. The years I shared with your father were worth every bit of heartbreak. Plus, I got you and that's worth everything."

I shook my head. "This whole conversation seems premature. We've only been on one date and I'm not even sure she wants to go out again."

"Do *you* want to go out with her again?"

I replayed the evening in my head, minus the rocky start and the abysmal finish. It was the first time I'd had an actual conversation with a woman in forever. I told Penny about my dad, and that was huge. Rule number one when I dated was no personal details. They weren't going to be around long enough to earn the right to know me on a deeper level. The fact that I'd overshared a fuckton with her meant something. I couldn't believe how easily the words flowed from my lips. "Yeah, I do."

"I've never known anything to hold you back. When you're focused on business, you give it a hundred and ten percent. You're fearless. But when it comes to your heart"—she rested her hand on my chest—"it's like you're that eighteen-year-old kid all over again. Give yourself a chance to feel. Anything worth having is worth taking a risk."

Chapter 9
Penny

A sadist invented yoga. I was sure of it.

It seemed so easy on television but let me tell you, it was a lot more difficult than it looked.

"Grab your heels and gently lift them off the floor while leaning back. Find your center and balance." The instructor effortlessly rocked back on her butt.

I looked around as everyone followed her directions. I seemed to be the only one struggling. "Don't worry about everyone else. Just do your best," Bea whispered, giving me a thumbs-up.

Giving her a thumbs-up back and huffing out a breath, I grabbed my feet and lifted them from the floor. Thank goodness I had a big butt. It was the only thing keeping me from falling over as I wobbled back and forth.

"Now, still holding your heels, stretch your legs out. Back straight, chest to the ceiling. Keep balancing."

She had to be fucking kidding. There was no way. The room was a gynecologist's wet dream. Legs spread in the air with cooches front and center.

But I was nothing if not devoted to this journey. I tentatively tried to lift my legs, but I could only get them up to my shoulders. This was the most unnatural position I'd ever been in, arms stretched out and back hunched over. My body was not made to be contorted like this. I lasted about three seconds before falling on my back and imitating an overturned crab. Letting go of my feet, I collapsed on the mat and stared at my sister. Her long legs pointed at the ceiling and her back was perfectly straight. She appeared graceful and effortless. I couldn't believe she did this for fun.

As if she sensed my eyes on her, she turned in my direction. "Don't give up. You're doing so good."

Good? I was the exact opposite of good. I was downright awful, and I would have quit if I didn't remember my bigger goal. There was a dress I needed to fit into and a man I wanted to see me as sexy. Although last night he didn't seem to be bothered by my size. It was definitely the wine. Nothing else made sense.

This class was torture, but I pushed forward and followed along. The rest of the positions weren't as challenging. I stopped competing with everyone and focused on myself. I could touch my toes, so I counted that as a win. Downward dog, cat, cow... why were all these poses named after animals? Without a doubt, my favorite was the corpse pose because, by the end of the class, that's exactly what I felt like... a damn corpse. I'd strained and stretched muscles I didn't even know existed, so I closed my eyes and let my limbs sink into the mat. My mind went blank as I drifted into a comatose state. It was so peaceful I considered staying there for the foreseeable future.

"Are you alright?" Bea nudged my leg with her toe.

I cracked an eye open. "Do I look alright?"

"You'll survive." She reached down and pulled me to my feet. "It wasn't that bad."

"Says the girl who took dance lessons her entire life." Bea had always been the most athletic of the three of us. Loretta was a cheerleader in high school, although I think she only did it for the short skirts and boys they attracted. Neither of my sisters ever had a problem drawing the attention of the opposite sex.

I used to think I was dropped on my parents' doorstep by a stork because I just didn't fit. I liked books, facts, and numbers. Boring. I was the girl you came to if you had problems with your chemistry homework, not a date for the winter dance. Everybody's friend, but nobody's girlfriend.

"It'll get easier. Give it a chance," Bea said as she pulled a shirt on over her sports bra.

I wished I had her confidence. "You mean I have to do this again?" I groaned.

"You don't have to, but I'll hound your ass if you don't."

I groaned again.

"You wanted help? This is me helping. I'll be your motivation when yours is gone."

It was sweet. As her big sister, I should have been the one encouraging her, not the other way around. My arms wrapped around her shoulders. "Thank you. I'm only being crabby because you put me through torture, but I appreciate it."

"That's what sisters are for," she said, returning the hug. "How's your diet going?"

"Actually, pretty good. Between the meals Mom helped me prepare and throwing out my junk food, plus getting on the treadmill every day, I've lost three pounds."

Bea hooked her arm in mine, tugging me out of the classroom and over to the juice bar. "That's great! I'm so proud of you."

"It could have been four, but I splurged last night. I had the most divine chocolate dessert at Le Coucou."

She spun me around. "Stop it! You went to Le Coucou?"

"Yeah. I had a date."

"How was it?"

"The food was to die for. A little snooty for my taste, but the view was fantastic," I said as I remembered looking at Brett across the table and how handsome he was with his hair tousled and his beard trimmed short. I spent

59

most of the evening wondering what his scruff would feel like against my skin.

Bea smacked me on the shoulder. "Not Le Coucou, you dimwit. I meant the date. Who is he? Where did you meet him? Did you… you know?" Her eyebrows waggled.

I laughed. I wasn't used to telling my sister about my love life, mostly because I didn't have one. It might have been normal for sisters to dish on all the dirty details, but it wasn't something we'd ever engaged in. "I'm gonna need hydration first."

"Don't even think about holding out on me." Bea dragged me over to the cooler, where she pulled out two bottles of protein water. Who even knew such a thing existed? I would have rather had a fruit smoothie, but water was the smarter choice. After paying, we found a small table in the corner.

"What do you want to know?"

Bea leaned on the table and batted her eyelashes at me. "Tell me everything."

I uncapped my water and took a sip, surprised by the fruity taste. "His name is Brett. I met him through work. He's my new boss's boss's best friend."

"You mean Trent Dorsey. I thought you hated him. How did you meet his friend?"

I sighed. "Long story short, Gia and I went to The Rabbit Hole last Friday after work. Trent showed up with Brett, and although it wasn't planned, the four of us ended up sitting together for most of the night. Brett offered to help me with this giant fundraiser we're planning, and it sort of happened from there."

"Interesting. So, does this Brett guy work at Mystique too?"

I shook my head. "Nah. He works in mergers and acquisitions. I think he owns his own company, but I'm not sure. We didn't talk that much about his job, but he must do well because he drives a Ferrari."

Bea spat her water on the table. "What?"

Using the napkins in the center of the table, I sopped up the mess. "It's just a car, Bea. Don't get me wrong, it's nice, but money doesn't mean that much to me."

"That's because we don't have any."

"We do fine. We work hard for everything we have. That's how Mom and Dad raised us."

"True, but don't tell me it wouldn't be nice not to worry about every little dollar we spend."

"It would be nice. Did you know Le Coucou doesn't even have prices on its menu? It was way out of my league. And so is he. I'm still not even sure why he asked me out, but it might have been a pity date."

"A pity date? Oh, Penny, Le Coucou is not a pity date. Did he put the moves on you?"

I remembered the suggestive words that rolled off his tongue and the way his hand ran up my thigh. My head wobbled back and forth. "Yes and no. He was a bit tipsy, so I don't even know if it counts. I sent him on his way at the end of the night with a kiss on the cheek."

Bea's eyes widened. "You didn't!"

"I did. I may have wanted what he was offering, but it was better nothing happened, even if I'm already in love with the guy. You know me. I fall in love with every man I'm even remotely interested in, and it never pans out. I saved myself the heartbreak this time."

She scowled. "We need to work on your self-confidence. You have a lot to offer a man. What's this Prince Charming's last name?"

"Kingston." She spat her water out again. "Really?" I grabbed another handful of napkins and wiped the table.

"Brett Kingston?"

"That's what I said." I frowned at her as I continued to clean up the mess.

Bea laughed. It started as a chuckle and then turned into full-blown hysteria. She shook her head at me. "Only you, Penny. You have no idea, do you?"

I was getting annoyed. "Apparently, I'm missing the punch line."

My little sister pulled her phone out of her bag and typed in the search engine. Then she held it up to my face. "Read this."

I pulled my glasses from my purse and began reading the article from the *Las Vegas Not So Confidential*, a notorious gossip column about the who's who of Vegas.

Billionaire Bachelor in Vegas

Hello, ladies. I have a juicy scoop for you today. Although there's no shortage of handsome, wealthy men in Vegas, it seems there's a billionaire living among us. And here's the exciting part... he's single and ready to mingle.

Brett Kingston is hella hot and hella rich. Taking over Kingston Enterprises after his father's untimely death two years ago has made him the wealthiest single man in Nevada at age thirty-two. And we're not talking a little rich. We're talking billionaire rich. Like swimming in a pool full of money rich.

Rumor has it he's a viper in the boardroom and a tiger in the bedroom. But more than that, he's a slippery little rabbit. Many a woman has tried to sink their claws into his impressive biceps, but none has been able to make them stick. Seems Brett Kingston is as good at evading relationships as the slots are at avoiding making payouts. Many may play, but few will be granted the elusive second date.

My sources tell me Kingston will treat you like a queen, lavishing you with all the things a woman could want, including food, drinks, and toe-curling, earth-shattering desserts (wink, wink). "The man is a god between the sheets," one source said. "I'd give up chocolate to have another night with Brett, but I never heard from him again. He made it clear we were one and done. However, the memory will last a lifetime. My future husband has a lot to live up to."

Judging by the photos from recent events, it seems Mr. Kingston has a very particular type. I just wonder if any of them will have what it takes to tame the tiger and get him to settle down. It seems the cards are stacked against us, but if you don't play, you can't win. Much like the Hunger Games, *the challenge is on, and I, for one, am ready to play. Good luck and may the odds be ever in your favor.*

Underneath the story was a collage of pictures from various red-carpet events. In each one, he had his arm wrapped around the waist of some gorgeous woman who beamed for the camera. They all had one thing in common, a size-twenty-two waist and thirty-six boobs. They were tall, elegant, beautiful, and dressed to kill. If they couldn't keep his attention…

My heart sank. The article was disgusting, treating Brett like a piece of filet mignon. How could they write this shit about him? Didn't they know he was an actual person who had feelings and a life, not a trophy to be won? It was exactly why I stayed away from the salacious column, but it also confirmed the thing I feared the most. Last night was a one-time deal. There would be no second date.

The thought both depressed and relieved me. I tossed Bea's phone on the table. "Well, I guess that's it."

Her brows furrowed. "What do you mean?"

"Bea, be real. If these women couldn't hold his attention, what makes you think I could?"

"Because you're not a shallow, gold-digging hooker."

I laughed. "No, I've never been accused of being a hooker, but look at them and look at me. I think it's best not to get my hopes up." Although, truth be told, I was mentally already picking out wedding invitations and naming our future children. One boy and one girl. A modest house with a pool. Family vacations on the coast of California. Every detail of our lives was planned out in my head. Just like I'd done with a dozen other guys over the years. Damn my stupid heart. It was too gullible for its own good.

"There's no harm in holding out hope. You're a catch, and he'd be stupid not to think so."

"You have to say that because it's sister code. I'm not blind, Bea, and neither is he. I'm an ordinary girl from an ordinary family. I don't have anything to offer him."

She frowned and took my hands in hers. "That's where you're wrong. If you don't have faith in yourself, I'll have enough for both of us."

It was sweet and supportive and everything I could ask for from my sister, but I couldn't help thinking she'd read more romantic fairy tales than I had.

After yoga, I went to see my parents at Between the Covers Café. They started the bookstore and coffee shop when we were kids. I would cuddle up with a book on a beanbag chair for hours, getting lost in the pages. When I was old enough, I helped stock shelves, serve treats from the café, and do anything else they needed. Nowadays, I mostly managed their social media and marketing. For a family-owned business, it did surprisingly well. My parents would never be rich, but they were doing alright, keeping their heads above water, which is more than I could say for most small businesses in the area.

The bell above the door rang when I walked in, grabbing my dad's attention. "There's my favorite girl," he said, pulling me in for a hug. He called all of us his favorites, including my mom, but it always made me feel special anyway.

"How's business?"

"Meh. You know. The online stores are killing us, but we still have a loyal following. What we need are ways to get new customers through the door."

So perhaps it wasn't going as well as I thought. My dad never really discussed the finances with my sisters and me, so I assumed all was good.

"I'll start brainstorming some ideas. We could host theme nights or get authors in to do book signings. That would help."

"That's why you're my favorite. This brain is brilliant," he said, poking me in the temple. "I know you'll come up with something amazing."

No pressure or anything. It was only my parents' livelihood at stake. "I'll do my best and we'll get customers flooding through the doors." I might have overestimated my abilities, but the look of happiness on my dad's face was worth it. This store was his dream, and for over twenty years, he'd lived it. How many people could actually say that? If I had my way, the next twenty years would be even more successful. It would kill me if my mom and dad had to give this up and find another way to make ends meet.

I strolled around the store gathering inspiration and taking notes on my phone. Cooking. Magic. History. Finance. Mystery. Romance. Each type of book had my brain spinning with ideas of how to get more customers into the store.

"How was yoga with Bea?" My mom snuck up behind me and shoved a paper cup in my hand.

"It was torture, but I'm doing it again."

"Good for you."

It was easy for her to say. She wasn't the one twisting her body into a pretzel. "What is this?" I asked, sniffing the contents of the cup.

"Herbal tea. Drink up. It'll get all those nasty toxins out of your body."

I took a small sip and cringed. It was goddamn awful. "My body is not full of toxins. I don't need this," I said, shoving the cup back at her.

Ignoring me, my mother sighed and rolled her eyes. "We all have toxins. Trust me, you need it, especially after I saw all the crap in your cupboards. It'll help with your diet."

She tossed my bag of M&M's right into the garbage when she saw it hiding in the back of my pantry. Why did being healthy have to be so damn miserable? I was more about the destination than the journey. There had to be something that could boost my weight loss without drinking awful teas and pushing my body to the limit. I hated that damn treadmill more than I hated yoga.

After choking down the herbal concoction my mother forced on me, I stopped at the drugstore, then headed home with ideas swimming in my head for Between the Covers Café. There was no shortage of magicians in Vegas. Perhaps we could get one to do a demonstration. We'd make it family-friendly and push the how-to magic books, as well as magic-inspired fiction. Kids loved magic and tricks that seemed impossible. It was a theme better suited for Halloween, but we needed the business now.

Once I parked, I typed everything into my phone while it was fresh in my head. The idea of planning an event on my own gave me a little thrill. I could do things the way I wanted without conforming to the wants of my boss. Something that was just mine.

Walking up to my door, I saw a white box sitting on the mat. I hadn't ordered anything. As I got closer, I noticed the blue printing on the box from a local florist. It was probably delivered to the wrong address. My elderly neighbor recently had surgery, so surely it was meant for her. I scooped it up and headed to her door, then stopped abruptly. The label read *Penny Quinn.* Doing an about-face, I dug my keys out of my purse and tried to calm my racing heart.

There was no way.

It couldn't be.

Why would he?

The thoughts ping-ponged through my head so fast that my hand shook as I tried to get my key in the door. When I finally got it open, I tossed my purse and shopping bag on the couch and carried the box to the counter. Standing back, I eyed it suspiciously, like it might jump out and bite me. Fred, the brave boy he was, hopped on the counter and batted the box with his paw, checking to see if it was safe. When nothing happened, he sat and stared at me.

"Oh, alright already." I grabbed the scissors, cut the tape along the top, and opened the flaps. Reaching inside, I pulled out a crystal vase filled with at least two dozen pink roses. Nobody had ever bought me roses. Hell, nobody ever bought me any kind of flowers. My heart swooned even though my brain was telling me to be cautious.

They had to be from Brett. Who else could it be? I pulled the card from the bouquet without reading it. "Good news or bad news?" I asked Fred. Flowers were generally a positive gesture, but it was entirely possible they were an it-was-fun-but-have-a-good-life gesture. Another apology. I gently opened the tiny envelope and slid the card out.

Penny~
Thank you for a wonderful evening. I'd like to see you again.

I stuffed the card back in the envelope, elated and perplexed.

My romantic heart jumped up and down in my chest, doing a cheer with triple back handsprings, but my rational brain called a time-out.

Even before I read the article Bea shoved in my face, I knew we were a mismatch. It's not like our date ended spectacularly. I hadn't even let him kiss me last night... a necessary but regretful decision.

Tossing the card on the counter, I picked up my shopping bag from the drugstore. If I had any chance at making Brett fall in love with me, three pounds a week wasn't going to cut it. Nor was it going to help me fit into my bridesmaid dress for Loretta's wedding. Taking the bottle out of the bag, I read the directions. *Take two times a day before your two main meals.* Seemed easy enough. Millions of people took diet pills, so they had to work. One thing was for sure, it wouldn't hurt. I was willing to try anything to get the weight off.

I opened the bottle and tossed two into my mouth. Picking up the card again, I held it to my chest. *The* Hunger Games, *indeed. I'm coming for you, Brett, but this time it'll be on my terms.*

67

Chapter 10
Brett

This was not what I had in mind when I asked Penny on a second date. She said she knew the perfect place and to dress casual. When I asked more questions, she refused to be forthcoming and insisted on picking me up. That's how I ended up standing on the sidewalk outside my building in a pair of jeans and a golf shirt like I was waiting for a taxi.

"Shall I get your car, Mr. Kingston?" Stanley, the valet attendant, asked. "I didn't receive a request, or I'd have had it ready."

"Not today, Stanley, but thank you. I'm actually waiting for someone."

"Very well, sir." He tipped his hat at me and went about his business.

I had my own personal chauffeur on call, but usually, I preferred to drive myself. I liked the control and the power of being behind the wheel of a souped-up engine.

The current situation was a first for me. No woman had ever picked me up for a date. Under any other conditions, I wouldn't have allowed it, but she was adamant and that made me curious. I'd never met anyone quite like Penny.

I scrolled through my social media, ignoring the other residents that came and went from my building. Amanda's sleek, white Porsche pulled into the circular drive in front of the entrance. I watched as she exited the car looking like she'd come straight from the country club for Sunday brunch. Which she probably did.

Amanda handed her keys to Stanley and strolled over to me in her three-inch heels. "I knocked on your door last night," she whispered as she ran her fingers along my shoulder.

I stepped away, afraid Penny would see Amanda's outward show of affection. "Sorry. I crashed last night. It's been a long week." I should have told her I was seeing somebody, but I wasn't sure if that was the truth. This whole thing with Penny could be over before it even started. It'd been so long since I'd been in a relationship I didn't know what that looked like anymore. Or if Penny wanted to be in a relationship. Or if *I* wanted to be in a relationship. Today was testing the waters. A daytime adventure that wouldn't lead to being tangled in the sheets. Keeping my options open with Amanda was the safe thing to do.

"Some other time. I'll be home all night," she purred with a wink as she walked away.

Damn, she was beautiful, and on any other day, I'd take her up on the invitation. She was a sure thing, unlike the quirky brunette who I hadn't been able to erase from my mind since The Rabbit Hole. It was so unlike me to become obsessed with a woman. I enjoyed them, of course, but usually, it was the sex that drew me in.

And I had a feeling sex was not part of Penny's secret excursion.

A pale-blue Corolla pulled up to the curb. Penny leaned across the front seat toward the open window. "Get in, Fancy Pants."

I scowled at her name for me, and I wasn't a scowler or a snobby prick with a stick up his ass. She brought all my emotions to the surface, and it unsettled me. "Hardy har har." I opened the door and squeezed myself into the passenger seat with my long legs squished into the dashboard.

Penny laughed. "There's a lever on the side to slide the seat back."

I stuck my hand between the seat and the door, searching for the lever. When my fingers managed to wrap around it and give a good yank, the seat careened backward, nearly giving me whiplash.

"Sorry about that. No one as tall as you have ever sat in my car. How was your morning?" she asked, acting like my neck didn't almost snap off. She pulled away from the curb with a squeal of rubber on concrete.

I held on to the oh-shit bar. "It was fine." Letting her drive was a big concession for me. It meant a lack of control and I was starting to regret acquiescing to her request.

"Am I making you nervous?"

"A bit."

"I assure you, I'm a great driver. Never been in an accident and there's not so much as a ding on my car. You can let go of the handle. You're safe with me."

"I'm not so sure about that." I let go of the handle anyway and settled into the seat, taking my first good look at her. Her hair was up in a ponytail with a scarf tied around it and she had on a sleeveless, polka-dot blouse knotted at the waist. She looked adorable but also five years younger than she did on Friday night and it had me rethinking the entire situation. "Where are we going on this mystery date?"

Penny took her eyes off the road and wagged her finger at me. "I'm not telling. You'll find out soon enough. It's killing you, isn't it? Not being in charge? Sit back and relax. Enjoy the ride."

I wished I could, but it wasn't in my nature. Instead, I listened to Penny talk nonstop about the events she was planning for the bookstore her parents owned. Little by little, my shoulders loosened, and my heart stopped racing. "When is the first event?"

"Two weeks if I can find a magician on short notice. It should be plenty of time to build some buzz on social media."

I let out a low whistle. "That's cutting it close, but I might know a guy who can help."

"Of course you do. You know everybody. But I can't hire someone who's going to charge an arm and a leg. The whole point is to bring money into the bookstore. I'm sure I can find a local guy who wouldn't mind doing it on the cheap."

"Cheap isn't going to bring in business. You need someone with a decent reputation and following." She sped through a yellow light and my heart jumped again.

"I don't disagree, but we've got a budget and it isn't big."

"Let me make a call and see what I can work out." The guy owed me a favor and he could use it as a tax-write-off. If push came to shove, I'd pay for it out of my own pocket. She was so excited, and I didn't want to see the event flop.

"Fine," she grumped. "And thank you. I don't like asking for favors, but we really need this."

"You didn't ask. I offered and it's okay to ask for help."

Penny waved me off. "I know. Ever since Gia started trusting me with more responsibility at work, I've found a new purpose. I don't want to be an assistant forever and I feel like planning some things on my own might push me in the right direction. It would build my résumé. I mean… I'm not thinking about making any changes soon, but eventually. I might even take classes at the community college."

A feeling of pride welled up inside me, which was funny because I didn't know her well enough to have that emotion, but her enthusiasm tugged at me. "I think it's great. Sounds as if you've been doing a lot of thinking. I bet if I could see inside your head, it would be an explosion of confetti."

She laughed. "You have no idea. My brain is a crazy place." She made a right turn into a parking lot and pulled into a space. "We're here."

I looked at the sign above the building. "You're kidding me, right?"

"Not even a little bit. I did Le Coucou with you; you can do this with me," she said, opening her door and getting out.

I had no choice but to follow her lead. After exiting her car, I leaned on the roof of it. "You didn't like Le Coucou?"

Penny rose up on her tiptoes so she could see me over the car. "Oh, I thoroughly enjoyed it." She walked around to the trunk, popped it open, and pulled her bowling bag from inside. "But that was your world, and this is mine. If we're going to be trying this out"—she pointed between the two of us—"whatever it is, I need to know you can hang with beer and nachos. What's the worst that can happen? If you don't have fun, then we'll go our separate ways... no hard feelings."

She was right. Although I didn't want to admit it, I was as much out of my comfort zone bowling as she had been at an expensive French restaurant. "The last time I bowled, I was in college."

She closed the trunk with one hand. "Then I'll take pleasure in kicking your butt."

I chuckled and grabbed the bowling bag from her. "Look at you, all competitive." Her sassiness added another layer of adorability when she already looked cute as a button in her sandals, cropped pants, and polka dot blouse. "You have your own equipment; I'm at a severe disadvantage, Ms. Quinn."

"It's not about who wins. It's how you play the game. Are you up to the challenge, or are you going to wimp out?"

The gauntlet was thrown down. I didn't like to lose, and I rarely did. "I'm still here, aren't I?"

She giggled while I opened the door for her. "Only because I kind of kidnapped you."

"True, but I could find a way home if I wanted to." We made our way to the counter, where Penny rented us a lane and a pair of shoes for me. When I whipped out my credit card, she pushed it back at me. I grumbled my displeasure as the young kid behind the register plopped a pair of size-thirteen shoes on the counter. They were scuffed, ragged, and highly unsanitary. Did they really expect me to stick my feet into those things?

Penny snagged the shoes from the counter and began walking toward our assigned lane. "They're disinfected with antibacterial spray. If it grosses you out, I'm sure you could buy a pair in the pro shop."

"I'll do that." I took the shoes from Penny and returned them to the counter, getting a refund of her money. Once inside the pro shop, I went a bit crazy, getting not only a pair of shoes but a bowling ball, a bag, a towel, and anything else the eager salesperson stuck in front of me.

Penny looked down at my new shoes. "Well, don't you look professional now?"

"Just evening the playing field."

"It's going to take more than expensive shoes to beat me." She sat on the bench and changed into her bowling shoes which looked more like sneakers, while I put our balls on the rack. Then she sat in front of the monitor and stared at the screen. Biting her lip and letting out a huff, she reached into her purse and pulled out a pair of glasses. Without looking at me, she slid them on her face and entered our names. The glasses had red frames that flared at the corners like cat eyes with little rhinestones at the tips. They were as unique as her. "I didn't know you wore glasses."

She quickly pulled them off and stuck them back in her purse. "I only need them for up close. I'm farsighted."

I thought back to the two times we'd been to restaurants together. "You didn't use them to read the menus."

Her cheeks turned pink. "I memorized the menus so I wouldn't have to wear them."

Now that I thought about it, I remembered Penny barely glanced at the menu at Le Coucou before she ordered. I sat down next to her. "Why?"

"I didn't want you to see me in them. They make me look nerdy."

I frowned. Did I really make her feel so uncomfortable around me? That needed correcting. "You don't look nerdy in them. They give you that naughty librarian vibe, which, in case you didn't know, guys tend to find rather sexy. Also… I'm a fellow nerd." I pointed to my eyes. "Contacts since I was thirteen. Nearsighted. I can't see shit without them, and my glasses aren't half as cute as yours."

"Really?"

"Yep, so no more hiding your glasses or memorizing menus. Just be you."

She smiled. "Okay. Be warned… *just me* is ready to kick your heinie."

Penny grabbed her ball off the rack and stepped onto the approach. She did the tiniest wiggle of her ass before taking the few steps toward the foul line and letting the ball go. It smoothly sailed down the lane and hit right in the pocket. With a pump of her arm, she yelled, "Yes! Strike."

73

"Why do I feel like I've been set up?"

She shrugged. "I have no idea what you're talking about."

I pinched her round cheek. "I think you do."

"Your turn." Penny playfully patted me on the ass. The action was innocent, but it sent a current of electricity right to my cock.

Down, boy. Now was not the time to get aroused. With my new ball in hand, I stepped onto the approach. It'd been a while since I'd done this, and I hoped I wouldn't embarrass myself too much. Taking a few steps toward the line, I threw the ball down the lane. It looked good. Really good. When the pins stopped spinning around, only one was left standing. It wasn't a strike, but it wasn't terrible either.

"Nice one."

When the ball returned, I repeated the process. The ball rolled toward the lone pin. *Come on, come on, come on!* Then it skimmed right by and fell in the gutter.

"Good try. That was really close."

"Close only counts in hand grenades and horseshoes," I grumped.

"It's the first ball you've thrown in... what? Like ten years?"

"Approximately."

"Give yourself a break. Besides, getting nine pins is really good." Penny picked up her ball, did that little wiggle again, and threw it down the alley. This time she only hit eight but picked up the spare.

My next few balls were awful, splits and one humiliating gutter ball. In the end, I broke a hundred, but barely. Penny scored a one fifty-seven. "I think I'm ready for that beer now. You want one?"

"Yes, please. Michelob Ultra if they have it. And nachos?" She scrunched up her face like she shouldn't have asked.

"Definitely nachos." I headed to the snack counter, glad Penny didn't insist on paying. The young girl took my order and kept sneaking peeks at me as she pulled the two beers.

"Are you Brett Kingston?"

I'd gotten asked that a lot since that stupid article in the *Las Vegas Not So Confidential* blabbed my business all over town. "Nope."

"Really? You look like him. Are you related?"

"No."

"Darn. I thought I was finally meeting someone famous."

I laughed. "The guy's a hack. I'd hardly call him famous." Deflection was always the best route.

"Famous enough," she said, setting the beer glasses on the counter. "Cute too, like you."

The girl couldn't be much older than eighteen. "I'll take that as a compliment," I said, handing over some bills. "I heard he's a jerk though." The article certainly didn't shed me in a flattering light. It made me sound like an emotionless womanizer who was only interested in sex. It didn't mention my stellar education, the work I put into Kingston Enterprises, or the money I donated to charities. Nope. Those weren't the juicy bits that attracted readers. Sex sold and they sold the shit out of that article.

"With looks like that and the money he's got... who cares? We'd travel to New York, Paris, Rome..." she said with a dreamy look in her eyes. When I didn't answer, she added, "I'll bring your nachos out when they're ready."

"Thanks." I carried the drinks back to our table, where Penny was already clearing the scores from our last game.

She smiled up at me with her glasses firmly on her face. "Rematch?"

Penny didn't seem to care about New York, Paris, or Rome. The only thing she asked for was bowling. I don't know how she did it, but somehow, she'd dug herself under my skin and I couldn't refuse. "Absolutely."

Chapter 11
Penny

When I dropped Brett off, he palmed the back of my head and brought me in for a kiss. He'd only had one beer, so I knew he wasn't tipsy this time. It was better than I imagined. His lips were gentle and controlling at the same time, taking from me what I'd denied him the other night. His tongue ran along the seam of my lips and pushed inside. I let my tongue briefly touch his before I got too lost in his kiss. And damn, he smelled good. My senses were overloaded with everything that was Brett.

"No more cheek kisses," he said as he tucked a stray hair back into my ponytail. "I had fun today and would like to see you tonight."

"It's a work night."

"I won't stay too late, and you can kick me out when you want."

"You want to come to my place?" I looked at his apartment building and the valet attendant standing out front who was pretending he didn't see the kiss we exchanged. "Why?"

"Are you questioning my intentions?"

"A little. I don't understand. You could have anyone." Of course, I wanted him, but I couldn't understand why he would be interested in me. Plain Jane Penny. I wasn't anything special. As a matter of fact, I was the opposite of special. I was the girl you had a drink with after work, not the girl you took home at the end of the night.

"I don't want just anyone. I want to spend time with you. You make me laugh and smile and you spark a lightness in me I haven't seen in a really long time. You asked me before if I was happy. I'm happy with you."

"We're not having sex tonight," I blurted and then immediately wanted to crawl underneath the seat. Why would I think he wanted to have sex with me? We'd barely kissed. It was a long stretch from touching lips to him putting his penis inside me. My nether regions clenched at the thought. I wanted it. I really did, but I wasn't ready for the force of nature that was Brett Kingston.

He buried his head in my neck while he laughed. "Only you, Penny. No sex, I promise. But I can't guarantee I won't want to kiss you again. Is that okay?"

I nodded. Yes… it was more than okay. It was a dream come true. A storyline from one of my romance novels. Something made for other people… not me. "I have to get home to feed Fred."

"I don't want to piss him off, so I'll let you go. But I'll come by in a couple hours and bring dinner. How does that sound?"

"No snails."

He laughed. "Absolutely no snails."

"Okay." My tongue was tied in a knot and my brain short-circuited. All intelligent thoughts vanished, and I was only capable of one-word answers.

He reached for the door handle, then changed his mind and kissed me again before he left. A quick peck that I was barely ready for. "Later."

"Later." I raised my hand and wiggled my fingers at him. It was all I could manage, seeing as my brain had completely disconnected from my body. I watched Brett nod to the doorman as he disappeared from my view.

A million different questions popped into my head. *How much did it cost to live here? What did his apartment look like? Was it a penthouse or more modest? Did it have hardwood floors or carpet? Would I ever see the inside?*

"Ma'am, do you need something?"

I'd totally spaced out. Blinking my eyes, I realized the doorman was standing at my open window. "No." I pointed to the drive ahead. "I'm just gonna... I'm leaving."

"Very well. Have a wonderful rest of your day." He tipped his hat at me.

"You too," I looked at his nametag, "Stanley."

The drive home seemed to last forever. I couldn't remember if I'd made my bed this morning or cleaned Fred's litter box. There was so much to do.

I pulled into my driveway and raced inside. Fred met me at the door, meowing like crazy. It wasn't quite dinnertime, but I fed him anyway.

I loaded the dishes from the sink into the dishwasher, wiped down all the counters, and ran a dry cloth over the floor, trying to get as much of Fred's hair as possible. Next was the vacuum. I ran the hose over the couch and chairs. I loved my furry little beast but didn't think Brett would be as forgiving as I was when it came to cat hair.

I scurried around my condo, putting everything in order. Fred's litter box and toys. The bathroom. And finally, my bedroom. The bed was indeed left unmade. I was ninety-nine percent sure Brett would not be seeing my bedroom tonight, but there was that measly one percent. He'd promised no sex, but promises were made to be broken. And deep down, didn't I want him to break it anyway?

Yes. Yes, I did.

I ripped the sheets from the bed and tossed them in the hamper, along with the bras hanging on the doorknob. Better to be safe than sorry. If there was any chance we were going to end up in this love nest that had yet to see any action, I wanted it to be perfect. Or as close to perfect as my discount department store bedding could be.

The doorbell rang and I quickly glanced at myself in the mirror and groaned. This ponytail made me look every bit of twenty-five, if not younger. It was a poor decision on my part, but there was little to be done about it now. I puffed up the ponytail and swiped gloss across my lips before hurrying to the door.

A flash of ginger scampered past me and into the kitchen. "Be on your best behavior, Fred. Brett could be my future husband." He twitched his whiskers at me. "Okay, that probably isn't true, but a girl can dream." I patted him on the head. "Be good."

Pulling my shirt down to cover my belly, I opened the door and gawked at the man standing there with his arms full. "Hey."

"Hey yourself." His smile was gorgeous, and I was hypnotized. "Can I come in?"

Breaking out of my trance, I grabbed one of the bags from his arms and moved out of the way. "I'm sorry. I didn't expect you to have so many bags. What the heck are we eating? This looks like enough to feed a third-world country."

He laughed and followed me to the kitchen. "Only part of this is food. The rest is for Fred."

I quirked an eyebrow. "You have me curious."

Fred ambled over and wound himself around Brett's legs as we set everything on the table. "It is for Fred, but it's for me too."

"Now, I'm really curious. Did you get matching shirts or something?"

Brett knelt and rubbed Fred's head. "They have shirts for cats? Is that a thing?"

"Oh yes. Cat clothes are a thing. It's a booming business. I mean… why should dogs have all the fun? They get all the cute costumes at Halloween and have been wearing clothes for decades. You should see the stuff people post on social media. I could spend hours scrolling through the craziness." I pressed my lips together to stop the rambling. He didn't give two shits about pets in sunglasses and hats.

"It's not matching shirts," he said, giving my feisty feline a final rub. "But I think Fred will like it even better." He reached for the biggest bag and pulled out a box. "It's an automatic feeder, so he doesn't have to wait for you to get home to eat."

My insides turned to mush. "That's probably one of the most thoughtful things anyone has ever bought me." My hand pressed on my chest to stop the erratic beating. "Or Fred."

He used a finger to lift my chin and look into my eyes. "That's just sad, but like I said, it wasn't totally unselfish. I plan on spending more time with you and don't want you to worry about Fred getting his dinner."

If my insides were mush before, now they melted into a gooey mess. "You do?"

He nodded. "If that's alright with you."

Again, I was reduced to one-word answers. "Yes." The word flowed from my lips like he'd dropped to one knee and asked for my hand in marriage. And for a brief moment, the image flitted through my mind. *Him in a tux and me in a flowy wedding dress, standing on a beach with the breeze tousling my dark hair. Waves crashed against the shore and birds sang as he wrapped me in his arms and proclaimed his love for me. He dipped me low and pressed his lips to mine.*

"Perfect." He clapped his hands together, startling me out of my daydream. "I wasn't sure what kind of food he ate, but the store assured me this was the best." Brett pulled out a bag of premium cat food that I would have never splurged on. I loved Fred, but my love for him was deeper than my pockets. "Also, catnip toys. Figured I couldn't go wrong with that."

I looked at the array of supplies laid out on the table. "You did all this for Fred? I don't know what to say." Who was this man? And where had he been all my life?

Brett chuckled. "Fred may be the beneficiary, but I did it for you. It's nothing, really."

Nothing to him, but everything to me. "Thank you. You've made both of us truly happy. You shouldn't be spending your money on us." Dinner was one thing, but that feeder cost a pretty penny. I'd looked them up online before. It wasn't generic. It came with all kinds of fancy settings and capabilities.

He kissed me on the forehead. "Don't you worry about that. I have plenty and I'll spend it as I like. Should we try it out?"

There went the goo again. "Yes."

Brett pulled the feeder from its packaging as I read the instruction manual. We had it set up in no time, and although Fred already had his dinner, he was more than willing to have a second. "Well, I'd say that's a success," Brett said as he watched my frisky feline devour the premium kibble. "Now to feed my girl."

I liked the way it sounded coming from his lips, even if he threw it out casually as if it were the most natural thing in the world. "What's on the menu?"

He pulled two plastic take-out containers from the remaining bag. "We splurged on nachos today, so I thought we should go with something a bit healthier. I got us garden salads with grilled chicken on top. I hope that's okay."

It was more than okay. "It's wonderful." I pulled plates from the cupboard and grabbed silverware from the drawer. "Thank you for dinner and everything you bought for Fred. It was unnecessary but greatly appreciated."

We dug into the salads and began eating. Brett pointed his fork at me. "I've got good news too."

"Better than an automatic cat feeder?"

"That was hard to beat, but I think I topped it."

"Seems like a tall order."

"Tall but not impossible."

"Lay it on me." I liked this easy back-and-forth between us. It felt natural. Not like he was a billionaire, and I was, well… not even close to being in the same tax bracket. I always assumed billionaires would be stuffy. Maybe Brett wasn't the norm, but he definitely wasn't stuffy with an overinflated ego. We were just two people sharing a meal and it was nice. More than nice.

"I spoke to my friend, the magician, and he's in for doing your show."

My fork stopped halfway to my mouth. "Wow. That was fast. Who is it and what is it going to cost me?" I was thankful for the help, but our budget was limited.

"It won't cost you a dime. He owes me a favor," he said, cutting his chicken like he didn't throw me a huge lifeline.

My eyes bulged. "That's amazing and very generous. Who is it? Anyone I might have heard of?" Not that it mattered. I was confident Brett wouldn't hook me up with a two-bit hack.

"Maybe. Ever heard of Mind Bender?"

My fork dropped and clattered on the plate. "Shut the fuck up!"

He quirked a brow at me, and his lips turned up on one side. "So, you *have* heard of him?"

"Heard of him? His shows are sold out six months in advance. I've seen him on YouTube, and the stuff he does is seriously freaky. He's more than a magician. He's a legend! When you said you knew a guy, I never imagined it would be him. Oh my god! How do you know him?"

"We went to high school together. You should've seen the pranks he used to pull on our teachers. It was funny shit, although they didn't think so. He was told being the class clown wouldn't get him anywhere in life. That he needed to get serious and figure out what he wanted to do to earn a real living."

I giggled. "I bet his teachers are eating their words now."

"He definitely proved them wrong."

"I can't believe you know him, but even more, I can't believe he agreed to do a show at a family bookstore. It seems beneath him, so I have to ask… why is he doing it? And why is he willing to do it for free?" This tremendous gift was too much to ask for. There had to be a catch.

Brett continued to eat as if it were nothing. "I helped him out with a financial situation. It's not a big deal. He's happy to help and is expecting to hear from you in the next couple of days with details. I'll forward you his contact info."

Mind blown.

This was going to be big for Between the Covers Café. Huge. The marketing would be fast and furious, although once the word got out, I expected it to spread like wildfire. It would practically sell itself. I grabbed a pad of sticky notes from the counter, pushed my food to the side, and began scribbling a to-do list. "I'm sorry. I need to get this out of my head, or it'll fester in there until my brain explodes."

"No problem. I'm happy I could help."

Setting my pen down, I went to him and wrapped my arms around his shoulders. "Thank you so much for this. You have no idea how much it helps. I think the store is struggling, though my dad won't admit it. I can't say thank you enough." I begrudgingly unwrapped my arms and kissed him on the cheek.

As I retreated to my own chair, his fingers wrapped around my wrist and pulled me onto his lap. "That's all I get? A peck on the cheek? Surely you can do better than that."

He was asking for more when more was exactly what I wanted to give him. More kisses. More hugs. Much, much more. After all, I was already in love with him. "I can do better."

"Show me." His husky voice sent tingles down my spine and between my legs.

"You want me to kiss you?" I whispered. I felt as if the lights had dimmed and there was a giant spotlight aimed right at us. This was my moment to shine, and I was utterly unprepared. It wasn't that I hadn't ever been kissed, but a man like Brett was oceans away from other men I'd dated. *Were we even dating?* I wasn't sure, but this seemed like a step in the right direction.

"I do, and I think you want it too."

Oh god, I did. I wanted it so much. I leaned forward and pressed my unpracticed lips to his. Brett ran his tongue along the seam, and I cautiously opened to let him in. That was all he needed to take control of the kiss. One hand splayed on the back of my head while his other wrapped around my waist. He leaned me back, holding me securely in his arms as his tongue tangled with mine.

Fireworks exploded and I was gone.

Lost.

Floating on cloud nine as my arms roped around his neck and pulled him in even closer. It was, without a doubt, the most amazing, fantabulous, erotic moment of my life.

His fingers brushed against the side of my breast. "Stop me now if you don't want me to touch you."

"I want you to touch me." My voice sounded raspy and breathless to my own ears. "Please." I wasn't a beggar, but damn, I wanted his touch.

He gently squeezed my breast and let out a growl. "Your tits are fantastic." Brett kissed down the column of my neck and across the tops of my breasts that peeked out from my open blouse. Wetness pooled between my thighs when I felt his erection beneath me. It lit a spark of excitement at how our make-out session affected him.

Me.

Penny Quinn.

My fingers raked through his hair and tugged on the short hairs at the nape of his neck. I wiggled on his lap, wanting to feel more of him.

His gold-flecked eyes snapped to mine with a lustful gaze. "You're a naughty girl, teasing me with that delicious ass of yours. I may have to punish you for that."

Liquid fire shot through my veins. The idea of punishment shouldn't have been appealing, but I was sure Brett would make it quite delightful, so I wiggled again.

He growled. "You make me want to do bad things to you."

My panties were soaked. "Start with the good and we'll work up to the bad," I said with more vibrato than I felt.

He began unbuttoning my blouse. "Trust me. Good or bad, you'll enjoy every minute of it."

It was a declaration. A promise. A guarantee I was certain he could deliver on.

His lips followed the trail of undone buttons, kissing between my breasts and over the lace of my bra. Pulling the flimsy fabric to the side, he licked my nipple. My body turned into mush under his skillful tongue, and I wondered what it could do to other parts of me.

Bang! Bang! Bang!

My heart thumped out of my chest as he continued his ministrations. The fantasy playing out in my kitchen was the best thing that had happened to me… ever.

Bang! Bang! Bang!

"Do you want to get the door?"

"No," I gasped. "Keep going." There was nothing that could tear me away from this moment. Whoever it was would eventually go away.

Bang! Bang! Bang!

"Penny, open up. I know you're home," my mother's voice echoed from the other side of the door.

"Fuck," I grumbled while twisting out of Brett's arms.

"Is that your mom?"

"Yes. She has impeccable timing as always." I rebuttoned my blouse and smoothed down the front of it. "I'll get rid of her. How do I look?"

"You mean, do you look like I just had your tit in my mouth? No, you look fine. She'll never know," he said with a wink and picked up his fork to dig back into his salad.

Rolling my eyes, I let out a huff. As quick as the moment had started, it ended. My insides clenched with frustration and disappointment.

I opened the door to find my mother standing there with a jug in one hand and a cooler in the other. "Hi, Mom."

"Oh, thank goodness." She held out the jug for me to take, then crinkled her brows and put her free hand on my forehead. "Are you feeling alright? You look flushed."

Of course I did. I was in the middle of getting sexed up. I removed her hand from my head. "I'm fine."

"Oh good." She pushed her way through the open door without invitation. "I brought more of the detox tea. Only drink one glass a day, or you'll be pooping like crazy."

And just like that, every good feeling I had disintegrated into ash on the floor. There was no way Brett didn't hear her.

"I also did meal prepping for you," she continued, holding up the cooler. "Thought I'd save you some time. You've got to stick with it."

It was incredibly thoughtful, yet terribly bad timing. "Thank you."

I reached for the cooler. She pulled it away. "I got it," she said as she continued to the kitchen.

"Mom…" I tried to stop her, but it was too late. She was on a mission. When Brett came into view, she stopped in her tracks. "Oh… hello there. Penny didn't say she had company."

Looking exceptionally calm and not like he'd had my tit in his mouth two minutes ago, Brett reached for the cooler with one hand and took my mother's hand in the other. "You must be Penny's mom. I'm Brett."

She looked him up and down like he was the newest exhibit at the zoo. "Lillian. I'm so sorry to intrude. Penny doesn't often have guests."

Any shred of confidence I had left evaporated like a wisp of smoke in the wind.

He placed the cooler on the counter. "Well, that's about to change. I plan on spending lots of time with your daughter." Scraping the remnants of his dinner into the trash, he rinsed the dish and put it in the dishwasher. "I'll give you two some time together." Brett kissed me on the forehead. "Call me later."

I followed him to the door. "I'm sorry about my mother."

"It's okay. My mom can be overbearing at times too."

"You don't have to leave."

"It's better if I do. Otherwise, I might ravage you right there in the center of the kitchen. Audience or not."

"You wouldn't dare." I laughed.

"Obviously you don't know me well enough yet, but you will." He gave me a chaste kiss. "Good night, Penny."

"Good night, Brett." I closed the door behind him and leaned against it with a sigh.

"He's handsome," my mother said.

"He is." That's all I had left. Mentally I was still on his lap with his lips all over me.

"Was that his Ferrari in the parking lot?"

I nodded.

"Jesus, Penny. Is it serious?"

I let him suck on my breast. In my world, that was serious. According to the article I read about his rotating door of women, I wasn't sure it meant serious to him. But I had gotten the elusive second date, so that was something. "I'm not sure yet."

Chapter 12
Brett

My date on Sunday escalated quickly and deflated just as fast. It was the first time since high school that a woman's mother interrupted my moves.

However strange the night ended and no matter how horrified Penny was, I found the entire event somewhat endearing. I could see my own mother showing up on my doorstep with a cooler full of food for fear that I wasn't eating properly. If she didn't know I had a personal chef, she'd do exactly that.

What I couldn't get out of my mind was the way Penny kissed. There was a hesitant eagerness to her. My guess was that rendezvous like today weren't the norm for her. What she lacked in experience, she more than made up for in enthusiasm. She was like a delicate flower, and I couldn't wait to peel back her petals and watch her bloom. To show her how she should be treated by a man. To corrupt her in the very best way. To give her the pleasure she deserved.

Had her mother not arrived, I would have put her on the kitchen table and feasted on her pussy. It was better this way though. Built the anticipation. Gave me something to look forward to. Kept her needy and wanting.

I was more of an instant gratification type of guy, but this was nice for a change. Women were more than willing to ride my dick without much wooing on my part, hoping it would help them get into my wallet. It never did. I'd treat them like a queen for the night, but that's where it ended.

No complications.

No strings.

No attachments.

I rarely had a compulsion to see them again. Second dates only solidified the reasons I didn't do second dates.

These thoughts filled my head as I waited in the small café for my best friend. Trent and I had known each other since we were eleven. We were both fucked up when it came to love.

Over the years, we'd seduced dozens of women together, giving them a night they would never forget. Vegas was the perfect playground. Tourists came and went. The anonymity allowed us to keep our activities discreet.

That was until Gia showed up. I would have paid money to see the look on Trent's face when she showed up in his office on Monday as his new events coordinator.

Mystique's newest employee was perfect for Trent. She challenged him and sparked something I hadn't seen in my best friend in years. He could deny it all he wanted, but the attraction was there.

The only problem I had with Gia had nothing to do with her. It was all about Penny. I didn't need Penny to know I fucked her boss. The evening meant nothing to me beyond mutual orgasms and pleasure. However, I was sure Penny wouldn't see it that way and the last thing I wanted to do was hurt her, even if this obsession between us turned out to be nothing but a fling.

Trent finally showed up and took the seat across from me, looking less broody than usual. The waitress came and took our orders, though she probably had them memorized from all the times we ate here. I steepled my fingers and focused on my friend. "So, did you make a move on Gia yet?"

The scowl I was so familiar with was back. "I told you I'm not into her like that. Besides, we work together; it's a bad idea."

I shook my head. "It's more excuses. Why can't you admit she's perfect for you?"

"I would if she was, but she's not."

"You're a fucking liar," I said, tossing my straw wrapper at him.

He picked it up and tossed it back at me. "Why do you fucking care if Gia and I get together?"

"Because I'd like to see you happy for a change instead of barking at everyone and ripping their heads off."

"I don't do that."

The waitress placed our orders on the table and left the bill, knowing we had limited time for lunch. "The only time you've seemed happy lately is when your dick is buried in pussy, or you talk about Gia. You get this little sparkle in your eye." I fluttered my lashes at him.

"Fuck you. I don't sparkle, dipshit." He took a bite of his sandwich with one hand and flipped me off with the other.

"Well, you're not a grumpy fuck, so it's as good as a sparkle."

This time he flipped me off with both fingers. "Drop it."

I knew when I'd pushed his limits, so I held my hands up in surrender. "Okay, okay. I have a serious question though." His brow went up as he waited for me to continue. "Gia won't say anything to Penny about what went down with the three of us, will she?"

"Not a chance. She doesn't want anyone knowing about that. She'd be mortified if it ever got out around the office."

I nodded. "That's what I thought, but I needed to make sure our little triangle of trust was intact."

Trent narrowed his eyes at me. "You're not going after Penny."

I narrowed mine right back. "First of all, you're not my father. Second, I don't like how you said *going after* like I'm a fucking predator. Third, we've been texting since I helped her out with the guest list for *your* fundraiser. You're welcome, by the way." No need to give him all the details. "And finally, why the fuck not?"

He sighed. "She's not your type. Penny's not a fuck and run. She's a nice girl who deserves more than that."

"So, I'm not good enough for her?" I pushed.

"It's not that. Any woman would be lucky to have you if you were capable of an actual relationship."

I crossed my arms over my chest. "Which one of us is the pot and which is the kettle?"

"When's the last time you had a girlfriend? I can only remember one and that was in high school."

"That's totally irrelevant." Bringing Katy into this was a low blow, and he knew it. "I'm capable of a committed relationship. I just haven't wanted one."

"And you do now? With Penny?"

I shrugged one shoulder. "I want to take a chance and try it out."

"She's not even your type."

The time we spent together over the weekend replayed in my mind: the little wiggle of her ass at the bowling alley, her fist pump when she beat me, how cute she was in her glasses, and the way she responded when I kissed her. "Maybe she is now."

"You better not hurt her."

"Why are you so protective all of a sudden?"

He sighed. "Listen, Gia really likes her. If you screw Penny over and drama bleeds into my office space, I'm going to have to deal with emotional women and I don't need that headache."

I understood his reasoning, but it wasn't good enough to keep me from pursuing Penny. "In case you haven't met me, I'm charming as fuck. Hurting her isn't on my agenda and it's insulting that you'd insinuate it was."

"I'm not insinuating anything."

"Fine."

"Fine."

That was the end of our conversation about Penny. We had never let a woman come between us and it wouldn't happen now.

Maryanne, my personal assistant, poked her head in my office. "You haven't RSVP'd for the investors' party on Saturday."

I groaned. "I don't want to go."

She smiled. "You kind of have to." Maryanne worked for my father for years. She was old enough to be my mother and had a soft spot for my bullshit.

"I haven't even decided if we're taking on the project yet. Why do I have to go?"

She stepped into my office and closed the door behind her. "Brett Jamison Kingston, you know this is an important meeting. The mall project is huge. Go there to show them that you don't take any crap and you're as good at this job as your father was. You need to be the face of the company and uphold its prestige."

"It's going to be a schmoozefest."

"Of course it is, so put a smile on that charming face of yours and let them schmooze you. Then you schmooze them back. That's how this business works. Let them feel important for one night. If you decide to take on this job, you're going to need those investors."

Everything she said was true, I just wasn't in the mood. It was all so contrived and fake. No one actually cared about your family or golf game or any other bullshit they chitchatted about. The only thing they really cared about was your money and what it could do to make them more money. It would be much easier to cut to the chase without all the bogus bullshit.

"Fine. RSVP for me."

"Good choice," Maryanne said with a smile. "At least you know the food and drinks will be good."

I hated these things, but an idea popped into my head that would make me hate it a little less. "On second thought, RSVP for two."

"Two?" She tapped her fingers against her lips in rapid succession. I knew that look. "Go ahead. Say it."

"I don't think it's a good idea. This isn't the type of event where you take a date. What if someone tries to engage her in conversation? No one is going to care about her Instagram feed."

I chuckled. "I'm not sure she's even on Instagram, but I have confidence she can hold her own."

Maryanne quirked a brow. "Someone new?"

"Very."

She looked at me again and tilted her head to the side. "Oh, my goodness! You're smitten."

"Pfft! I'm not smitten." Yes, I liked Penny, but I'd hardly call myself smitten. It was so... high schoolish.

"Whatever you say," Maryanne sang as she walked away.

I shook my head. Normally I wouldn't be so keen on someone commenting about my personal life, but Maryanne was the exception. She'd known me since I was a kid, showing up at the office with my mom to bring Dad lunch. She used to give me lollipops on the sly back then. It was difficult to get annoyed with someone like her, especially when she had good intentions and looked out for my best interest.

Before I could change my mind, my phone was pressed to my ear. When her sweet voice came through the line, a tiny spark lit in my chest. Damn... maybe I was smitten. "Hello, beautiful."

"Hello to you too."

"I was wondering how Fred likes his new feeder."

"He loves it. Keeps staring at it like it's a vending machine and food will drop at any minute. Thank you, again, from both of us."

"You're very welcome. Sooner or later, his wish will come true," I said with a lightness I rarely felt at the office. "Like I said, my intentions were purely selfish. I'd like you to attend a work function with me on Saturday. It's appetizers, drinks, and dozens of boring investors."

"Wow... way to sell it."

"I'm not too thrilled about it myself, but I thought with you by my side, we could make the best of it together. There'll be lots of people watching." She laughed. "That's the best you can do? Brett, I don't know the first thing about acquisitions and mergers. I'll be useless."

I frowned through the phone. "You could never be useless. You're an intelligent woman who can hold an intelligent conversation."

"What if I ramble?"

"Oh god, I hope you do. It would be such sweet revenge for having to listen to their endless bragging and overinflated egos."

"What if I embarrass you?"

"Highly unlikely. Please, Penny. I'm begging you." That was a new phrase. I didn't beg women. They begged me.

"Fine," she huffed. "What shall I wear to this soiree?"

I let out a breath of relief. "Thank you. Wear that little black dress you wore to Le Coucou. It'll be perfect."

"I gotta let you go," she whispered. "Trent gave me the evil eye on his way to Gia's office. Talk to you later."

The line went dead in my hand, and I smiled despite myself. Getting hung up on would have pissed me off if it happened with anyone else, but with Penny, it was one of her peculiar habits I was becoming accustomed to.

With my plus-one solidified, I picked up the prospectus for the mall project. When I was first approached with the idea, I rejected it on principle. It wasn't what we did. Although Kingston Enterprises had a solid portfolio of companies we'd acquired, we were often hired as a third party to broker mergers and acquisitions for other multimillion-dollar companies.

This project didn't fit into either of those categories. It was a land development project from a company that wanted us to be the major investor and manage the financial oversight. It was a billion-dollar mall based on the concept of the Mall of America. Vegas definitely had the wealth to support it. The developer wanted to fill it with high-end fashion, dining, wine bars, and adventure experiences. It had promise.

As I read through the prospectus again, I made a list of questions that would make or break this deal for me. If I decided this job was right for us,

I wanted full control. Putting the Kingston name on the line wasn't a responsibility I took lightly. Jeopardizing my father's years of dedication and hard work wasn't an option, but if I could push Kingston Enterprises into the future and secure financial wealth for my children... that was worth entertaining.

I threw my pen down and leaned back in the leather chair.

My children?

Where the hell had that thought come from?

As I stared out at the Vegas skyline, my eyes homed in on one particular hotel. Mystique.

I knew exactly where that thought had come from and, for the first time, it wasn't altogether unpleasant.

Chapter 13
Penny

I stared at myself in the full-length mirror and pinched my sides. There was definitely a little less fat between my fingers. I lost another five pounds. The diet, exercise, and pills were working. It wasn't easy. I craved a juicy burger and fries, the detox tea tasted like shit, and I despised the treadmill. It took me longer to talk myself into getting on the damn thing than I actually spent walking on it. The yoga classes with Bea were tolerable, but I did them more to spend time with my sister than anything else. I upped my intake of pills, doubling the recommended dose. I didn't have months to lose the weight. I had weeks.

Regardless of how much I hated my quest to lose weight, the results were undeniable. The approaching date for Loretta's wedding loomed in my mind like a neon sign reminding me of the dress I needed to fit into.

And then there was Brett.

I couldn't erase the images of him next to beautiful, skinny women who looked like they belonged on the cover of Vogue. That would never be me. No matter how much weight I lost, I would never be mistaken for a model.

Yet, he asked me to accompany him tonight. That had to count for something. An indication that we were more than just friends.

I didn't need more friends.

I needed someone who could give me orgasms that weren't self-induced. Someone to fulfill all my romantic fantasies. I wanted to be blindfolded, caressed, and kissed from my head to my toes. I wanted my legs spread open and his tongue between my thighs before his cock sank deep in my pussy. I wanted to writhe with pleasure so consuming I saw stars.

Well, fuck!

Now I was horny.

Checking the time, I crawled on the bed and pulled out my vibrator. One orgasm to take the edge off. That's all I needed.

I closed my eyes and imagined Brett between my legs. *"Do you want me to lick your pussy, Penny? Look at you all wet for me."* *He kissed up the inside of my thigh and down the other one. His tongue licked my slit from my ass to my clit. He spread my lips apart and feasted on me. My hips pressed up into his face to increase the pressure. It was so good. So pleasing. He tickled my clit with the tip of his tongue as his fingers curled inside me. I wasn't going to last long. Clenching my walls, I let the pressure build to a crescendo before I fell over the edge and endorphins spread through my body like fire through my veins.*

That was fucking intense. When I came back down, I took a breath I didn't know I was holding and opened my eyes.

Fred sat perched on the pillow next to my head, staring at me and cocking his head to the side. Irrational embarrassment crept in. "You're not supposed to watch me do that," I whispered, then quickly stashed my vibrator back in the nightstand drawer.

I rushed to the bathroom, touched up my makeup, and twirled my curls around my fingers. Except for the slight blush to my cheeks, he'd never know I got myself off before he arrived. The thought of him knowing what I'd been up to mortified me.

Squeezing my body into my Spanx, I finished getting dressed and strapped my heels on. I grabbed my knockoff designer clutch and stood by the front window to wait. I didn't dare sit for fear of getting Fred's hair on

96

my dress. I wished I had something else to wear, but it was the fanciest dress I owned and buying another wasn't in my current budget, especially not knowing if I'd ever get to wear it again.

We were standing at the bar and my heart was in my throat. I'd eaten exactly two shrimp and I could feel them churning in my empty stomach, wanting to make a reappearance. When I agreed to this date, I had no idea it would be so formal. So stuffy. These were not my people.

"Would you like a drink, beautiful?"

To say I was out of my comfort zone would be an understatement. "I think I need one." We'd already made the rounds and I stayed quiet. My goal was not to embarrass myself or Brett. Be seen and not heard. Wasn't that the old adage?

Brett signaled the bartender. "Two bourbons. Neat."

I'd never had bourbon, but at that point, I didn't feel it was something I should point out.

The bartender returned with two rock glasses filled with a splash of amber liquor. I wasn't sure of the etiquette, but I lifted the glass to my lips and tossed it back. The caramel-flavored liquid coated my tongue and slid down my throat easier than it should have.

Brett quirked a brow at me. "You were supposed to sip that."

I licked my lips, savoring the taste. "My mistake. I'll have another."

Within seconds, another glass was placed on the bar in front of me. I lifted it to my lips and took a tiny sip. "Better?"

"I'm not criticizing, but trust me, you'll need to pace yourself."

My eyes narrowed. I wasn't a child that needed to be schooled on the effects of alcohol. I may not have been sophisticated, but that didn't mean I couldn't handle my booze. "Point taken." One drink to calm my nerves wouldn't hurt.

Several more men approached us during the night. I could smell the money oozing from their pores. Attempting to appear as if I was listening attentively, I occasionally asked a question to seem as if I had a clue what they were discussing. One thing I learned was that rich men loved to talk about themselves and their accomplishments. The women hanging on their arms were beautiful and statuesque. Most of them didn't wear wedding rings. Either these men were single, or they'd left their wives at home. The women didn't seem to care, as they were too busy devouring Brett with their eyes and handsy gestures.

When we were finally alone again, I turned to Brett. "Tell me more about this mall project. I've gathered bits and pieces, but give me the whole picture."

"So you were listening. I thought maybe you'd tuned out. Lord knows I was trying to."

I patted him on the chest. "I'm not sure that's an option for you. Seems like you're the star attraction here."

He kissed me on the temple. "Everybody wants something from me. I'm used to it."

It was sad, but he wasn't wrong. I saw firsthand the way people schmoozed him with compliments and offers of golf at their fancy country clubs. He could buy and sell these people a dozen times over, yet he never slighted one of them. He kept a smile on his face and indulged their egos.

Brett led me over to the model of the new mall. I'd seen it when we came in but didn't get a chance to really check it out. "This is Vegas Vista. Its design is inspired by the Mall of America. The idea is to make the mall a destination on its own."

I inspected the model on all sides, with its white walls and tiny glass windows. No expense had been spared in its preparation. Parts were cut away to provide a view of the inside, complete with escalators, little tables in the food court, and miniaturized clothing racks in the stores. The outside was just as detailed, with yellow lines denoting the parking spaces and palm trees as landscaping.

"It's huge," I gasped.

An attractive older man with ample silver decorating his temples approached us. "It's amazing, isn't it? I'm Frank, the mastermind of this beauty."

"And humble," the woman attached to his arm said. She was quite a bit older than me, maybe late forties. Regardless of her age, she was stunning.

"It is amazing," I agreed. "Where would it be built?"

Frank tapped his finger on one of the palm trees. "We haven't figured out all the logistics yet, but the goal is to extend Vegas tourism beyond the Strip. Help to build up the older neighborhoods. Gentrification, if you will."

"So out with the old and in with the new," I clarified.

"Exactly," he said with a snap of his fingers.

"But what about the people who already live there?"

The man furrowed his brows. "We don't have a location yet, but we'll cross that bridge when we get there. There's plenty of prime real estate in the area."

I was a little taken aback by his quick dismissal of my question. These men saw numbers and the color green. I saw hardworking people being dislocated from their homes. I'd seen it before when big businesses came in with their money and new ventures.

"Don't be so dismissive," his wife, I assumed by the size of the rock on her hand, scolded him. It was the first time all night I'd seen a woman contradict her man, and it gave me a shred of hope that not all these women were brainless zombies. "It's a valid concern."

He patted her hand that was wrapped around his arm. "You're right, dear." Then he turned to me. "I apologize if I seemed insensitive, but there isn't a solid plan in place yet. I'm hoping Brett can help us with that. Having Kingston Enterprises on board would be a dream come true."

I nodded. "Well, one thing I know about Brett is he gives everything he does abundant consideration. You'd be lucky to have him."

My insecurities set in, and I wondered if I'd said too much or if I shouldn't have spoken at all. "I'm going to run to the restroom," I whispered in Brett's ear. He gave me a nod and pressed his lips to my forehead.

My feet rushed down the long hallway to the ladies' room. Once safely inside, I leaned against the door, glad to be out of the stifling atmosphere. I took my first full breath since we'd entered the party. I didn't belong here. What was I thinking when I agreed to this?

I quickly did my business and washed my hands. The stunning woman with Frank entered the bathroom and pulled a tube of lipstick from her purse. As she traced her pouty lips, her eyes zeroed in on me.

"You're new."

It was an observation and an accusation rolled into one. I waved my hands under the paper towel dispenser and grabbed the sheets that appeared. "It's my first time at one of these events."

She twisted the lipstick back into the tube and tucked it into her purse. "You're not like the others. I see the way he looks at you."

It wasn't what I expected, but she had my attention. "What does that mean?"

"You're not one of his bubble-gum Barbies. He seems to actually care about you. What do you do, darling?"

"I'm in marketing and public relations." It was the truth, just not the whole truth. No one would be impressed that I was a personal assistant.

"I knew it. You have more to offer than being arm candy."

"I do?"

"Of course. My husband uses big words like *gentrification* to feel superior. He's a genius with a blueprint, but his social game needs some work. He made you feel small for asking a very relevant question."

"I probably shouldn't have said anything. It wasn't my place."

"It very much is your place. The fact that you're more interested in people than a new Gucci store speaks volumes. You're not some dim-witted bimbo, so stand tall and command attention. Women like us are more dangerous than all the men in that room put together. If you act like a mouse, they'll treat you like one. Nothing is sexier than a woman who knows her worth. Go out there and insist they respect you. Trust me, you'll be thanking me at the end of the night. It's better to be an asset than a liability."

They were wise words, and I ingested every one of them. Swallowing down the lump in my throat, I asked, "Why are you telling me this?"

She laughed and tucked a stray blond hair into her updo. "This isn't my first rodeo. It's boring as shit, but at the end of the day, my husband respects me. He knows what I bring to the table and it's more than a quick blow job in the back of a limo. Intelligent men need equally intelligent women by their side. We can make or break them."

Not knowing what to say, I simply nodded.

She surprised me by wrapping her arms around my shoulders. "Us women need to stick together instead of tearing each other down. Twenty years ago, I was you and I wish someone had given me the same advice."

"Thank you," I murmured.

"Come join me at the bar. Let's let the men wonder where we've gotten off too. They get big heads if we hang on their arms all night," she said with a smirk.

"I like the way you think." I held my hand out to her. "I'm Penny."

"Valerie. And we're way beyond a handshake." She looped her arm through mine and led me back to the party. "Let's see what kind of trouble we can find."

It was amazing the amount of attention two women alone at the bar garnered. A steady stream of people approached us, and we indulged in small talk while our men attended to business. I felt a bit bad about abandoning Brett, but I'd done my due diligence at this snoozefest. Hanging out with Valerie was much more enjoyable.

Eventually, Brett wrapped an arm around my waist. "I was wondering where you'd gotten off to." He planted a possessive kiss on my lips.

My heart beat erratically, threatening to thump right out of my chest. Looked like Valerie was right. "We were just having a little woman time."

"You ready to get out of here?" he growled in my ear.

"Only if you are."

"I'm more than ready. Good night, Valerie. A pleasure, as always." He chastely kissed her cheek. "Frank, I'll be talking to you soon." He shook her husband's hand.

I gave Frank a wave of my fingers and Valerie a quick hug. "It was nice meeting you both."

"I hope to see you again, Penny."

Brett whisked me out to the waiting limo and into the back seat. "My place," he instructed the driver and powered the divider up to give us privacy.

"Are you going to take on the mall project?" I asked.

He pulled me to straddle his lap, and I gripped his shoulders for balance.

"I don't give a fuck about that project right now. I'm more interested in you."

Alrighty then.

Chapter 14
Brett

"What are you doing?"

"What I've wanted to do since the first time I saw you in this dress. How much did you have to drink?"

"Not that much," she whispered.

"Are you drunk?"

She lightly shook her head so her curls bounced. "Pleasantly buzzed but nowhere near drunk. Why?"

"Because I want to ravage you and I need to know you're okay with that." I pulled her hips down onto my rock-hard cock. "Do you feel what you do to me?"

She gasped. "Yes. Kiss me... please."

The sound of that one word got me even harder. A woman begging for what I could give her drove me insane. She didn't need to ask twice. I took her face between my hands and kissed her stupid, devouring her lips and letting my tongue dip in and out of her mouth.

Penny returned the kiss with a hunger I happily obliged. We were like two teenagers in the back of my dad's car, and I couldn't remember the last time I felt this much passion. My hand skimmed up the back of her neck and under her dark hair, gripping the strands at the base of her skull in my fist and tilting her head back. My teeth nipped at the column of her throat. The little moans escaping from her lips drove me crazy as she rocked against my dick. When I met her at The Rabbit Hole, I thought she was cute. I had no idea she was such a temptress and a tease, although she didn't realize she was either of those things.

All I could think about was the tiny taste of her tits I got a week ago. It was enough for her to take up permanent residence in my brain. When we weren't talking or texting, all I could do was think about her. The fluttery feeling in my chest wouldn't go away. It was totally inconvenient yet somewhat addicting.

I licked across her collarbone and down between her breasts. Brushing the fabric of her dress back, my tongue swiped across the lace of her bra and over her hard nipple. In the dim light, I could barely see her, but my mouth remembered all I needed to know.

"Brett..." The plea poured from her pretty lips.

"I got you, baby." With one arm wrapped around her waist, I swiveled us on the seat and laid her down against the soft leather. It was a little cramped, but I didn't give a fuck. I'd waited all night to get her alone. Pulling the lace aside, I traced the tip of her nipple. Penny's back arched off the seat and her head fell back.

If she was this responsive when I sucked on her breasts, I couldn't wait to find out how she'd respond to what else I had planned. Reaching inside my suit jacket, I pulled the tiny vibrator from the pocket. Slipping it on my finger, my hand ran up her thigh and under her dress.

Damn her. I let out a chuckle.

"What?"

I snapped the elastic on her thigh. "Surely you don't think this contraption is enough to keep me out." I was well acquainted with women's undergarments. I'd seen everything from adhesive bras to crotchless panties to leather corsets to the body suit Penny was wearing. It was the most practical but least sexy undergarment a woman could wear. A woman wearing Spanx was trying to hide her imperfections. Little did she know that her plentiful curves turned me the fuck on.

"I didn't plan on this happening," she gasped.

"Yet, it is. Don't you worry. I can work around it." I flipped the switch on the vibrator and ran it over the spandex covering her thigh to the juncture of her legs.

"You have a vibrator? You kept that thing in your coat pocket all night?"

"Never know when it might come in handy." I pressed it to her pussy as I nibbled on one breast and then the other. "You like that, don't you?"

"Yes… yes. God, yes!" she whispered, probably afraid my driver would hear us. He was paid well enough to forget anything he might overhear. It was a necessity.

"You want more?"

"Please."

It was a tight fit, but I spread her legs wider until one was hanging off the seat and poked my finger through the opening at the bottom of her bodysuit. She was soaked. I found her clit and held the nubs of the small vibrator against it. She squirmed beneath me, trying to get away and get closer at the same time. I wouldn't let her get away until her sweet little pussy came all over my hand.

"Sweet Jesus!" A string of incoherent words left her mouth as her entire body pulsed underneath me. I swallowed her scream, kissing her until her body relaxed. "That was the best experience of my life," she gasped, trying to catch her breath.

Wishing I could see the blush on her pretty cheeks, I brushed her hair behind her ear. "Oh, Penny, what kind of men have you been dating?"

She pulled her top back in place and sat up on the seat. "Not the kind that do that."

I gripped her chin and turned her face to mine. "That's just sad. What I did was foreplay. It's nothing compared to what you deserve or what I have planned for you. You need a good dicking down, and lucky for you, it happens to be my specialty."

105

Penny pulled her knees up on the seat, smoothing her dress over them, and leaned against the door. "I feel like I need to be honest with you, even if I might regret it later."

She did a one-eighty from the sexy minx who was writhing on the seat beneath me a few moments ago. I turned on the overhead light so I could see her face more clearly. "I'm listening." If she told me she wanted money or anything else from me, she was going to be sorely disappointed. This was why I didn't do relationships or get attached. Finding a genuine human being seemed to be getting more difficult by the day. Most were more interested in my bank account than me. I thought Penny was different, but maybe I judged too quickly.

She took a nervous breath. "After we went to Le Coucou, I told my sister about it, and she showed me an article about you in the *Las Vegas Not So Confidential*. I didn't want you to think that's why I went out with you. Although I'd be lying if I said I didn't enjoy the glitz and glam, I don't really care much about money. That's not how I was raised." She dropped her face into her hands. "This is the really embarrassing part."

I pulled her hands away. "So far, I've appreciated your honesty. I've never thought you were with me for the money. What else?"

"I'm not like those women in the photographs. I don't look like them and I'm not"—she swallowed—"experienced. I mean… I've had sex, but most of what I know I've learned by reading romance novels. I guess I don't understand why you keep calling me and taking me out. I'm the piece of the puzzle that doesn't fit."

Wow! That wasn't at all what I expected from the feisty woman who loved to bust my balls every chance she got. I pulled her close and tucked her into my side. "Penny, you're a very attractive woman and I very much enjoy your company. You've got things none of those other women have… like a brain, and a heart, and an opinion. I like it when you question and challenge me. It's refreshing to have someone by my side who does more than giggle and nod." I tilted her chin up. "As for the sex… well, that means I'll have to teach you and trust me, I'm looking forward to it. There's a lot to explore. I'm going to take you to heights you've never been to before."

She bit her lip. "Why does that excite me and scare me at the same time?"

Despite the serious conversation we were having, I couldn't help but lighten the mood. I remembered exactly what that article said about my bedroom skills. "Because you've never tangled with a tiger before." I held up my hand like a claw and pawed at her. "*Rawr.*"

Penny pushed my hand down and laughed. "Oh, heavens. You did *not* just roar."

I shrugged. "Hey, I read the article too. Apparently, I have a reputation to uphold."

"So it's true?" she asked.

It was such a loaded question. Me being a billionaire? My prowess in the bedroom? The dozens of women I dated? That article covered all the bases yet said nothing about me. It was completely superficial. "Which part?"

"The no second dates part?"

My head wobbled back and forth. "Sort of. I have gone on second dates, but it's a rarity." What I didn't say was that I'd had more one-night stands than I had socks. Somehow, I didn't think that would endear me to Penny. She didn't seem like a one-night-stand kinda woman.

"I see."

Her wheels were turning and what started as a steamy night in the back of my limo turned into an inquisition I wasn't prepared for. I should have known from the beginning. Should have listened to Trent. *Penny isn't a fuck and run.*

The crazy thing was... I had no desire to run. What I wanted to do was take Penny back to my place and show her, repeatedly, what a proper orgasm was, then fall asleep with her cuddled into my side. I wasn't a cuddler, but the thought of Penny snuggling into my chest was extremely appealing.

"You have questions." It was a statement and although I wasn't particularly fond of baring my soul, I'd endure them for her.

"One... well, several, actually... but only one that matters at this moment. What date number are we on? Do you start counting before sex or after? I need to know how to prepare myself mentally. If tonight is all I get, then I'll deal with it. I don't want to set myself up with false expectations. Romance novels will do that to you, you know? The heroine knows what she's getting herself into, yet she thinks she's the one who can change him. And lo and behold... bam!" She clapped her hands together. "She is the one to change him and he falls madly in love with her, and they live happily ever after with two-point-five kids and a dog... or cat. Of course, a cat, because of Fred, but that's not real life. I know that, but I still want it someday, even if it's not..."

I put a finger on her lips to keep her from rambling. "Four."

Her eyebrows went up.

"This is our fourth date. I can't promise you two-point-five kids or a dog, but I can promise I'll want to see you again after tonight. Does that help?"

She nodded. "It does actually."

We'd been parked in front of my apartment building for the last ten minutes. The lust-filled moment had passed, and my stomach rumbled. Those tiny appetizers were a joke. Even if they weren't, I'd barely had a moment to myself to indulge in canapés and shrimp. Whoever even heard of putting shrimp on a cucumber? I found it ridiculous and pretentious, and I'd been around wealthy people my entire life. Rich or not, people needed to eat, especially when the drinks were flowing, like we were at the Gatsby estate.

"Are you hungry?"

"Starving. Are *you* hungry?"

"Famished." I lowered the privacy partition. "Maurice, there's been a change of plans. Could you take us to Tico's Tacos?"

"Of course, Mr. Kingston." The barrier slid back into place, though I doubted we'd need it.

"What's Tico's Tacos?"

My eyes bulged. "You've never been to Tico's Tacos?" She shook her head. "Only the best food truck in all of Vegas. Seriously, how have you lived here your whole life and never had Tico's Tacos?"

"I don't know, but the way you're going on about it, I feel like I've missed out."

"Oh, you definitely have," I said, pulling my tie off and unbuttoning the collar of my shirt. The jacket came off next. I laid it across the seat before undoing my cuffs and rolling my shirtsleeves up.

Penny laughed. "These tacos must be serious business."

"The most serious," I deadpanned. "Listen. I should never have taken you to that boring party. The food was crap, and the conversation was even worse, so consider tacos my apology."

She waved off my apology like it was no big deal. "I didn't mind. Besides, the night wasn't a complete bust. I did get a toe-curling orgasm out of it."

I ran a finger along her jaw. "There's more where that came from."

Tilting her chin down, she bit the tip of my finger. "Tempting, but tacos first."

The lightness I felt with Penny was like nothing I'd ever experienced. She made me forget about mind-numbing meetings, overzealous investors, and potential projects worth billions. After college, my whole life was dedicated to Kingston Enterprises, learning the business and taking over when my father died. There were high expectations from everyone, but none of them were higher than my own. The need to prove myself over and over again was a compulsion I couldn't let go of. The board had questioned whether I was ready to take the reins of Kingston Enterprises at thirty. I was set on ensuring their decision to take a chance on me was the right one. I was the only acceptable replacement.

But when I was with Penny, all of that faded into the background. All I could see or hear was her. She reminded me there was more to life than work, like bowling and laughing and flirty late-night conversations… and tacos. "A woman must have priorities and the tacos are amazing, so I can't really blame you."

The car stopped at the edge of a lot lit up by dozens of colored lanterns. I exited without waiting for Maurice, taking Penny's hand and leading her to the most fantastic food truck that ever existed. Latino dance music floated through the air, giving it a festive feel as people swayed and danced to the beat.

"It's so crowded!" Penny exclaimed as her nose lifted. "And it smells so good. How did I not know this existed?"

We were way overdressed and stuck out among the crowd of twentysomethings partying on a Saturday night. "No idea. Come on, you're in for a treat." I tugged her toward the truck.

Penny struggled to keep up as her tall heels crunched on the gravel. The gentleman in me wrapped an arm around her waist and practically carried her to the open window.

Today's specials were written in bright colors on a chalkboard menu. In addition to tacos, Tico's had enchiladas, burritos, fajitas, chimichangas, and nachos, all served with your choice of beef, chicken, or pork. It was a Mexican food wet dream. My stomach rumbled above the music.

Penny patted it. "Whoa. You weren't kidding, were you?"

I stared down at her. "I never joke about Tico's. The food is an existential experience."

"Okaaay. What's your favorite?"

"That's a tough question. Everything is excellent. We'll get the taco trio and the combo platter. That way, you can try a bit of everything."

She grimaced. "I can't be eating that much."

"You barely ate anything all night. Trust me, your stomach will thank you." I placed our order and moved us to the side to wait for our food.

"I ate before you picked me up. I don't need that much," she insisted.

"Tacos aren't about need; they're about want. And believe me, you're going to want to eat all the tacos." Our order was ready in a flash, and we carried it to one of the picnic tables scattered around the lot.

Penny sat across from me and took a long whiff of the food between us. "They do smell delicious." She picked up a beef taco and took a bite. "Oh my god! My taste buds are singing."

"Told ya," I said, picking up my own taco. She took another bite and a dribble of sauce dripped down her chin. I wiped it away with my finger and licked the sauce off. "You had a little something." I tapped my chin.

She wiped her mouth with a napkin and finished off the taco. Picking up a fork, she pointed to the plate with it. "I don't know what to start with. It all looks so good."

I pushed the plate toward her. "No matter the choice, you can't go wrong. Try a bit of everything."

Penny poked and prodded the plate, taking the tiniest bites of the enchilada, burrito, and chimichanga. She pushed it back at me. "It's too good, and if I don't stop myself, I'll eat the whole plate."

I pushed it back toward her. "You can have as much as you like."

"I wish that were true, but I have a bridesmaid dress to fit into. My sister, Loretta, is getting married."

I dug into the burrito with gusto. "It can't be that bad. I'm sure you'll look great."

She blew out a breath. "You haven't met my sisters. People have been comparing us our whole lives."

Come to think of it, Penny had picked at her food every time we ate together. Her comment in the car echoed in my head. *I'm the piece of the puzzle that doesn't fit.* Also, the spandex bodysuit hiding under her dress. Penny Quinn was insecure about her figure.

Why had it taken me so long to figure that out? No, she wasn't the stick-thin-model type. She had more cushioning around her middle and hips, but it suited her. In a society where every other commercial was about weight loss and women flaunted their perfect bodies all over social media, how could she not be self-conscious? Lots of women had body issues, but the ones I slept with had no problem stripping down and prancing around naked. I didn't foresee any prancing where Penny was concerned.

Was I a shallow asshole? A man who contributed to the low self-esteem of women? Maybe I was. But maybe it was because I never saw anything with those women besides sex and pleasure. I hadn't been looking for someone to spend my life with, not that I was with Penny, but it was the most time I'd spent with a woman without having sex. That meant something, right?

"I wouldn't mind meeting your sisters. Do you have a date for this wedding?" *God, what was I doing?*

Penny's eyes bulged. "Did you just invite yourself to my sister's wedding?"

Seemed I did. Scooping more of the spicy goodness from the plate, I shoved it into my mouth. After an exorbitant amount of time chewing, I tried to pull back my faux pas. "It's okay if you don't want me to go or if you already have a date. I just thought…" I shrugged my shoulders. "I don't really know what I was thinking."

She side-eyed me. "Actually, I don't have a date. I was planning on going alone or maybe conning Tom into going with me."

I scowled. The thought of Tom spending the evening with her rubbed me the wrong way. "Well, I'm throwing it out there. I'd love to be your escort for the night."

"It'll be a lot of family time and there will be dancing."

"I'm good with family and I'm an excellent dancer. I do a mean chicken dance." I held up my hands and clapped my fingers together like beaks, then flapped my arms.

She laughed. "Oh, jeez. This I've got to see, but for the record, Loretta has banned the chicken dance from her reception."

I snapped my fingers. "Damn. I was looking forward to showing off my moves."

"No better time than the present. How about you give me a little sample right now? This music makes me want to shimmy my shoulders and shake my hips." She stood from the table and backed into the crowd of people already dancing. When I shook my head, she beckoned me with a finger.

"Oh, hell. Why the fuck not?" I murmured to myself. Penny shook her hips to the beat as I prowled toward her. She might have been the one who initiated this impromptu dance session, but I wouldn't let her forget who was in charge.

My hands clamped onto her wide hips and pulled her flush with my body. Her arms hung loosely on my shoulders as our bodies pressed together and moved to the music. She stared up at me with those big green eyes that first captured my attention. "You're good at this."

"Dancing is sex standing up. Of course, I'm good at it."

Her cheeks blushed crimson. "What are we doing, Brett?"

"Dancing. Foreplay. Call it what you want." I leaned down and captured her lips with mine, sliding my tongue into her smart mouth. Her tits felt good pressed against me. I'd never dated anyone as short as her and all I could think about was how close she was to my dick. The thought of it created a steel rod in my pants I was sure she couldn't miss.

"I'm not talking about the dancing."

"I don't fucking know, but what I do know is you're not taking fucking Tom to that wedding with you," I growled.

Her eyebrows hiked up. "Is that jealousy I hear?"

"Possessiveness. You're mine for the foreseeable future. No other man will be taking you anywhere."

"And does that go both ways? No other women?"

"All I can see is you. I don't need anyone else." *What the fuck was I doing?* I didn't do relationships. Penny had me breaking all my rules for her and I didn't give a damn. All I knew was the thought of another man putting his hands on her made me twitchy. "Come home with me."

"It's late." She blinked up at me.

"Do you have a curfew?"

"No, but I have Fred. I've never left him alone before."

I pressed a kiss to the corner of her mouth. "He has an automatic feeder." I knew that purchase was a wise one.

"I have yoga with my sister in the morning and I have to go to the bookstore."

"I'll make sure you're home early."

"I don't have a toothbrush."

"I have an extra. No more excuses. Come home with me, Penelope Quinn."

She gulped. "What if I'm not… what you need?"

My hips pressed into her stomach. "In case you haven't noticed, you're exactly what I need." I brushed her hair over her ear. "Don't make me beg. Come home with me."

"Okay," she whispered.

Not giving her a chance to change her mind, I pulled her through the throng of people and to the waiting car. I attacked her mouth in the back seat with my hand up her skirt and over her voluptuous ass, squeezing and kneading. My first priority would be to strip her of the cockblocking Spanx.

113

The ride back to my penthouse seemed like an eternity and my patience was wearing thin. I was half tempted to tear the garment from her body; consequences be damned.

Chapter 15
Penny

I barely noticed the ornate lobby with chandeliers and marble floors as Brett whisked me away to the elevators. He scanned a key card and the doors shut while he backed me against the wall, burying his head in my hair at the nape of my neck.

I'd dreamed about a moment like this my entire life. Fantasized about it. Got myself off to it. I tried to hike my leg up on his hip, but he was too damn tall. Instead, I wrapped my leg around his, pulling him closer with my heeled foot. He bent his knees and pushed his cock into my pelvis. Good Lord, he was going to destroy my body with that thing.

"Can't wait to get you naked. This dress hides all your best parts."

And that's when the panic set in. Not only was my dress coming off, but the Spanx too. Every bit of extra fat and ripple of cellulite would be on full display. Apparently, my undergarment worked too well at concealing my imperfections. It was too late to turn back. I'd already set this train in motion and stopping it would take an act of God. I might have been a lot of things, but a tease was not one of them.

It was dark. My best hope was he'd opt not to turn the lights on.

The elevator doors slid open, and in seconds, we were in his apartment. "This is where you live?" It wasn't an apartment at all. It was as if an entire mansion had been crammed into the space. It had two sets of stairs, floor-to-ceiling windows with a view of the city, and so much open space we could have had the fundraiser here. And was that a pool I saw through the glass?

"I'll give you a tour later."

Right. He brought me here to fuck, not to sightsee.

Brett caged me against the door with his arms. My pulse raced from the desire in his eyes. For me. Penny Quinn. Plain Jane, who'd taken a back seat to love. "Are you nervous?" he asked.

"A bit. You're very intense and it sets off my warning bells."

He ran the back of his fingers along my jaw. "I'll never do anything you don't consent to. I may push your limits, but you're free to stop me at any time."

"I tend to get in my head."

"When we're together, the last thing you'll be doing is thinking. I want to make it so good that all you can do is feel. Understood?"

I nodded. "I'm feeling like I want to keep the lights off." It was a plea more than a request.

He smirked down at me. "For tonight. No promises beyond that."

It was a fair compromise. After all, it implied there would be a *beyond tonight* and that made my foolish heart beat double time. I was in so deep with this man. He'd made no promises, but I saw them in every look, every word, every meaningless gesture. A man like Brett would never settle down with a woman like me. If he settled down at all. I was setting myself up for heartbreak, but I couldn't help it. The fantasy was too good to let go of, and I was going to indulge in it for as long as possible.

"Show me your bedroom."

He took me by the hand and led me down a long hallway to a set of double doors. On the other side was a king-size bed covered by a black satin duvet. My whole condo could fit in this single room.

"I've been waiting all night to get you out of this dress. And by the looks of the men eye fucking you at the bar, I wasn't the only one."

"It was probably Valerie that attracted the attention." No one was looking at me. Men never undressed me with their eyes… or hands, for that matter.

Brett put a finger to my lips. "You really have no idea, do you?"

Speechless, I shook my head.

"Let me show you what you do to me." He took my hand and placed it on his erection, rubbing it along the length. My fingers involuntarily squeezed to get a better feel. "Does that seem like I'm lying to you?"

"I need to feel more of you." Before I had time to second-guess myself, I unbuckled his belt and pants and had his zipper down. My hand slipped between the soft cotton of his briefs and his hard abs, claiming his cock like it was a prize I'd won.

"God, baby, you're killing me."

I was about to drop to my knees on his plush carpet and quickly realized the logistics wouldn't work. With my free hand on his chest, I pushed him back toward an upholstered armchair. "Sit," I commanded, using the bravado Valerie had instilled in me.

He lowered his dress pants to his hips and wrapped his hand around mine, stroking his cock in tandem. "You gonna suck my cock?"

"Tell me how you like it," I said as I dropped to my knees between his spread legs. My blow job skills were limited at best, but I'd read enough fellatio scenes that I figured I couldn't go too wrong.

Brett ran his hands through my hair and gathered it on top of my head. "With your sassy mouth on my dick." With the slightest of pressure, he pressed my head down until my mouth hovered over the crown, where a drop of his arousal glistened. "Lick it."

I wrapped both hands around his erection and closed my eyes. My tongue darted out and lapped up the bead of liquid, then ran along the rim of the crown. Lowering my head, I took him as deep as I could and let my hands handle the rest. There was no way all of him would fit in my mouth, even if I was brave enough to try, which I wasn't. He was too long and too thick, and I wondered how all of it was going to fit inside my pussy.

117

That thought made me wetter and urged me to double down my efforts. I swirled my tongue on the underside of his cock and hollowed out my cheeks like a seasoned porn star. His groans let me know he was enjoying it. With one hand, I ran my nails under his balls until he stiffened and grabbed my wrist.

"You naughty girl. You're trying to make me come, but I don't play that way. I'll always make sure you come before me."

I gulped around his cock, and he burst from the chair, his dick bobbing before me. "Stand up, baby."

"Did I do something wrong?" I asked, rising to my feet.

He let out a breath, pulling his pants up his hips. "Just the opposite. I almost blew down that pretty throat of yours. Turn around."

I slowly turned, so I was facing the bed, waiting for what was coming next. The unzipping of my dress sent me into a fresh wave of panic. There was no sexy lingerie for him to admire or a revealing thong for him to rip off. I looked like I was wearing my great-grandmother's bathing suit.

I quickly grabbed the front of the dress and held it to my chest. "Brett," I whispered.

"Let me see you," he whispered back, gently taking my hands and removing them. He slipped the dress off my shoulders and let it pool around my ankles. "Step out." I did, and he picked up my dress and laid it over the chair.

My arms crossed over my body, not knowing which parts I wanted to cover the most. I didn't have enough hands to properly do the job.

He started under my arms and smoothed his large hands down over each one of my generous curves. "I'm already in love with your body. You don't need to hide it from me." He cupped my breasts. "Your tits are amazing." Then he grabbed a handful of my butt. "And this ass... Mmmm... makes me want to spank it."

I stiffened under his hands. *Spanking?* Good Lord, what had I gotten myself into?

"Relax," he whispered in my ear. "We'll save that for another night. Tonight, I'm going to eat your pussy until you come all over my face and then I'm going to fuck you like you've never been fucked before."

A shiver ran down my spine. "You're intense."

He gripped my chin and turned it toward him. "You already knew that. It doesn't matter if it's negotiating a deal or fucking you senseless, I'm the best at what I do. Now strip."

I straightened my spine and tried to muster some confidence. "You first. I'm already halfway there and you're fully dressed." Anything to put off the inevitable and reveal myself to him.

He shook his head at me. "Only you, Penny Quinn." Brett stood in front of me and began unbuttoning his shirt, revealing a sculpted chest with a light smattering of hair I found extremely sexy. He shrugged it off his broad shoulders, revealing a barrage of tattoos I didn't know existed, and threw it to the side. "Better?"

The urge to lick the lines on his chest made my tongue poke out. "Pants next," I demanded.

He chuckled as he slid his belt through the loops, grabbing it in both hands and giving it a good snap before dropping it to the floor. "You're testing my patience." Brett toed his shoes off and slid his pants down his legs, removing his socks in the process and kicking the pile of material away, leaving him in only his boxer briefs.

"No more excuses." He stepped toward me and hooked his fingers in the straps at my shoulders, slowly sliding them down my arms. When my breasts popped out, he groaned but kept moving the spandex down my body and over my hips, which put my pussy at eye level. He placed a gentle kiss on my bare pelvis, then continued pushing the fabric down my legs to my ankles, lifting each one and pulling my feet through the holes.

"My shoes…"

"Are staying on." His hands skimmed up my legs with the most delicate touch. When he got to my pussy, he parted my lips and ran his tongue through the seam, stopping to nibble on my clit.

I almost came from the unexpected onslaught. Wetness dripped down my thighs in anticipation of what was to come. A little moan escaped my lips. "Yesss."

Brett stood and parted my legs with his knee. He started with one finger in my pussy while his other hand kneaded my breast and he nuzzled on my neck. Another finger and a come-hither motion had me whimpering.

"You're so tight."

"You have big hands."

"I have big everything, baby."

"Don't break me," I pleaded.

"You'll take every…" A kiss to my jaw. "Inch." Another kiss to the corner of my mouth. "Of me." He attacked my mouth with a vengeance as I grabbed the back of his head and tugged him closer. He pulled his fingers from me and hiked my leg up on his hip. His other hand grabbed me under the ass and lifted me off the ground, carrying me to the bed.

We crashed onto the black duvet, still devouring each other with a passion I'd never felt before. All my insecurities drifted away as lust took over. My hand snaked down the back of his boxers and grabbed his ass. It was firm and tight like I'd imagined. I traced the flexing muscles of his back and ran my fingers through his hair. He was everything I dreamed he'd be.

Brett pulled back from the kiss. He was handsome as fuck. Illuminated only by the lights of the city and the moon, I could barely make out the green in his hazel eyes as he stared down at me. "You're a pleasant surprise, Miss Quinn. I think you're a little minx who's been waiting to be unleashed your whole life."

"I am." I giggled. "Now, I think you promised you were going to eat my pussy."

"That sounds so sexy coming from your lips." He grabbed both my wrists and held them above my head with one hand as he licked down my neck, between my breasts, and over my soft stomach. Sliding down my body, he parted my thighs and propped my legs over his shoulders.

Then he feasted.

His tongue dove deep inside me, sucking up all my juices. That talented tongue attacked my clit next, flicking it with the power of my favorite vibrator.

My head swam from the endorphins rushing through my body. This was a bliss I'd never experienced before. Just like he promised... all I could do was feel.

His lips latched around my clit and began to suck while still tickling it with the tip of his tongue.

The sensation began low in my belly and the tingles spread through my extremities like sparklers. My back arched off the mattress and Brett slid his hands under my butt and lifted me closer to his face, increasing the intensity tenfold. My walls clenched, and my body tightened to the point of being painful. The orgasm was right there, waiting to break and push me over the edge. Bright spots danced beneath my eyelids as my head dropped back and a scream stuck in my throat.

And when I thought I couldn't climb any higher, he stuck his fingers inside me and hit that magic spot no other man had ever bothered to find. I exploded and the scream broke free. Brett's mouth and fingers worked overtime. The waves of pleasure kept coming, one after another until I was nothing but a spineless pile of goo.

He kissed along my body, stopping to suck on my nipples until his lips met mine. I tasted myself on his tongue and that turned me on even more.

"Your pussy is dripping for me." He reached down, pushing his boxer briefs to his ankles and kicking them away. His cock bobbed, smacking his belly button, and I worried for a second it wouldn't fit. It was irrational, but none of my vibrators were that big. He smoothed the lines on my forehead with his thumb. "I'll need to make you come harder next time because you're still thinking. Get out of your head."

I tapped my fingers against my temple. "It's a busy place in there."

"Then let me give you something else to think about." He straddled my shoulders and held his cock out to me. "Suck."

Chapter 16
Brett

For a woman with minimal experience, Penny came like a dream and sucked cock like a queen. My dick slid in and out of her mouth at a leisurely pace. There was no rush to the finish line. That would come when I was deep inside her sweet pussy. She gently tugged on my balls and massaged the place behind them. It felt too damn good, but there was no way I was coming in her mouth.

I pulled back and leaned over to the nightstand, pulling a condom from the drawer. "Are you ready for me?"

She nodded. "I'm nervous."

"Don't be. I'll take very good care of you," I assured her as my thumb caressed her jaw. Rolling the condom on, I kneeled between her open legs. Lining myself up with her pussy, I nudged in the tip and caged her in with my arms. "You good?"

"Yes. I trust you." She grabbed hold of my arms and pushed her pelvis toward mine.

I slipped in a little more. She was so wet; it was taking all my self-control not to go hard and fast. But that wasn't what she needed. She needed to feel safe and secure in the promise I made to take care of her. I gave her another minute to adjust, then pushed in a little farther. Her pussy was so tight it felt like a warm, wet glove gripping my cock.

"Are you in?" she asked coyly, and it was so damn cute.

I chuckled. "About halfway." What kind of men had she been with? Obviously, the dinky dick variety.

Her eyes bulged. "I already feel full. You're going to split me in half."

"Am I hurting you?"

She shook her head.

"Don't anticipate the pain. Anticipate the pleasure because I assure you if you're not getting off, neither am I." I gave her another couple inches and kissed her pretty lips. I wasn't necessarily big on kissing. It was personal, and usually, when I fucked, it was anything but. It was important to send the right message from the beginning, or a woman could get clingy.

But with Penny, everything was different. I wanted second, third, and fourth dates. I wanted bowling on a Sunday afternoon and late-night phone calls. I wanted to kiss her because, deep down, I wanted to keep her. This was more than a lust-fueled fuck. It was personal.

With one final push, I was deep inside her. "You feel like heaven wrapped around my cock."

"Oh god! I never knew it could be like this," she said, her voice breathy and sexy as hell. Those tiny hands gripped my ass and squeezed. "Need you to move now, tiger."

I chuckled. Even pinned beneath me, she was bossy. There was only one boss in my bedroom, and I intended to prove it wasn't her. I rocked my hips, starting with slow, short thrusts. She wasn't the type of woman you fucked fast and furious the first time. We'd get there, but it wouldn't be tonight.

This was a gentle fuck. The kind I avoided. Again, because it was personal.

My hips rolled, each time giving her a little more of me. Another inch out, another inch in. Her pussy was so soft, so wet, so warm... I wanted to live inside it. Her hands roamed my back from shoulders to ass as if committing it to memory. The soft, little moans that escaped her lips were a welcome sign of pleasure. Apparently, the way to get her to quit rambling was by fucking her because, for once, she was at a loss for words. I grabbed her thigh and hiked it up to my waist to get deeper as I swiveled my hips.

Her back arched and I nipped at her tits, sucking one, then the other. "Oh god, so good. Don't stop," she moaned.

"I'm not stopping until you come on my cock, baby." Switching the angle, I rubbed against her clit with every push and every pull. She was close, I just needed to take her over the edge. The tingles started at the base of my spine. I wasn't going to last much longer, but I needed to get her there first.

Her hand crept between us, heading for her clit. I pushed it away. "Nuh-uh. That's my job. The only time you get to play with your pussy is if I let you. I own your orgasms. Understood?"

"Please," she begged.

I loved seeing her like this… desperate and needy for what I could give her. Using my thumb, I rubbed circles on the sensitive nub while rocking my hips faster, chasing both our orgasms.

Her walls began to pulse around my cock with every thrust. "Come, Penny. Come all over my cock." She fisted the comforter with her tiny hands and jolted up off the mattress as she screamed my name. Her walls squeezed me so damn hard I exploded. All thoughts of being gentle ceased to exist as I pounded into her hard and fast, gripping her hips with enough force to leave bruises.

It'd been a long time since I'd come that hard. Sweat dripped down my forehead and landed in tiny droplets on her stomach. Penny's chest heaved up and down, her tits bouncing as she tried to recover from how I'd wrecked her. "Are you okay? I didn't mean to get so rough," I asked as I brushed her hair away from her face and kissed her temple.

"I'm more than okay," she said, cracking open her pretty green eyes. "I feel like I'm still floating. What the hell did you do to me?"

"Fucked you the way you deserve to be fucked."

"Mmmm," she hummed. "I like it."

"I'm glad to be of service because I plan on doing it again and again. Don't move a muscle," I said as I got up to dispose of the condom. Tossing it in the bathroom trash, I grabbed a clean washcloth and ran it under warm water. She might not have realized it yet, but when those endorphins subsided, she was going to be sore.

Penny stretched, her fingers brushing the spindles on the headboard. She was going to look phenomenal tied to them. Soon.

I kneeled on the bottom of the bed, unbuckling the strap of one of her shoes and kissing the inside of her ankle, then did the same to the other foot. She pointed her toes and wiggled them. "Oh my gosh, that feels so much better. I'll probably have to go home barefoot tomorrow."

Gliding the washcloth up the inside of one thigh, I pried her legs apart and began to clean her. "Are you sure you can't stay for breakfast?" She tried to grab the washcloth from my hand, but I pulled it away. "I got you. Let me."

Penny dropped her arms over her face. "This is embarrassing."

"No," I insisted. "It's me taking care of you. Get used to it." I finished wiping her down and threw the cloth into the bathroom. Crawling up on the bed next to her, I pried her arms away from her face and kissed her plump lips. "Now, about breakfast?"

"I have yoga with Bea at ten."

"I see." Usually, I was the one eager to get away. Sex was just sex. It didn't include sleepovers or breakfast in the morning. "Let me get you some water. It's important to stay hydrated."

"That would be nice," she said sheepishly.

"I'll be right back." I rolled from the bed and snagged my briefs from the floor, stepping into them.

When I returned from the kitchen with two bottles of water, I found Penny dressed in my discarded shirt, standing at the window with her hands pressed up against the glass, silhouetted by the lights of the city. The shirt dwarfed her small figure, hitting her midthigh and swallowing up her arms. She was drowning in it. I set the bottles on the dresser and snuck up behind her, lifting the shirt up her hips and rubbing the full globes of her ass.

She panicked, trying to pull it down. "Someone will see me."

"The glass is tinted. No one can see you but me." I took both her hands in one of mine and held them above her head on the glass. With my other hand, I slowly undid the buttons, exposing her breasts. With a gentle hand on her back, I pressed her tits to the window. Her nipples pebbled against the cold glass. "You look beautiful like this."

"I feel exposed," she whispered.

"I would never let anyone look at you unless you wanted it." Her eyebrows rose to her hairline, and I could practically see the gears in her head turning, but for once, she stayed quiet. "Arch your back for me," I breathed in her ear.

Without arguing, she stepped up on her toes and lifted her hips.

"Absolutely gorgeous." I kneeled behind her and spread her legs apart. The first swipe of my tongue against her pussy sent a shiver down her spine and a moan tumbling from her lips. "I can't seem to get enough of you. This pussy is so sweet I could eat you all night." I spread her open with my thumbs and she gasped.

"Brett..."

"You don't like it?"

"I didn't say that."

"Then let me fuck you with my tongue." I feasted on her until her legs were shaking with need. When she finally came, Penny collapsed against the glass.

I carried her to the bed, her arms wrapped around my neck, and placed her in the middle, then handed her a bottle of water. "Thank you," she said, sucking down half the water in one gulp. She pulled the shirt closed across her chest and began buttoning it.

I put my hand over hers. "Leave it. You look sexy like that."

She looked up at me from under her long lashes. "No one has ever called me sexy before."

Tilting her chin up with my fingers, I looked into her eyes. "You are. I adore your curves and everything that makes you who you are."

She snuggled into my chest. "That might be one of the nicest things anyone has ever said to me." Closing her eyes, she burrowed in deeper.

Within minutes she was asleep. I pulled back the covers and tucked us both under the comforter. Pulling her back to my chest, I nuzzled into the soft place between her neck and shoulder and breathed in the scent of strawberries. It was sweet and innocent, like the woman who'd unexpectedly captured my attention. With her in my arms, it was the best I'd slept in years.

Chapter 17
Penny

I woke with the woodsy scent of Brett's cologne surrounding me. Hugging the pillow, I took a deep whiff to make sure I wasn't dreaming. Last night had been everything I had ever dreamed of. It was hard to believe that I, Penelope Quinn, was waking up in his bed after a night filled with multiple orgasms and the most amazing sex I'd ever had.

The *Las Vegas Not So Confidential* hadn't been lying when it said he was a god between the sheets. A girl could get used to that kind of attention.

But the article also pointed out that no woman had been able to tame the playboy. I cringed when I thought about the pictures of the beautiful women he'd dated. He might be temporarily obsessed with me, but how long could it last? He'd said all the right words last night, but there was a part of me that didn't believe him.

I wanted to.

God, how I wanted to drink up every compliment he gave me and accept it as the truth. I may have been inexperienced, but I wasn't naive. A woman like me was an interlude to tide him over before the next gorgeous woman caught his eye.

With a sigh, I rolled over and found the space next to me empty. The sun barely lit up the skyline, turning everything purple and pink, promising a new day where dreams ended and reality took their place.

I sat on the edge of the bed, pulling Brett's crumpled shirt around me, and rushed into the bathroom, snagging my Spanx that had been carefully laid over the chair next to my dress. The mirror proved everything I already knew was true. My curls were out of control, sticking out at odd angles, and I had mascara smudged beneath my eyes. Perhaps it was a good thing I didn't wake up next to Brett after all.

Searching through the drawers of the vanity, I found a new toothbrush. After brushing my teeth, taming my wild hair, and wiping at last night's makeup, I felt a bit more human. The space between my legs was sore but in a good way. A reminder last night wasn't a dream.

I picked up my undergarment and held it out in front of me. The last thing I felt like doing was squeezing myself into the contraption first thing in the morning. Instead, I smoothed out the shirt I was wearing and buttoned everything except the top two buttons. Rolling the sleeves to my elbows, I turned in front of the mirror and inspected myself. I didn't want Brett to see me in the light of day. The shirt practically came to my knees and although I wasn't wearing underwear, everything was sufficiently covered.

Feeling a bit awkward wandering through Brett's home alone, I tiptoed down the hallway. The place was huge, with tall ceilings, white walls, and dark accents. Very chic, very modern, very masculine. Exactly what I'd expect of a billionaire's penthouse. The walls were lined with black-and-white photographs depicting some of the most famous cities in the world. I wondered if he'd visited them and if maybe someday I would too. Highly unlikely for a middle-class girl who was a lowly personal assistant, but I'd never been one to say no to a fantasy.

The smell of fresh coffee filled the air, leading me to the kitchen I hadn't got a peek of last night. Brett stood at the stove in only a pair of cotton shorts, surrounded by stainless steel appliances and granite countertops. The kitchen was massive, with a large island in the middle. It was the kind of place I'd only seen on TV, and although I was dying to check out the full amenities, all I could focus on was the sculpted muscles of Brett's back and how they rippled as he moved. My fingers twitched at the thought of rubbing all over them like I had last night.

Waiting a few more moments to let my presence be known, I looked around, taking in every detail. A large sitting area, complete with a black wraparound sofa and wide-screen television, took up the majority of the space. There was a dining room table big enough for eight with a vase of fresh flowers on it. The two sets of black metal stairs led to a loft, which I was sure housed other secret rooms.

But what stole the show was the view. Outside the floor-to-ceiling windows was a patio, complete with a built-in pool. And if that wasn't enough, beyond the city skyline were mountains tinged with the bright colors of the sunrise. It was the most fabulous thing I'd ever seen in my entire life.

"It's amazing, isn't it?" Brett handed me a cup of coffee.

I hadn't realized I'd migrated to the window and pressed my nose against it. I took the mug from him and wiped the nose print with the sleeve of his shirt. "It's beautiful."

He pushed my hair over my ear and kissed my temple. "You sure are."

I blushed. I didn't think I'd ever get used to the compliments Brett handed out so freely.

"I know you said you didn't have time for breakfast, but I made scrambled eggs in the hope that you'd change your mind."

"What time is it?"

"Just after seven. You have time." With a hand on my lower back, Brett led me to the kitchen island, where he already had two plates of eggs set out. I hopped up on the stool and sniffed. My belly rumbled loud enough for him to hear. "See? You are hungry. I wouldn't be much of a man if I sent you off to yoga without properly feeding you first."

I picked up the fork. "Thank you. I feel like I'm being spoiled."

He sat down next to me. "Not spoiled. Taken care of."

Lifting a bite of food to my lips, I hummed at the goodness. "Same thing." I pointed my fork at the plate. "Did you put cheese in these?"

"Of course. Cheese makes everything better," he said, scooping his own eggs into his mouth.

"No truer words have ever been spoken." After finishing my breakfast, I pushed the plate away. "I'm not sure that I ever properly thanked you for setting me up with Mind Bender. I'm meeting with him at the bookstore later today to firm up some details for next Saturday. He wanted to see the space."

"It was my pleasure. I hope it all works out well."

"How could it not? He's Mind Bender. My social media posts have been blowing up. I know people will come because it's a free performance, but I hope they buy books too."

He rubbed my back in small circles. "They will."

I frowned. "What do I call him? Mr. Bender? That's weird."

Brett laughed. "His name is actually Walter. Walter Bender."

"For real?"

He nodded.

"Yeah, Mind Bender sounds cooler. It's amazing the difference one word can make."

"He went by Wally when we were in school. Now he refers to himself in the third person. He's all Mind Bender did this, or Mind Bender said that. Says it makes a statement." He shrugged.

"I guess it doesn't matter. It seems to be working for him." I pushed myself away from the counter. "I should get dressed and call for a Lyft." Last night was fun, but I didn't know where we stood. I didn't want to make assumptions I shouldn't be making.

"Don't be ridiculous. I'm driving you," he said as if my words personally offended him.

I was about to argue when a brisk knock came at the door. I tugged at the hem of the shirt I was wearing, suddenly very aware I had no panties on. "Are you expecting company?"

"No." His brows furrowed. He seemed annoyed and didn't make any move to answer the door.

The knock came again. "Are you going to see who it is?"

Brett put his hand on my shoulder with a sigh. "Stay here."

131

He didn't have to ask me twice. The last thing I planned on doing was flashing some stranger at the door, but that didn't keep me from eavesdropping.

"*Amanda? What are you doing here?*"

"*I smelled the coffee and figured you were awake. I feel like I haven't seen you in forever.*"

"*I've been busy.*"

Amanda? Now I was curious. Slipping off the chair, I tiptoed to the corner and peeked around the wall.

She was beautiful. Dressed in running pants and a sweat-soaked sports bra with earbuds draped over her shoulders, she'd obviously just returned from a run. She didn't have on any makeup, and her hair was pulled back in a sleek ponytail, yet she looked flawless. Her legs were long and toned, and her stomach… I'd bet you could bounce a quarter off that thing.

I pushed at my own stomach through the oversized shirt. With my luck, said quarter would get stuck between my fat rolls. We were nothing alike.

"Too busy to see me? I thought maybe we could hook up later. It's been a while," she said as she ran a manicured nail down his bare chest.

Hook up? In other words, have sex. My happy heart practically dropped out of my chest. Of course, they were hooking up. She looked like that, and I was, well… me. I knew this was too good to be true, I'd just hoped it would last a little longer.

"I'm kind of seeing somebody." He ran a hand through his hair nervously.

Amanda propped a hand on her hip. "What does *kind of* mean? Is it serious?" *Yes, Brett, I'd like to know the answer to those questions too.* Her eyes scanned the open room and landed on… me. "She spent the night?"

My sneaky sleuth skills sucked, and it was too late to slink back into the kitchen with both Brett's and Amanda's eyes drilling holes into me.

Letting out a sigh, Brett waved me over. I walked as gracefully as I could to the door, holding the edge of the shirt against my thighs. Brett wrapped his arm around my shoulder like we were pals. "Penny, meet Amanda, my only neighbor on the floor."

Neighbor? I gave her a little wave. "Nice to meet you."

132

Amanda barely acknowledged my existence. "Well, isn't she adorable? Let me know when you have some free time. I'd love to get caught up." She walked across the hall and let her door slam behind her.

"I should get dressed." Twisting out from under Brett's arm, I hurried down the hallway, grabbed my clothes from the bedroom, and locked myself in the bathroom. It didn't escape me that Brett hadn't explained our relationship to Amanda or confirmed if we were serious. I flopped down on the closed toilet lid.

I was a fucking idiot.

How could I have fooled myself into thinking last night had meant anything? That the late-night chitchats and silly memes sent back and forth were the basis of a relationship?

I pounded the side of my head with my palm. "Dumb, Penny. Dumb, dumb, dumb." It was sex. That was it. If he didn't get it from me, he'd get it from someone else. I knew his reputation, yet I'd convinced myself it didn't apply to me.

A soft knock echoed in the large bathroom. "It's not what you think, Penny."

I wasn't stupid. It was exactly what I thought. "I'll be out in a minute." Quickly pulling on my Spanx, I stepped into my dress and pulled the zipper up. If I was going to have a breakdown, it would be in the privacy of my own home, preferably with Fred cuddled on my lap.

Opening the door, I rushed past Brett, grabbed my shoes, and searched for my purse. There was no telling where I'd dropped it last night. The front hall was the most likely place, seeing as we'd only made it to the entryway before he whisked me off to his bedroom.

I acted like a whore last night. In the dark, it seemed like a good idea to sleep with a man who had a history of being a playboy. In the light of day, I realized I was just another in a long line of women who'd come before me. No matter how special he had made me feel… I wasn't.

"It's right here," Brett said, holding my purse out to me. I went to reach for it, and he pulled it back. "Can we talk?"

Talk? Talk about what?

About the fool I'd made of myself?

About me pushing myself up against the glass last night like some kind of porno queen?

About the glamazon that showed up on his doorstep this morning?

"I don't think we have much to talk about. Thank you for breakfast." Thanking someone for breakfast wasn't nearly as pathetic as thanking them for sex. I snatched my purse from his hand and headed toward the door.

I'd barely gotten it open an inch when his palm smacked against it and pushed it closed again. He hovered over the top of me. "Whatever is going through your head is wrong. Let me explain."

My neck craned back to look up at him. "There's no need for explanations. I really need to get home."

"Let me take you."

I put my hand on his chest. "Let's not pretend this is something it isn't. I need some time alone. Please." My voice cracked on the last word. If I didn't get out of here soon, I was going to make a fool out of myself for a second time.

Brett kissed me on the forehead and took a step back, sticking his hands in the pockets of his shorts. "If it's time you need, then it's time I'll give you. Last night wasn't just another fuck for me. I've never let a woman spend the night before. Nor have I made them breakfast. Thought you should know."

It was too much information to process all at once. Like a coward, I opened the door and rushed to the elevator, pushing the call button like a madwoman. Stepping into the car, I hoped no one else got on. Nothing said *walk of shame* like last night's dress and bare feet.

When the elevator stopped in the lobby, I rushed for the front doors, planning to wait until I got to the street to call for a ride, but at the curb sat a very familiar limo. Maurice opened the back door for me. "Miss Quinn."

Without hesitation, I slid into the back seat, both embarrassed and relieved. As the door closed, I stared out the window and up at the building. Was Brett up there watching me?

Now that I was safely away from him, I wasn't sure bolting was the right decision. I let his parting words marinate in my brain. Yes, he could have defended me to Amanda, but I could have listened to him. Maybe I acted immaturely. Maybe I overreacted. Maybe I got in my own head.

The tears I'd been holding back ran down my cheeks, and I couldn't help but wonder who had messed up more.

Brett?

Or me?

Chapter 18
Brett

"Goddammit!" My hand smacked the back of the door repeatedly.

It was one thing for Penny to read a stupid article about me in a gossip rag and quite another for it to be thrown in her face while still wearing my shirt from the night before.

Why hadn't I told Amanda the truth? *Seeing somebody* wasn't the same as being in a relationship. Seeing somebody didn't imply exclusivity. It was vague. It was an escape hatch waiting to be used.

Was that what I wanted with Penny? An escape hatch?

Although I'd dirtied her up quite nicely last night, she was sweet. Naive. Pure.

Those weren't words I'd use to describe my normal hookups. Those women were with me for two reasons, sex and money. It was easy.

With Penny, it was different.

This got me back to my original question. Why hadn't I told Amanda what Penny was to me? We hadn't defined it. I revolted against it. But somehow, it'd happened without my consent.

I'd caught feelings for the quirky brunette.

Relationships meant commitment, something I'd been able to happily avoid for more than a decade. I didn't owe anybody anything.

I should have been relieved that Penny had left but instead I felt lonely.

Relationships also meant companionship for more than a night or two. Someone to share your thoughts, bed, and breakfast with. I couldn't remember the last time I'd shared breakfast with a woman.

Somehow over the past few weeks, I'd become accustomed to her random texts and sassy sense of humor. She made me laugh more than anyone else. And there were tacos.

I imagined the look on Amanda's face if I tried to take her to Tico's Tacos. She'd think I'd lost my mind. She'd bitch about the gravel parking lot, the less-than-five-star Michelin kitchen, and the shoddy picnic tables. She wouldn't have laughed or danced or eaten a damn thing that came out of that truck.

When I was with Penny, she made me feel light and spontaneous. Even the obligatory business function last night was tolerable. When I wasn't with her, I was thinking about her.

I'd broken my own rules for her.

And that scared the shit out of me.

I threw on my running clothes and headed to the park. A good run would give me time to think and gain perspective. Then I'd come home and drown myself in work.

If she wanted time, I'd give it to her.

Just not too much time.

Chapter 19
Penny

After giving Fred a good cuddle and apologizing for my absence, I took a shower while he watched me from the bathroom counter. I had zero privacy, but I didn't mind. Before Fred, I was lonely. Now, I had a shadow that bordered on stalking.

With myself pulled together and the events of the morning behind me, I met Bea at the yoga studio. She pointed to the place she'd saved for me to lay my mat. Although I was sad inside, I wasn't going to let that dampen my time with my sister.

"Hey," I said with a smile and rolled the mat out.

"Hey yourself." She nudged me with her shoulder. "Any more dates with the billionaire?"

I rolled my eyes. That's what most people saw when they looked at Brett, but to me, it wasn't even in the top five on the list of things I liked about him. Underneath all the money, he was a normal guy. Well, maybe not normal, but…

"Last night." I reached for my toes like going out with Brett wasn't a big deal.

Bea pulled her mat closer to mine. "And?"

"And what?"

She nudged me again. "You know. What did you do?" Bea waggled her eyebrows at me.

The instructor clapped her hands and began the class. Yoga wasn't a time for talking. It was about finding clarity and peace, and I desperately needed both today.

Did you have sex? She mouthed to me.

What? I mouthed back with a hand to my ear.

Bea rolled her eyes at me as she moved her lips. *S-E-X.*

Even though the morning hadn't gone great, I couldn't deny last night was everything I dreamed about. The way he touched me was divine. It wasn't rushed or rough. He'd taken his time with me, making sure I was completely satisfied. And for that experience alone, no matter where it went from here, I was thankful.

My sister hadn't taken her eyes off me, waiting for a response. I gave a little nod and couldn't help the way my lips turned up.

"Yes," she whisper-shouted with a pump of her arm, nearly falling out of her pose.

"Focus, ladies," the instructor scolded.

When the class ended, Bea dragged me out to a private table and huddled close to me. "Tell me everything."

I wrinkled my nose. "Eww. No. I'm not going to kiss and tell."

"Fine," she huffed. "Just tell me one thing. Was the article true about his skills in the bedroom?"

This time I gave her a wide smile. "Every word."

"Eeep!" Bea squealed, attracting the attention of everyone in the fitness center. She grabbed me around the shoulders and jumped up and down, bouncing me along with her. "Did you ask him to the wedding?"

"No." Technically, it wasn't a lie because he'd invited himself. I had no idea if we were even going to see each other again after what transpired this morning.

"Why not?"

I sighed. "Because I don't know what this is between us. I'm afraid I'm setting myself up for disappointment. He doesn't do relationships and it'd be silly to think I could change a man who doesn't want to be changed."

She held her hands up and twisted her fingers together. "I'm keeping my fingers crossed. And my toes, for extra luck. Not that you need it, but it can't hurt."

I crossed mine too. Why did I have to fall in love so easily? If I didn't, it wouldn't hurt so much.

My meeting with Mind Bender went better than I expected. He was a weird dude, who did, in fact, refer to himself in the third person, but he was nice. Kind of shy, which surprised me the most. I thanked him again for helping us out and introduced him to my parents, who were tickled pink to meet him.

After he left, I redid one of the window displays with the newest best sellers. My mom normally did the displays, but I'd suddenly found myself with time on my hands and a brain that wouldn't shut off. Brett's words replayed over and over in my head. *"Last night wasn't just another fuck for me. I've never let a woman spend the night before. Nor have I made them breakfast. Thought you should know."* Keeping busy helped quiet the noise.

This whole thing was about more than sex to me. I'd already gambled my heart the first time I met him. With each date, each conversation, each compliment he gave me, it upped the ante. I was all in when we had sex. I don't know what I expected to win—a commitment, a reciprocation, some type of loyalty—but I lost. *Sort of seeing someone* wasn't any of those things.

It was mostly on me. I knew that. Lots of people had meaningless sex. I simply wasn't one of them.

He might have cared about me, but that was miles away from claiming me.

It was best to move on from the ridiculous fantasy I'd conjured up in my mind and go back to standing with both feet planted firmly on the ground.

I thought about sending him a check for the fancy cat feeder, but I highly doubted he was going to care about a measly hundred dollars. I didn't want to feel like I owed him anything. There was the favor he called in with Mind Bender, but after next Saturday, I'd put it in the rearview mirror.

The storeroom was packed with boxes for the Reading is Magic event. I began opening them and organizing the contents into piles around the room, seeing what had arrived and setting things aside for the other window display and the table displays. The magician was the draw, but people needed to actually buy things for the event to work.

Going to my dad's desk, I shuffled through file folders to find the invoices for the remaining orders. For a longtime business owner, his organizational system left little to be desired. He was old school, so he kept paper copies of everything. I'd offered to scan the paperwork into the computer for him, but he nixed the idea immediately, saying he knew where everything was. It worked for him, so who was I to judge?

When I opened the third folder, my eyes bugged out.

"What are you looking for? I'm sure I can help you find it," my dad said with a chuckle from the doorway.

I held up the papers with red stamps across them. "Dad, what is this?"

His face dropped and he quickly swiped the papers from my hand, shoving them back into the file. "You weren't supposed to see those."

"You said the store was doing okay. I knew business was slow, but what the hell, Dad?" I motioned to the overdue notices in his hand.

He wrapped an arm around my shoulders and pulled me into his side. "I don't want you to worry about it."

"I do worry," I said, hugging him back.

"Once Loretta's wedding is over, things will go back to normal."

I pulled back. "What?"

He sighed and sat on the edge of the desk. "I didn't lie when I said we were doing okay. We're not bringing in the bucks we used to, but we're keeping afloat. I had to take some money out of the business to pay for the wedding."

"Jesus, Dad," I said, running both hands over my face. "Loretta and Beau have great jobs. Surely they can help pay for their own damn wedding."

"I'm sure they could, but I'm a proud man. I'm not going to let them, his parents, or anyone else think I can't take care of my own family. If I can't, then what the hell have I been doing all these years? It would mean your mom and my dream of owning this store was a waste."

I saw the resignation on his face. There was nothing I could say to change his mind. "Okay. This event on Saturday should help, and I'll come up with some other ideas too."

He kissed me on top of my head. "I know you will. Out of my three girls, you've always been the most headstrong."

"I'll do whatever I can to help."

"Thank you. And if you don't mind, I'd like to keep this conversation between us. Your sisters don't need to know we're struggling."

I nodded. Keeping this from my sisters seemed wrong, but honestly, what help would it be if they knew? My parents worked their whole damn life for this store, and I'd be damned if I let it go up in flames. I knew what it was like to dream and what it felt like when that dream came true... even if it was short-lived.

Chapter 20
Brett

The lights nearly blinded me as she pulled into the lot. I'd been sitting in the dark on this stoop for almost two hours. Penny hadn't answered my calls or texts, so I took matters into my own hands. I wasn't a man who waited around for things to happen. I was a man who made things happen.

"What are you doing here?" Penny asked as she walked toward me, sitting in front of her door. Wearing purple leggings and an oversized T-shirt, she looked darn cute, but not as cute as she had looked wearing my dress shirt.

"I missed you."

"You saw me this morning." There was no lightness in her voice as she walked past me up the steps. This was a side of Penny I hadn't seen before.

"You didn't answer my calls." People didn't ignore me. If anything, they clamored for my attention, so I wasn't quite sure what to do in the current situation.

She put her key in the lock and turned it. "I said I needed time. The world doesn't revolve around you."

Ouch! That was harsh. "I gave you time."

Penny leaned against the closed door. "It's been a few hours, Brett. When I said I needed time, I meant it."

I took the duffel bag from her shoulder. "Can we please talk?"

"Fine," she huffed, opening the door and going inside. I followed behind her and set the bag on the couch next to Fred, who let out a big yawn, showing me all his teeth. Penny scooped him into her arms and held him against her chest protectively. "What do you want to talk about?"

"Us."

She scoffed. "I wasn't aware there was an us. We're just *kind of* seeing each other. It's casual, right?"

Repeating my words back to me stung. This was going nowhere. "You're mad," I accused.

Fred jumped out of her arms when the feeder went off, leaving a fluff of fur in his wake. Penny ignored the hair floating around her face and crossed her arms. "I'm not mad. I'm disappointed, not in you, but in myself. I should have never had sex with you. I can't do casual."

I stepped toward her and ran my thumb along her jaw. "What makes you think this is casual?"

"How would you feel if, after the greatest sex of your life, some guy showed up at my door and propositioned me?"

The picture she painted was infuriating, but I focused on the important part. "It was great sex, wasn't it?"

She pushed me away with a hand on my chest. "It was, but you're missing the point. This morning, when Amanda showed up, I felt as insignificant as a gnat. Like a floozy you brought home and were done with." With a finger pointed at her chest, she continued, "I'm not that girl. I can't have sex with you knowing it didn't mean anything to you."

I clasped my hands around her cheeks and bent down to look into her green eyes. "It meant something to me. I told you I don't let women spend the night and I certainly don't make them breakfast. As a matter of fact, that was the first time I've ever made a woman breakfast in my life. I should have handled the situation with Amanda better, but I'll fix it."

144

Her lips turned down into a pout. "I don't want to feel like a cheap whore."

"You're the furthest thing from it. I'm sorry if that's how I made you feel." I pressed a kiss to her forehead. "What can I do to make it better?"

"Promise not to sleep with other women while you're *kind of* seeing me. I'm not expecting any promises of a future, just monogamy."

The thought should have scared me to death, but it didn't. Since I'd taken Penny to dinner at the French restaurant, I hadn't had the urge to see anyone else. "Done."

"Thank you," she said, pulling my hands from her cheeks and holding them in hers. "I'm sorry I ran out on you this morning."

"I'm sorry I made you feel like you had to." I slid my hands over her hips and under her ass, lifting her up.

Penny's legs immediately locked around me like a koala as she hung on to my shoulders. "I'm too heavy for you to hold like this," she whispered.

"You're not," I said as I carried her to the couch. She tried to crawl away, but I planted my hands firmly on her thighs to keep her on my lap. "You owe me some time. You teased me by wearing my shirt with no panties. You didn't think I'd notice, but I did. Do you think that was very nice?"

Her body stiffened beneath my palms. "I wasn't trying to tease you."

"Yet you did. I went all day with a stiff cock because you denied me your pussy."

A beautiful shade of pink blossomed at her neck and rose into her cheeks. "I'm... sorry?"

"You should be. Arms up." Penny raised her arms above her head, sticking her tits out. I reached for the hem of her shirt and pulled it up her body, revealing one inch of flesh at a time, the softness of her skin stirring my cock. Her tits were tucked away beneath a sports bra that barely kept them contained. I ran the backs of my fingers over her hard nipples as I continued to pull the material of the shirt up and off her body.

Her tongue came out to wet her lip before she pulled it between her teeth. She had no idea how sexy she was, looking all innocent when she was a dirty girl beneath the facade. This was a side of her others didn't get to

145

see. It felt special... only for me. I couldn't wait to see what other filthy things she would let me do to her.

"Are you going to kiss me?"

God, that breathy voice killed me every time. I pulled her mouth to mine and devoured her lips. Our tongues tangled, twisting together in heated passion. My fingers wove into the hair at the base of her scalp. I gave it a gentle pull and angled her head back, exposing the column of her throat, and nipped down her neck to the tops of her abundant breasts. Kissing along the edge of her bra, I eased the fabric down bit by bit.

She leaned back and brushed my hands away. "Nuh-uh. I'm not getting naked before you." Her dainty fingers grasped the bottom of my shirt and pulled. I grabbed the T-shirt by the back of the collar, whipping it over my head. "Damn... you're hot. Let's go to the bedroom."

I chuckled. "Somebody's impatient."

"It's your fault. You and your dirty mouth," she said, rocking her center against my cock.

I watched her as she shamelessly sought her own pleasure by rubbing her clit on me. Fuck, it turned me on, but I wouldn't let her steal an orgasm when the one I could give her would be so much better. "Do you want to come, Penelope?"

"So bad," she gasped, squirming on my lap.

I gripped her hips, stopping her from rocking. "I told you before... I own your orgasms. Ask me nicely."

She pouted. "You know I really don't need your permission, right? I'm very capable of getting myself off."

And that right there was what drew me to her. The subtle defiance. The sass. The challenge. It was all very appealing.

I held her tiny wrists behind her back with one hand as I rubbed her clit through her leggings with the other, teasing her without any relief. "Oh, I'm well aware. However, when you're with me, that won't be necessary, nor will it be tolerated. The only time you'll touch this pussy is when I give you permission. You see, not only do I happen to be very talented in pleasing a woman, but I enjoy it immensely. I love the way you taste, the sounds you

146

make, and the look on your face when I've brought you to ecstasy. I will not be deprived of the experience. Understood?"

I'd done the impossible and left her speechless. Her mouth opened several times, but no words came out. Instead, she twisted her lips to the side and wiggled against my hand, trying to steal it anyway. "Oops."

If it was a game she wanted to play, then I was more than amenable and so was my dick. "And to think I thought you were a good girl when we met. But you've proven to be a very naughty one." In one quick move, I had her over my shoulder on the way to her bedroom.

"Brett, put me down," she squealed. "You're going to throw your damn back out."

That earned her a swift smack to her ass. Actually, I made it two because I was sick of hearing her degrade herself and I liked the feeling of her ass under my palm.

She gasped. "You just spanked me. Oh my word!"

I tossed her in the middle of the bed. "You were naughty, and I can't let that go without some type of repercussion." I turned on the lamp on her nightstand and grabbed her by the ankles, removing one shoe and then the other.

Penny scrambled toward the lamp to turn it off. "I'd rather keep it off."

I blocked her access to the lamp. "And I'd rather have it on. I want to fully see you when I fuck you."

She groaned. "I'd rather you not."

"Why?"

"You know why."

"I know that you're hard on yourself, and for some reason, you think I won't be attracted to you."

"It's a valid concern," she said, reaching for the light again.

The playful banter was gone. With just a few sentences, we were deep into serious territory. Never had I been with a woman so reluctant to strip her clothes off for me. I reached for her hand. "Come here." I pulled her off the bed and over to the full-length mirror. "Tell me what you see."

She turned her head away from the reflection. "I don't want to do this. You should leave."

147

I stood behind her and rested my chin on the top of her head while holding her hips. "I'm not leaving. Not until you see yourself the way I do."

"Fine. My boobs are big, but they're not exactly perky." She pulled on the straps of the sports bra to lift them a little, then she poked her exposed stomach. "This is soft and squishy. No matter if I work out or not, it'll always be squishy." She ran her hands over her butt and thighs. "My ass is huge, and my legs are no better. To make matters worse, I'm short, so I look stumpy. I've been trying to lose weight, but it's a slow process. I wear the Spanx because they suck everything in."

It was sad the way she berated herself. "You know what I see? I see a woman with curves other women would kill for and that turns me on." My hands ran up and down her body. "A woman who's worked hard to be independent and make a life for herself. A woman who cares for her family so much that after she's done with her own work, she goes to her family's business and puts in time there. A woman with a big heart who adopted a surly cat and gave him a loving home. A woman who made me stop to think about if I was really happy or not. The answer was no, but in the last few weeks I've been happy. And that's all because of you." I kissed her on the temple. "You can still try to lose weight, but do it for you, not because you think I find you unattractive."

Her eyes filled with unshed tears. "I don't know what to say."

"Say you'll let me see you and make you feel as beautiful as you are." I slipped off my shoes and kicked them to the side, then undid my pants and pushed them down my hips.

"What are you doing?" she whispered as the first tear fell.

"I'm going first." I wasn't ashamed of my body, not in the light or the dark or even the company of a third person. I intended to leave my briefs on, but they went too. If I expected her to be vulnerable, then I had to make myself completely vulnerable too. This wasn't one-sided.

I turned her around to face me, my cock hanging between us. Given the circumstances, it wasn't time to play yet, but I knew once I got her naked, he'd spring back to life. "It's your turn." My fingers slipped inside the elastic at her waist, and I began sliding the pants down her legs. Once they were

148

removed, I peppered kisses up each thigh. I was on my knees for her. "Was that so bad?"

Another tear fell as she stood there in lacy panties and a sports bra, with her nipples in hard points. She sucked in her stomach. "I have cellulite."

I put a finger to her lips. "Most women do, even those who have sticks for legs. It doesn't make you any less beautiful. I like a woman who is soft and curvy."

Penny covered her mouth as her lips turned up and another tear fell. "Then I guess I'm your girl."

"Yes, you are." I inched her panties down her legs and placed an open-mouth kiss on her bare pussy. My tongue made a pass through her slit. One taste was all I allowed myself before standing and removing the last bit of clothing that kept all of her from me.

I gently turned her to face the mirror again and wiped her tears. With one hand clutched around her throat, I forced her head back and devoured her mouth. My other hand traced over her nipples and then crept down her stomach and between her legs. When my fingers entered her pussy, she let out a moan that I swallowed with my own. Her body went from rigid to soft and pliant. I forced her to look in the mirror, my eyes connecting to hers. "Look at us. You can't tell me we don't look sexy." I nudged my now fully erect cock into her lower back. "Do you feel what you do to me? That's all because of you."

"I look sexy with you."

"Because you are." With a gentle squeeze of her throat, I directed her lips back to mine. I'd been starving for her all day and now that I'd seen every inch of her skin in the light, I wanted her even more.

She twisted in my arms and stared up at me. "Make me come, Brett. I want it so bad."

My cock twitched at the thought of tasting her again. Backing her up to lie on the bed, I hovered over the top of her. "You won't regret this." Last night had been more lust fueled than anything. Today was something different. I wasn't sure what, but it was definitely different. I felt the need to worship her. To let her know her body was perfect the way it was. For her to see herself the way I saw her.

Was she curvier than other women I'd dated? Absolutely. Yet those women only held my attention for a night or two.

With Penny, it was more. Much, much more.

Chapter 21
Penny

My back arched off the mattress and a scream tore from my throat as he hit that magic spot inside me. White lights flashed behind my eyelids and my body pulsed.

"Not yet." Brett flipped me over. With an arm around my waist, he hiked me up on my knees so I was up on all fours. Soft kisses cascaded down my spine. "You look amazing like this. Your tits hanging down and your pussy on display."

He began playing with my clit as his dick slipped back inside me, deeper than before. His fingers dug into my hip, and I was sure I'd have bruises in the morning. Little reminders that tonight was not a dream. My body could barely keep up with the fast and furious pace.

I fell to my elbows and my head dropped between my arms, resting against the sheets. He thrummed my clit like it was a high-end instrument and my body sang. My walls began to clench as the stirrings of another orgasm threatened to tear me apart. The pressure built to unbearable *proportions. It was almost painful, but I knew, on the other side, it would be sweet bliss.*

"Come for me, Penny. I want to feel your pussy squeeze my cock."

He thrust into me harder and pinched my clit. The orgasm hit me like a tsunami and...

"You're spacing out again." Gia snapped her fingers in front of my face.

"I'm sorry... what?" I squirmed on the chair. It might have been a daydream, but the throbbing between my legs was very real.

"I was asking about the letters for the silent auction."

"They're done and sent," I said, trying to focus. Reliving last night in Technicolor while sitting across from my boss wasn't ideal. I'd never been horny at work before, so the fact that I'd been caught daydreaming was a bit embarrassing.

Gia's eyebrows scrunched together. "Are you feeling alright? Your cheeks are all flushed, and you're totally distracted."

I shrugged out of my blazer. "It's hot in here, is all. Aren't you hot?"

"Penny, it's not hot in here. The air conditioning has been blasting. If anything, it's cold." She got up from her desk and sat in the chair next to me, placing her hand on my forehead. "Maybe you should go home early and get some rest."

"I had sex with Brett," I blurted, immediately slapping my hands over my mouth. If I was embarrassed before, now I was horrified. It was one thing to think dirty thoughts at work. It was completely another to let your boss know about it.

Gia's eyes bulged and her lips formed a little *o*.

Panicked, I waved my hands in front of her face in an erasing motion. "Forget I said that. Dammit, where's that little *Men in Black* device when you need it?"

Gia grabbed my flailing arms and set them on my lap. "He made you forget your own name, didn't he?" she asked with a smirk.

"Yeah." I sighed dreamily. "How'd you know?"

"Oh... umm... just look at him. A man that looks like Brett surely knows what he's doing in the bedroom. I mean, I've only met him once...

no, twice... I ran into him in Trent's office... but my guess is the sex would be good."

"It was. It really, really was. Do you think I'm setting myself up for heartbreak?"

She shook her head. "I don't think so. How many times have you two gone out?"

I counted on my fingers. "There was the lunch meeting, although I'm not sure that counts as a date. Then he took me to Le Coucou. I took him bowling, but that probably doesn't count either. Saturday night, he took me to a work function and then we got tacos and then...well, you know the rest." I held up four fingers. "Maybe four. Plus, he calls or texts me almost every night. That means something, right?"

"It definitely means something," she said with a smile. "I've got a good feeling about you two. Maybe he'll take you to the fundraiser and you won't need the tickets I was going to try to squeeze out of Trent for us to go to this fancy affair. I mean, we're doing all the planning. Shouldn't we automatically be invited?"

Gia and I worked our asses off planning the masquerade ball to benefit domestic violence. The New Orleans-themed event was going to be the best fundraiser Mystique had ever thrown. We'd commiserated on how neither of us could afford the tickets at five thousand dollars apiece. "It's a couple weeks away. I'm not holding my breath. Besides, I wouldn't even have anything to wear."

"Clothes are hardly an issue when you're dating a millionaire."

"Billionaire," I corrected.

"Well damn, girl. Then clothes definitely won't be an issue. Maybe he'll buy you designer shoes too." Gia twisted her foot in the air. "Wish I could afford real ones instead of these knockoffs."

I rolled my eyes. "Your shoes always look great." I tapped my fingers on the arm of the chair. "Speaking of Trent..."

"We weren't," Gia huffed.

The two of them were like oil and water. Trent wore a scowl as if someone pissed in his Cheerios every morning. Gia challenged and goaded him every chance she got. None of the bosses I had before her ever had the guts to stand up to him. "Have you two agreed on the food for the fundraiser?"

Gia flipped her hair over her shoulder. "He agreed to our original menu with a minor *modification*." The word stuck in her throat like it pained her to say it. "No chocolate fountain at the dessert bar."

"Booo! He's no fun, but I guess we should be happy he approved the rest of it."

"He approved it because what we picked is classy and delicious. The 'no chocolate fountain' was his way of getting in a dig. He wouldn't want me to think I have too much control being… you know… the event coordinator."

"Director of entertainment and events," I corrected. Trent shocked us both by giving Gia a fancy new title.

"Whatever. It's the same job."

"Regardless, he seems to be a lot less grouchy lately. Maybe he likes you," I said, waggling my eyebrows.

"Pfft! He definitely doesn't like me. We're just more cordial now. He's probably less grouchy because Hunter's been sent to Albuquerque. I mean, you've heard them fight."

I had. The whole office had. Trent's brother, Hunter, always seemed to be creeping around, sneaking up on you when you least expected it. I was glad when I heard he'd been transferred to a different hotel, even if it was temporary. "Well, whatever it is, he's been much more tolerable lately."

"That's good for both of us," she said dismissively.

I supposed it was.

Tom came over to my desk, carrying a stack of envelopes. He wore his signature bow tie and black-rimmed glasses. The Clark Kent image made me wonder if, under his buttoned-up exterior, he might be like Superman. Take off the sweater-vest, tie, and glasses and he'd be hot. I mean, he was already cute in a nerdy sort of way. Not that I was interested, just intrigued. I already had my own personal superhero whose power was the ability to give me multiple orgasms within minutes. A girl couldn't ask for much more than that.

Even though Tom and I were both personal assistants, we'd never had much reason to interact until Trent assigned him to help me with the fundraiser. Tom would always say hi to me in the break room, but that was about it.

"Hi, Penny. I brought you some of the RSVPs that started rolling in. Figured you were putting them into a spreadsheet." He neatly stacked them on the empty corner of my desk and pushed his glasses up his nose.

"You guessed right." I smiled up at him, clicking open the document on my computer.

"Whoa! That's a serious data bank," Tom said as he leaned over my shoulder to get a better look. "Is it weird that it turns me on a little?"

I laughed. "Totally weird, but I get it." The spreadsheet was color coded with about a dozen columns containing every bit of information we might need about each guest. "Organization is my thing. It's a lot of work up front, but it saves me a ton of time down the road."

"You're preaching to the choir," he said. "To keep up with Trent's demands, I need to be on top of everything. When he snaps his fingers, it means he wanted it done yesterday." Tom stuck his hands in his pockets and rocked back on his heels. "So... you're dating Brett Kingston?"

My neck nearly snapped with how hard it spun to stare him down. "What?" The only people I'd told were Gia and Bea. My mom knew too, but I hardly thought she'd blab. For the most part, I kept our relationship private because, deep down, I had no idea how long it would last. Breakups were bad, but being broken up with by a billionaire was a whole other level of bad.

He grimaced. "Is it true?"

I yanked him by the arm, nearly knocking the poor guy off balance, and pulled him closer to me so no one else would overhear. "Yes, but I haven't exactly advertised it."

Tom let out a long breath. "I hate to tell you this, but it's public information now."

"What do you mean?" Was there gossip going around the office? Were people talking about me behind my back? Who here would even know?

Tom pulled his phone out of his pocket and showed me the latest article in the *Las Vegas Not So Confidential*. "I'm sorry," he said before I grabbed it from his hand and began to read.

Who's That Girl?

Sad news today for the single women of Las Vegas. It seems our local billionaire bachelor, Brett Kingston, has broken his no-second-date rule for one lucky lady. Over the past couple weeks, we've caught him with the same brunette on more than one occasion.

There's just one burning question. Who's that girl?

One thing is for sure, she doesn't fit the mold of the other women Brett Kingston has been seen with. You won't find her walking a runway or gracing the cover of the latest fashion magazine. Perhaps modelesque females are not his cup of tea after all.

It leaves one to wonder... how long will this affair last? Is she another one of Mr. Kingston's playthings, or is she perhaps the future Mrs. Kingston? Only time will tell.

Never fear... we'll be watching to see where this goes. And if anyone can identify this mystery woman, let us know. We love gossip that's not so confidential.

What. The actual. Fuck!

I may not have been named in the article, but that sure as shit was my face in the pictures. Yes, pictures... as in multiple. One from Le Coucou. Another from the bowling alley. And a third from the work function I'd attended with Brett. In all honesty, not that I was thrilled my picture ended up in some gossip rag, but that picture was my favorite. Brett was ushering me into the back of the limo and the look on his face was pure lust. Any woman would give her last dime to be looked at like that.

But again, what the actual fuck? Me—Penny Quinn, personal assistant, a virtual nobody—was in the *Las Vegas Not So Confidential*. Not only was I in the article, but I'd been cast in a less-than-flattering light.

I felt exposed. All my flaws were right there on the page for everybody to see. *Doesn't fit the mold*… no crap. I knew my insecurities weren't in my head. I knew it, I knew it, I knew it. Now all of Vegas did too.

"You look like you're going to pass out," Tom said as he took his phone back.

"I might." Pushing away from my desk, I fought the urge to throw up on my way to the ladies' room. Cold water, a paper bag, and about a dozen Xanax. That's what I needed. Once safely tucked inside the bathroom, I let out a scream and banged my fists on the counter.

How could this have happened?

The old adage, *be careful what you wish for,* rang through my head. I'd wanted to be with Brett so badly I'd never stopped to think about what dating a billionaire entailed. I was now fair game.

The bathroom door creaked open, and Tom stuck his head inside. "Are you okay?"

I stared at myself in the mirror while letting out measured breaths. *Was I okay?*

Yep. Nope. Maybe?

Tom crept into the bathroom and shut the door behind him. "It's not as bad as you think."

"Really? Because it seems really fucking bad."

"Nobody even reads this stuff."

"You read it."

"Fair point," he said, pushing his glasses up again. "They're good pictures and at least they haven't put a name with your face yet. It's still kind of anonymous."

157

"And how long do you think it'll take them? I'm sure there's someone willing to make a buck by handing over my name. Maybe even somebody from this office." I pressed my palms into my eye sockets to stop the tears that threatened to fall. "They called me fat and ugly."

"Whoa! It did not say that."

I threw my arms into the air in frustration. "It didn't have to. Read between the lines, Tom."

He wrapped his arms around my shoulders and gave me a hug. "You're reading too much into it. Nobody in their right mind would ever call you fat or ugly. You're actually pretty damn adorable." Tom rubbed his hands up and down my back. "Don't worry. By tomorrow some Hollywood fuckboy will be caught pissing in a plant in one of the casinos and no one will even remember today's article. That's the thing about gossip. There's always a bigger, better story waiting to be told."

I pressed my head into his chest. "You think?"

"I'm positive," he said, giving me one last hug before letting me go. He hitched a thumb over his shoulder toward the door. "I should... um... probably get out of the ladies' room."

"Probably." I snuffed a very unladylike snuff. "Hey, Tom... thanks for being my friend today."

"I'm always your friend, Penny. Not just today. If you ever need me, I'll be here." And then he slipped out the door.

I'd never thought of Tom as a friend before. He was just a guy I worked with, someone I ran into when getting coffee, but today I was thankful for his friendship.

The thing that bothered me was why I found out about the article from Tom. Why hadn't Brett told me?

Maybe he didn't know about it.

Chapter 22
Brett

"Goddammit!" I yelled as I slammed the phone down.

I'd been in damage-control mode all morning. My team of lawyers couldn't find any legal grounds for having the article taken down from the website. Not that it mattered. Half of Vegas probably already read it, including Penny.

If she had, I could guarantee she was losing her shit.

I should have called and warned her, but I was hoping I could get the article erased before she ever saw it.

When my Google alert went off first thing this morning, I expected it to be about Kingston Enterprises or one of our holdings.

Never did I think they would go after Penny. Maybe I should have, but I didn't.

"Maryanne!" I barked.

She was at my door in less than five seconds. "Yes?"

"I need you to get," I looked at my computer screen, "Karla Blitzer on the phone."

"The writer from *Las Vegas Not So Confidential*?" she asked nervously.

"That's the one. I want to know who her boss is and her boss's boss. Every fucking contact you can get, I want it!" I shouldn't have been taking my frustration out on her. It wasn't Maryanne's fault the damn article was written.

"Brett?"

"What?" I barked.

She came in and shut the door. "I know you're mad, and rightfully so. However, you need to calm down before you attempt to talk to this woman. She's in the market for gossip and if you lose your cool, you'll give her more to write about. You need to charm her."

"You're right. I know you're right." I ran my hands through my hair and tugged on the ends. "It just pisses me off. Penny doesn't deserve this shit."

"I agree, but you'll get more with sugar than with salt. Be nice."

"I'm always nice," I growled.

Maryanne laughed. "Most of the time. You need to think of this as a business deal, not a personal attack. Negotiate with her."

I pounded my fist on my desk like an idiot. "I don't negotiate with terrorists."

"She's hardly a terrorist. She's a gossip columnist. Offer her something she can't get anywhere else."

I threw my hands in the air. "And what would that be?"

"I don't know. Get creative."

It wasn't a half-bad idea. "Fine."

Five minutes later, I had the wench on the phone. "Hello, Ms. Blitzer."

"Mr. Kingston, to what do I owe the pleasure?"

"Oh, don't be coy, Karla. I'm sure you have an inkling as to why I'm contacting you." The syrup in my own voice gagged me. If Maryanne insisted on sugar, I was going to lay it on thick in hopes of giving Ms. Blitzer a cavity.

She hummed on the other end of the line. "I didn't realize we were on a first-name basis. Yes, I do have an inkling, but you know what they say about assuming things. That would make me a very bad journalist and I wouldn't want to get the facts wrong."

160

Inside, I fumed. Journalist was a stretch. She cared about facts as much as I cared about the mating habits of pigeons. Not one flying fuck given. "Since you've taken it upon yourself to write about my sex life, I'd say that has earned me first-name privileges. I read your article this morning."

"Well, *I* feel privileged that a billionaire is among our loyal readers, *Brett*." She spat out my name like it felt foul on her tongue.

She was irritated with *me*? The woman had some balls that was for sure. "I have a vested interest in what people are saying about me. You can write whatever you like about me. However, when you attack someone I'm dating, then you've gone too far."

"So you're confirming that you and the mystery woman are in a relationship?"

I ground my molars. The last thing I wanted to do was give Karla Blitzer more fodder for her column. "I'm not confirming or denying anything."

"Hmmm. Then I guess I'll have to keep digging."

The woman was relentless. "She's off-limits," I snapped. "What you wrote was borderline nasty and I won't tolerate you disrespecting her in that way! If you don't have something nice to say, then don't say anything at all."

"Even you have to admit she's not your normal type. Inquiring minds want to know the scoop and I won't stop until I've appeased my readers. You can't blame a girl for doing her job."

"I'm warning you… keep her out of it!" *Was I threatening her now? How low had I sunken?*

Karla's nails tapped away in the background. "You're in love with her," she said as if it were the most obvious thing in the world.

Love? I hadn't been in love since high school. Love led to heartbreak. What I had with Penny was different. Love wasn't even on my radar. "I care about her. That's all. End of story."

She tsked me. "Oh, Mr. Kingston, something tells me that isn't the end of the story at all."

Be charming and negotiate. Remembering Maryanne's words, I sighed. "What do you want, Karla?"

"What every woman wants… all the juicy details. If you want me to stop writing about the woman you *care* about, then you'll have to give me something bigger and better. And before you whip out your checkbook, I don't want your money. You can't buy me. It would be totally unethical."

I growled. Now she was worried about ethics? I went into this negotiation totally unprepared. Usually, money was my biggest bargaining chip. What else could I possibly offer that would be of value to her?

"I'm waiting, Mr. Kingston."

"What about two tickets to Mystique's Unmask Domestic Violence fundraiser? It'll be the Who's Who of the year. Surely you can do something with that." Trent was going to kill me for inviting a reporter to the fundraiser, but he'd have to get over it. "Two tickets are worth ten grand. It's a generous offer," I added, hoping she'd take the bait.

Karla hummed. "It is the biggest ticket in town right now," she said as she mulled it over. "Perhaps there may be some useful tidbits of information there, but to be clear, this doesn't let you off the hook. I'm still going to follow you around and I'm still going to write a story if I find anything interesting. However, I will temper my words regarding your new lady friend."

"That's all I ask." Not quite true, but when negotiating with a woman like Ms. Blitzer, you took what you could get.

"Is there anything else I should know? Anything you'd like to share with my readers, like what the mystery woman's name is?"

I assured her of two tickets to the biggest event of the year, and she still pushed. "I'm not going to do your job for you, Karla. Do your research, but if I read one word that is less than flattering, my next offer won't be so generous. Trust me when I say my resources outweigh yours. Enjoy the fundraiser." I hung up the phone before I said anything I might regret.

I was dangerously close to threatening her livelihood, and for all I knew, she was taping our conversation. Seemed like something a gossip columnist would do and the last thing I needed was bad press, especially with the board watching my every move.

Which reminded me I had real work to do. The mall project was waiting for my approval. If all went well, I'd never have to prove myself again.

Maryanne poked her head in my office. "Miss Quinn is on the phone."

Penny had called my personal phone several times, and like a coward, I let them go to voice mail. I didn't know how to break the news to her about the article in the *Las Vegas Not So Confidential*. It was going to crush her already fragile self-esteem.

There was only one explanation as to why she'd call the office.

She knew about the article.

"Go ahead and put her through." When the phone rang, I took a deep breath and picked it up. "Hey, Penny."

She sniffed on the other end. "Brett... did you see it? The article?"

"I did, babe."

"Why? Why would they write that about me? They called me fat and ugly."

It was worse than I anticipated. Saying she wouldn't be a runway or cover model was rude and uncalled for, but it hit Penny way harder. "Hey, now... that's not what it said. Besides, those are great pictures of us."

"No, they're good pictures of *you*. I look... chubby."

I knew she would say that. She was so damn hard on herself. I was hoping I'd put her worries to rest, but the article reinforced everything she already believed about herself. "Penelope Quinn, you stop that right now. You're a beautiful woman, don't let anyone make you feel otherwise. I'm sorry about the article, but there's not much I can do about it. Trust me, I tried. After the last article they wrote about me, I should have foreseen this. I guess I never thought they'd stoop so low as to drag you through the mud with me."

"I'm so embarrassed," she whispered.

I tried to put a different spin on it. "You shouldn't be embarrassed. Do you know how many women are jealous of you right now? You've caught the billionaire."

She giggled and then snuffed again. "I guess I have, haven't I?"

"Listen… people suck. There's no way around it. If you have something other people want, they're going to try to tear you down. I wasn't exactly thrilled with the first article written about me, but what could I do? I'm somewhat of a public figure, so I guess I'm fair game."

"And now I am too."

"In a way, yes. You can't let what other people say define you. I'll protect you the best I can, but I can't guarantee no one will ever write about you or take your picture." My deal with Karla was fragile at best. She was a rabid dog who wouldn't be satisfied until she got what she wanted. I hoped ten thousand dollars would persuade her to treat Penny with some decency. It was a gamble.

"I know and I'm not blaming you. It took me by surprise, is all. I'm used to fading into the background and I'm comfortable there."

That was sad. A woman like Penny should never fade into the background. She was born to stand in the light where the world could see her vibrancy. "I don't believe that. From the first moment I met you, I was captivated. You're beautiful and smart and witty. Fuck anybody who says otherwise."

"Thank you," she said. "I needed to hear that today."

"It's the truth." And I meant it. Penny brought back feelings in me I never thought I'd feel again. I hadn't allowed myself to feel it because it felt like a betrayal.

But maybe, just maybe, Karla was right.

I didn't just care about Penelope Quinn.

Maybe I loved her.

Chapter 23
Penny

Brett made me feel a minuscule better, but I couldn't get the words from the awful article out of my head.

One thing is for sure, she doesn't fit the mold of the other women Brett Kingston has been seen with. You wouldn't find her walking along a runway or gracing the cover of the latest fashion magazine. Perhaps modelesque females are not his cup of tea after all.

And the pictures… weren't *that* bad. I mean, I did look happy. Happy yet still chubby.

I'd lost twelve pounds, but it wasn't enough. Every time I stepped on the scale, I covered my eyes, afraid gaining even one pound back would send me into a tailspin.

Brett said if I wanted to lose weight, I should be doing it for me, not for him or anyone else.

It sounded good in theory.

But that theory didn't hold true when my picture was spread across the internet for the world to see. Or when my sister, Loretta, scowled at me for not fitting into the dress for her wedding.

My weight issues weren't all in my head. There was proof that couldn't be denied. Reminders of my unhealthy relationship with food. Evidence that I'd been complacent my entire life.

If I was going to be photographed with Brett, there was no way I'd embarrass him by being the woman people talked about behind his back.

I'd do what I had to do to lose the weight.

"Hi, sweetie." My dad kissed my forehead. "Everything looks great. Thank you for organizing this."

I hugged my dad. "You're more than welcome. I hope it helps." I'd spent every night this week stopping into the bookstore to assure it was ready for the Reading is Magic event. We were stocked to the hilt with books and merchandise, and my mom had the café overflowing with sweet treats. Even though Mind Bender was a great draw, I still worried that people wouldn't show up. That all of this would be for nothing. That we'd lose more money than we made.

"It will," he said as he walked over to straighten some books on the shelf.

My mom sidled up to me and bumped my hip with hers. "I saw the pictures of you and your hunky new boyfriend."

"Ugh! Has everyone seen them?" It wouldn't take long until my name was splashed across the *Las Vegas Not So Confidential* too. Once that happened, I'd be mortified. I mean, what if the next picture was of me stuffing my mouth with nachos? I couldn't even imagine what they'd write about that.

"They're good pictures," my mom insisted. "The two of you are quite cute together. Are you going to invite him to the wedding?"

I pushed my hair behind my ear. "I already did, but honestly, Mom, we might not even be together by then. We haven't put a label on our relationship."

"But he's your boyfriend, right?"

I cringed. "Do you call a thirty-two-year-old man a boyfriend? It sounds childish." There were so many differences between Brett and me, and age was one of them. He was more mature, more polished. He'd handled the article about us as if it didn't bother him at all. I, on the other hand, had a major freak-out in the ladies' room.

"What would you like me to call him then? Your man friend?"

That sounded even worse. "I don't know. How about you just call him Brett?"

"Who's Brett?" my dad piped in.

"Penny's boyfriend. Or man friend. What are we calling him?"

"Brett. That's all." I made a slashing motion with my hand. Good Lord! If this is what having a boyfriend was like, maybe I'd dodged a bullet all these years.

"Is he coming to our event today?" my dad asked, hanging his arm over my shoulder. "I'd like to meet him and make sure he's suitable for my little girl."

"He drives a Ferrari," my mom whispered as if that was the most important detail about him.

I squirmed away from the both of them. "He's perfectly suitable and no, he won't be here. He's got a business meeting in San Jose, so I won't see him until tonight."

My mom whipped out her phone. "Want to see a picture of him?"

"Of course," my dad said as he leaned over her shoulder.

The bell over the door jangled and in walked Bea and Loretta. It was all hands on deck today. "Oh, thank goodness. Mom and Dad are making me crazy over Brett."

Bea pulled me in for a hug. "They're excited. Let them have their moment."

"Of course, they're excited." Loretta frowned, clearly wanting to be anywhere but here. She never loved the store like the rest of us. "It's the first guy you've ever dated. We were starting to worry you were going to become a crazy cat lady."

Guess she didn't count my prom date as a boyfriend. In all fairness, it only lasted two weeks. "What?"

"I wasn't worried," Bea interjected. "I knew some man would fall madly in love with you."

"I wouldn't say he's in love with me." Yeah, it was a little early for that kind of declaration.

"He will be. Just give it time." Bea held my hands while jumping up and down. "I'm so excited for you."

"I'm just happy you have a date for the wedding. It would be lame for my maid of honor to show up solo." Loretta picked up a children's magic kit and pretended to read the back of it. "How's the diet coming, by the way?"

I took the box out of her hand and placed it back on the display. "It's going well."

"I hope so. The next fitting is coming up soon. I pray it's not too late to order you a bigger dress."

I loved my sister and was honored when she asked me to be in her wedding, but I was starting to regret being a part of it. My whole life, I stood in her shadow. The sister of the cheerleading captain and Homecoming queen. No one ever paid attention to me because they were too busy fawning over her. "Don't worry about the dress. It'll fit," I said through gritted teeth.

"Good, because I don't want you looking like a stuffed sausage in all my wedding photos."

"Stop it, Loretta," Bea scolded, getting in her face. "You're being a bitch. Penny's been working really hard. Maybe instead of insulting her every chance you get and being a complete bridezilla, you could show a shred of humanity and be a supportive sister."

"I'm not supportive? That's a crock of crap..."

I cut them off before it turned into a full-blown war in the middle of the bookstore. With a hand on each of their chests, I squeezed between my sisters and pushed them apart. "It's fine. It's all good. Bea, I appreciate you defending me. And, Loretta, I'll fit in the dress. I wouldn't do anything to sabotage your wedding."

"Fine."

"Whatever."

They headed in opposite directions, and hopefully, that was the end of it. I hated being the cause of their arguing. When we were little, the three of us never fought. Somewhere in our teens, Loretta pulled away from us. Well, mostly she pulled away from me, which caused friction between her and Bea. I think I embarrassed Loretta by being more interested in books than boys.

It wasn't that I wasn't interested in boys. They weren't interested in me. Eventually, I realized the fictional men in my books would never let me down or judge me, unlike the real ones. I gave up on dating and put all my energy into my studies, praying one day I wouldn't need a man to validate me.

It worked for the most part, but I'd be lying if I said the praise Brett showered me with didn't make my toes tingle and my heart flutter. As much as I wanted to be independent, it was comforting to have someone who saw you for who you were and not what they wanted you to be. I felt that with Brett.

As it got closer to the time of Mind Bender's arrival, the store filled with customers. Loretta and my dad ran the registers. Mom managed the café. Bea and I helped on the store floor, assisting people in finding what they wanted. It was nice seeing us all work together toward a common goal, saving the bookstore, even if my sisters were clueless about how dire the situation had become.

Right at noon, Mind Bender walked through the front door wearing a pair of ripped-up jeans, a white T-shirt, and a black leather jacket. He looked as if he'd just rolled out of bed, his hair sticking up in every direction. There was a coolness about him as if he barely noticed the crowd that followed him into the store.

"Who's ready to get their mind bent?" he shouted.

And so it began.

Chapter 24
Brett

"You should have seen their faces. When he pulled that baby chick out of the lady's purse, I thought she was going to fall over. I mean, we all watched her dump everything out on the counter, and he showed us it was empty. How in the world do you think he got that chick in her purse? It was amazing, I'm telling you."

I'd gotten home later than I had planned from my meeting and offered to take Penny out, but she wanted to stay in. Honestly, I think she was worried about getting her picture taken again. It was reasonable, especially after I challenged Karla to do her research.

That's how we wound up sitting on Penny's couch eating Chinese food from take-out containers, her feet resting on my lap as she leaned back against the arm of the sofa. "I'm sorry I missed it."

She waved her chopsticks at me. "No worries. You have more important things to do than to watch one of your old classmates do magic, but you did miss out. He had this lady randomly select a book off the shelf without him seeing it, and then he read her mind and told her exactly what book it was.

Do you know how many books we have in the store? Thousands. I mean, what are the chances he'd know she picked *Great Expectations*? That book isn't even on anybody's radar. And then," she took a bite of her kung pao chicken and continued, "and then he took this guy's wedding ring and made it disappear. The guy was totally freaking out. But do you know where he found it?" I shook my head. "In the middle of a cheese Danish. That's where. How in the hell did he get the ring in a cheese Danish? Amazing. Absolutely amazing! Mind blown. Or maybe I should say bent. Yes, definitely mind bent."

Her enthusiasm was worth every dime I spent getting him there. When I called Wally, his response was, "Since we're friends, Mind Bender will do it for five grand." I didn't hesitate to send him the money that day. Seeing the look on Penny's face as she told me about his performance... I would have paid ten. No questions asked. "I'm glad it worked out. How did the sales go?"

Penny stuck her chopsticks into the cardboard box and set it on the coffee table. "That's the best part. We quadrupled what we usually make in a whole weekend. My mom's going to start having a story hour for kids on Saturday mornings and I've already lined up a couple of book signings with local authors. But if we can host events like today on a monthly basis, it'll help big time. They won't be exactly like today because he's freakin' Mind Bender, but I'll think of something."

"I'm proud of you," I said, putting my food on the table next to Penny's. "You've been working really hard to help your parents."

"It's their livelihood. I can't sit by and let Between the Covers Café fail. If I didn't do everything I could to help, I'd never forgive myself."

I picked up her foot from my lap and rubbed my thumb into the arch. "You're a good daughter."

"I'm trying," she said as she let out a moan. "You have no idea how good that feels."

"You worked hard today. You deserve it," I said, switching feet.

"I didn't work that hard, but please keep rubbing." She wiggled her toes. "How was your meeting in San Jose?"

"Good for me, good for them. It was a win-win."

"Tell me about it." Penny relaxed back on the couch and closed her eyes. "What kind of deal was it?"

"A small tech company. They're developing great stuff but were almost bankrupt. It has potential, so I bought the company."

She opened her eyes and stared at me. "Just like that? You bought a company today?"

I shrugged. "It's what I do."

"Wow! What about the mall project? Have you decided on that yet?"

"I signed the paperwork yesterday." I'd never dated a woman who cared about what I did or asked me how my day was. It was nice to share a part of my world with someone outside the office. I imagined what our lives would be like if we continued this relationship, talking about our days over breakfast or dinner. My parents were like that. No matter what was going on around them, they made time for one another. It wasn't always business; they had a lot of fun too. My dad never stopped dating my mom. He'd always do little things for her, like buying flowers or planning a getaway, to let her know she was his number one priority. Their marriage was as close to perfect as you could get. It made me want to be a better man for Penny. I wanted to treat her right.

She crawled onto my lap and wrapped her arms around my neck. "I'm proud of you, and your dad would be too."

I rubbed my hands up and down her sides. "I hope so. He built Kingston Enterprises from the ground up. I don't want to let him down."

"You won't," she said with a kiss on my lips. "Have you decided where the mall will be built?"

"We have several pieces of property we're looking at. Nothing has been decided for sure." Shifting gears, I twirled a lock of her hair around my finger. "About the fundraiser…"

"What about it?"

"I was wondering if you'd be my date?" It seemed like a formality at this point, but asking her properly was the right thing to do.

Her lips twisted to the side. "I didn't plan on attending."

Not what I was expecting. "Why not?"

Penny lifted her eyebrows. "I'm a PA. I don't have any business attending a five-thousand-dollar-a-plate dinner. Besides, what would I wear?"

Call it privilege, but I rarely thought about money. When you have lots of it, you don't even look at price tags anymore. Five dollars, five hundred dollars, five thousand dollars... it was all the same to me. Sometimes, I forgot to appreciate my own wealth. "You'd be my date, so you wouldn't be paying for a ticket." The fact that she thought I'd let her pay was absurd. I might not have been great at relationships, but I did know how to treat a lady right. My father taught me to be a gentleman.

She tapped her fingertips on my shoulders, contemplating my words. It should have been a no-brainer, but her wheels were spinning. "The fundraiser *is* going to be fantabulous. Gia and I have planned everything down to the very last detail. I would love to say yes, but..."

"Then say yes." It shouldn't have been this hard. I could have asked any woman off the street, and she would have said yes without hesitation.

"But... there's going to be photographers. I don't want to end up in the paper again."

Not only photographers but one very thirsty gossip columnist who I personally invited. Giving Karla those tickets was reckless. An impulsive, impetuous reaction to her threat of digging through Penny's life. I figured she'd find another target, but instead, I'd offered up my girl on a silver platter. I was expected to attend, but I wouldn't go without her. We had to spin the narrative.

"There will be photographers and probably some news outlets, so let's give them something to talk about. The more you hide, the deeper they'll dig."

"I don't have anything to wear," she whispered, tucking her chin and avoiding eye contact. "That black dress is the nicest thing I own and it's not exactly appropriate for a formal masquerade ball. I don't want to embarrass you."

I lifted her chin with my fingers and looked her in the eye. "First of all, I'd never be embarrassed to be seen with you. Secondly, you'll have the most exquisite dress of all the guests. I can promise you that. You'll walk into that fundraiser feeling like a queen."

"It's too much. I'm not a charity case."

"No, you're not. You're my girl, and nothing is too much for you."

Penny cracked a smile. "It doesn't feel real."

"What doesn't feel real?"

"You and me. That this is my life now."

The appreciation in her eyes melted me deep down inside. It'd been so long since I felt that feeling that it was foreign to my senses. A need to care for her, although she'd been doing fine taking care of herself. She was a giver, not a taker. She didn't have a selfish bone in her body. A dress was the least I could do for her. It was nothing to me, but it was everything to her. "Get used to it. I take care of what's mine."

Looking at Penny was my new favorite pastime. She sat out on the patio overlooking the city, a glass of wine in her hand and the ripples from the pool casting bands of light across her face as she sat in a lounger. Her smile was so bright the lights of Vegas didn't even compare.

After talking her into leaving Fred alone again, I convinced Penny to come over for dinner. My chef's chicken parmesan was to die for, yet she only ate half her serving. It was concerning. No matter how many times I told her to ignore that article, it was stuck in her brain. Running on repeat.

I intended to erase those nasty thoughts from her head.

I came up behind her, holding out the bottle of wine. "A bit more?"

She put her hand over her glass. "I shouldn't. I have to work in the morning."

"So do I, but a little more wine won't hurt."

"Oh, what the hell? Why not?" She held her glass out for me to top off. "You're a bad influence."

Moving her legs to the side, I sat at the bottom of the lounge chair. "I haven't even begun to corrupt you yet."

She lifted the glass to her lips. "I'm afraid to ask."

"It's better that you don't. That way, I'll get to see the look of surprise on your face."

"Are you trying to scare me?" she asked with a shiver.

"Scare you? No. Only if you're scared of having the best sex of your life."

"I thought I already did," she mumbled.

"Not even close." I took the glass from her hand and wrapped her fingers in mine. "Come in the pool with me?"

She looked down at her blouse and skirt. "I'm wearing my work clothes and I don't have a bathing suit."

I unbuttoned my shirt. "Look around. It's totally dark, and we're so high up, no one could see us if they wanted to." The shirt fell off my shoulders and dropped onto the concrete.

Penny gulped. "It is dark, but I've never... you know."

"Swam naked?" I stood, toeing off my shoes and pushing my dress pants down my legs. "It's fine. You can keep your underwear on. For now." Before she had a chance to refuse, I turned and dove into the pool in only my briefs, shaking the water from my hair as I emerged. Although the pool was a definite bonus when I bought this place, I didn't use it half as much as I should have.

Already barefoot, she stepped to the edge of the pool. "No one can see us?"

"Not a soul." That, I was sure of. Complete privacy was a must for this purchase.

She unzipped her skirt and slid it down her legs, kicking it to the side, then sat on the edge to dip her feet in. "The water's warm."

"Eighty-five degrees."

"Of course it is. Only the best for a billionaire."

My hands wrapped around her calves. "Only the best for you." I reached up and began unbuttoning her blouse. She looked around as if a photographer would jump out of the bushes. "It's safe. I promise."

175

Her throat bobbed before she said, "I trust you." Shrugging her blouse off, she leaned back on her hands and stared up at the sky. "It's so peaceful up here."

All I could do was look at her, back arched and tits pushed up. With a growl, I slipped my fingers into the sides of her panties. "Lift." She lifted her hips, and I slid the panties down her legs, placing them on the cement. "You need to get wet." Moving her round ass to the very edge of the pool, I stepped between her legs and spread them. "Hmmm. Looks like you already are."

"What are you doing?"

"Having my dessert. Lie back and relax."

Reaching for a towel from a nearby chair, she placed it under her head and lay down. I loved how she didn't fight me on every little thing anymore. A couple weeks ago, she would have balked at spreading her legs for me to see her pussy. Now she wanted it as much as I did. She'd come so far.

I placed her one foot on the edge of the pool and then the other, so her glistening, pink pussy was on full display.

She let out a whimper. "Brett…"

"Shhh. Let me." I kissed along the insides of her thighs, rubbing my beard along the sensitive skin. Tomorrow she'd remember who'd been between her legs. I'd make sure of it. I spread her lips with my thumbs and lapped at her pussy with a long stroke of my tongue. Then another. And another. She tasted so sweet, like sugar and honey melting on my tongue. All women had a unique taste and smell. I loved eating a woman's pussy, making her feel worshipped and having her come on my face, but I'd never become addicted to one in particular. Until now. I was addicted to Penny's pussy.

I loved the way she responded to my touch. Her little moans and quiet whimpers when she was lost to the feeling and the way her hips jutted up when I'd hit the right spot.

Poking my tongue out, I circled her clit in a figure-eight motion, flicking it back and forth slowly, teasing the sensitive bundle of nerves.

"Brett… more, please!"

176

Nothing was more beautiful than my name on her lips, begging to come. I flicked faster and nipped at her clit while sticking two fingers inside her and fucking her with them.

Her hips lifted and she pressed her pussy into my face. She was on the edge, but I wouldn't let her come yet. I rubbed her puckered hole with my thumb, and she clenched her cheeks. "Relax. Trust me to make you feel good, Penny."

Guarantee, she'd never been touched there, so I took it slow. One day I planned on fucking her ass, but she wasn't ready for that yet, so a finger would have to do. Wetting my thumb with her juices, I slowly circled the hole again and gently slipped it inside her ass while never once taking my tongue off her clit. I needed her to be distracted so all she could focus on was the pleasure. With both holes full of my fingers, I sucked on her clit and gave it a little bite.

Her whole body went stiff, and her pussy throbbed around my fingers. "Fuck... oh my...yes, yes, yes!"

When she came down from her orgasm, I lifted her from the edge of the pool and held her in my arms. Her legs immediately wrapped around my waist as she buried her head against my neck. I unclasped her bra and slid the material out from between us, setting it on the edge. Her large breasts were warm, pressed against my chest.

My cock strained against the material of my briefs. One little layer of cotton was all that prevented me from slipping my dick inside her. I'd never gone bare with a woman, but it was damn tempting with her naked pussy pressed up against me.

Penny lifted her head and looked me in the eyes. "Thank you for taking me swimming."

I chuckled because she damn well wasn't talking about swimming. "Any time." I walked her around the pool and over to the stairs that led to the attached hot tub, climbing up them and sinking us into the hot water.

"You still have your underwear on," she said, tugging at the waistband from where she was perched on my lap.

I lifted her up, removed my briefs, and set them on the side. "Happy?" My rock-hard cock ached for her warm, wet pussy. She tested my self-control at every turn.

She leaned back against the opposite side of the hot tub, gripping the edge with her arms and letting her legs float out in front of her. Her pink toes peeked up through the surface of the water. "Very. What's good for the goose is good for the gander."

I shook my head and pushed the wet strands back. "That's something my grandmother would have said."

She shrugged. "I'm an old soul. It's probably because my parents named me Penelope." She stuck out her tongue like she was gagging. "I've always hated my name. I don't know what my parents were thinking, naming their children Loretta, Penelope, and Beatrice. They could have named me Heather or Jenny or anything else from this century."

Pushing off the wall, I draped my body over hers and caged her in with my arms. "I love your name. Do you know why?" She shook her head. "Because it's unique to you. I've never gone out with a Penelope before."

"That's good. I've never dated a Brett before." Her legs came up and wrapped around my waist again as she smiled up at me. Her tits peeked out of the water, her skin all pink from the heat. I captured a nipple in my mouth and sucked, then did the same to the other. She rubbed her pussy along the length of my dick.

I had the urge to slip inside her, condom or not. "You're being a bad girl,"

She tilted her head to the side. "Then maybe you should spank me."

"A very bad girl," I growled, yanking her from the hot tub and carrying her through the house. I didn't give a damn about the water we dripped on the floor. All I cared about was being inside her.

Chapter 25
Penny

Gia and I were going over the schedule for the day when Trent poked his head into her office. "Good Morning, Miss Romano." He ignored me completely, like I wasn't right there in plain view.

"Good morning, Mr. Dorsey." Her voice was missing the I-want-to-chop-his-balls-off vibe it usually held.

"I'll need you in my office in ten minutes. Don't be late."

She lifted a manicured brow. "I rarely am."

He tapped on his watch and disappeared down the hallway. Weird. Normally he'd send Tom to get her. It was his go-to move to piss her off.

"Okay, I'm going to ask," I said, throwing my hands in the air. "What the hell is going on with you two? You've been acting weird for weeks."

Gia tapped a pen on the desk. "Weird how?"

I squinted my eyes at her. "Don't be coy with me, missy. I remember you threatening to poke his eyes out with a pen when you first started here. Now it's all... *Good morning, Mr. Dorsey. Right away, Mr. Dorsey. Of course, Mr. Dorsey.*"

She signed her name on the document in front of her and dropped the pen. "I told you. We've come to an agreement to be cordial for the purposes of work. It makes it much easier than wanting to strangle him."

"Uh-huh. Just as I suspected." I leaned back in my chair and crossed my arms.

"What is?"

"You two have the hots for each other, don't you?" All the bickering. The locked doors and private meetings. The late working hours. I'd been in this office for almost seven years, and I'd never seen Trent give any other employee as much attention as he'd given her. It made total sense.

She let out a sigh of exasperation. "You're being ridiculous. We've been nothing but professional."

"Too professional," I mused. Why hadn't I figured it out before? "You used to come in here and vent about him being an asshole, but for the last month... nothing. You haven't complained one bit about him being demanding or making unreasonable requests. Absolutely nothing. It's as fishy as the Shark Reef at Mandalay Bay."

"I've never been there, so I wouldn't know." She tapped the side of her head. "Think about it, Penny, you're dating his best friend. Don't you think he would have told Brett if we were involved?"

My lips scrunched to one side. "Maybe, but I still think you're hiding something." I mentioned my suspicions to Brett once and he dismissed it. Was it all in my head?

"Perhaps it's your own guilt," she said. "You've barely told me anything about you and Brett. You're the one who's hiding something and so you assume I am too."

I sagged. She was right. I'd given her the bare minimum, too embarrassed to tell her all the details. "What do you want to know?"

She folded her hands under her chin and leaned on her desk. "Only everything."

I double-checked the door to make sure we were alone. In all honesty, I'd been dying to confide in someone. The thought of telling my younger sister all the sordid details of my sex life felt wrong. Gia was the closest thing I had to a girlfriend, plus she knew Brett. Maybe she'd be able to give me some advice on what he'd like. She definitely had more experience than me.

I lowered my voice. "He likes to spank me."

Gia got up from her desk and dragged me over to the small couch in the corner of her office. I nearly tripped over my own feet and started to regret uttering the words. "Spank you?"

I covered my face with my hands and peeked out through my fingers while nodding. "Not hard or being mean." She pulled my hands away from my face. "Sometimes, when I'm on my knees and he's having sex with me from behind, he'll swat my butt. Says he likes to see his handprint on my ass. It doesn't hurt, just stings for a second or two. Then it feels good. Kind of turns me on."

Gia stared at me with her lips pressed together. The silence killed me. "You think I'm a freak."

"No, no, no. What kind of feminist would I be if I shamed you for what you like behind closed doors?"

"You don't think it's weird?" Ever since the first swat on my ass, I'd been feeling guilty. Like there was something wrong with me for wanting Brett to do it again.

My boss frowned. "There's nothing wrong with you. People like what they like. Honestly, I bet there are more women who like it than you know. They just don't talk about it."

I slapped a hand over my mouth and mumbled through my fingers, "I shouldn't have said anything."

Gia pulled my hand away from my face for the second time. "That's not what I'm saying. We're friends. You can tell me anything. No judgment. I promise."

"Can I ask you a question?"

"Of course."

I leaned in closer. The walls were fairly thick, but I wasn't taking any chances. "Have you ever had anal?"

Gia's face turned almost as red as her hair, and I felt bad for asking. "Only once."

"Did you like it? Cuz, I think Brett wants to. He stuck his finger"—I poked my index finger up—"you know, in there."

She blew out a measured breath. "I was scared at first, but once I got over the initial fear, I liked it. It was different, but different good, you know? I'd do it again."

"Was it with your ex-husband?" Not that it mattered. "You know what? That's none of my business." As a matter of fact, my whole line of questioning was totally inappropriate.

"It wasn't my ex-husband. It was a one-night stand." She looked at her watch and got to her feet. "Listen, maybe we can finish this conversation over drinks tonight. I don't want to keep Trent waiting. No sense in pissing him off since we've called a truce. I'll talk to you later." She strode from her office in her three-inch heels, leaving me sitting on the couch.

I couldn't help but think that I'd messed up. That I'd pushed over a line that I shouldn't have crossed. Two lines actually. First, accusing her of liking Trent and then telling her about my own sex life. Gia didn't seem upset, but she did seem uncomfortable.

Maybe I'd projected my need to fall in love onto Gia. Just because she and Trent were getting along didn't mean there was anything fishy going on.

"She lied to me."

Drinks with Gia ended up being drinks with Brett and Trent too. Trent and Gia confessed they were together, blindsiding Brett and me.

I was hurt. I thought Gia and I were friends. This whole time she'd been keeping a secret from me, even after I confided in her about my relationship. It felt like a betrayal.

Brett rolled toward me and propped himself up on one arm, smoothing out the lines on my forehead. "You're taking this too personally. Aren't you happy for them?"

"Of course, I'm happy for them. I might not understand falling for Trent because he's all *grrrr*," I held up my hands in claws, "but I want Gia to be happy."

"You're only saying that about Trent because you're used to seeing him in the office. I've known him since we were kids. He's that guy at work because that's who he has to be."

I rolled on my side and faced Brett, squishing my pillow under my head. "I get that, but it's not really the point."

"Then what is the point?"

How could he be so dense? I sat up against the headboard, pulled the sheet to cover me, and flipped the lamp on. "The point is I asked her if anything was going on between the two of them and she lied to my face. I thought we were friends."

Brett sat up next to me, letting the sheet fall to his waist. "They're trying to keep it on the down-low because they're afraid of losing their jobs, so I can't really blame them. I knew those two would be a good couple the first time I saw them together. Hell, I even encouraged it."

"You did?"

"Yes. Gia's exactly the type of woman he needs. Someone who's not afraid to put him in his place. And you know what? He didn't even tell me about their relationship. Am I mad? No. I was a bit irritated, but I'm not mad. Do you know why?"

"You should be mad. Why aren't you?"

"Because people are allowed to have secrets. They're allowed to have something that's private and just for them. I'm not going to let this one little thing ruin a twenty-year friendship. Everybody keeps secrets. I don't need to know every little thing about you or your past, just like you don't need to know about mine. It's in the past and has no bearing on the future. It's totally irrelevant."

Fred jumped up on the bed and crawled into my lap. I hadn't been giving him the attention he deserved lately, which is how we ended up back at my condo. He curled up into a ball and began to purr as I stroked his head. "I don't have any secrets."

Brett rolled his eyes. "Yes, you do. Everyone does. And that's okay."

I curled into his side without disturbing Fred. "What are your big secrets?"

He pulled down the sheet and plucked my nipple. "The past is the past. Let it go."

The whole idea that he was keeping secrets from me rubbed me the wrong way. So, I poked a little more. "Are they about women?"

Brett's brows furrowed and he sighed. "Do you really want to know about all the women I've slept with? Because I'm gonna be honest, I don't even know most of their names. Is this the road you want to go down?"

His snippy tone annoyed me. "How many people have you slept with?" I knew it was more than I had, but how many more?

He jumped out of bed and grabbed his boxer briefs from the floor. "How many men have you slept with, Penny?" he asked as he pulled them on.

I'd managed to piss him off, which was not my intent, and now he was shoving my inexperience in my face. "Including you? Four."

"Well, let's see…" He began silently counting on his fingers. When he held up a second hand, I got worried. "In the last fifteen years? Take your number and multiply it by fifty. And that doesn't include you." He stepped into his pants and grabbed his shirt.

I should have been concerned that he was leaving, but I was still in shock. "Two hundred?"

"Newsflash… I didn't go out with those women for the thrilling conversation. I did it for the sex. Don't ask questions you don't want to know the answers to."

I jumped out of bed and Fred scampered away, scared of my sudden movement. I grabbed my robe from the hook on the back of my closet and wrapped it around me. "So that's all this is to you? Sex?"

He roughed a hand over his beard. "Actually, with you, it was for the conversation. Just not *this* conversation. The sex, when we finally got to it, was a bonus." He picked up his keys and wallet and headed toward the door.

I followed him down the hallway. "Well, excuse me for not being up to your expectations! Sorry I didn't suck your dick on the first date! Maybe you can drive down the Strip and pick up some hooker!"

He stopped suddenly and turned, forcing me to crash into his chest. "FYI... I don't need hookers to get laid," he growled down at me.

"Of course you don't! Your Brett fucking Kingston. Women fall at your feet wherever you go."

He clenched his jaw and narrowed his eyes. "You sure did."

My hand connected with his face before I had a chance to think about it. "Get out! Get the fuck out!" How dare he use my love for him as a weapon? Like I was some foolish little whore who chased him around.

"Penny, I'm sorry. I didn't mean it." He tried to wrap his arms around me.

I pushed against his chest with all my might, only managing to knock him back an inch or two. "You need to leave."

Brett held his hands up in surrender. "I don't even know what we're fighting about."

"How about you being a self-centered dick?"

"Actually, it's more about you being insecure and trying to dig up a past that has nothing to do with us."

That hit a little too close to home. I walked to the door and held it open for him. "Please leave. I need some time alone."

"Gladly." He marched out the door to his fancy Ferrari and drove off.

I watched the taillights fade into the distance until they were nothing more than tiny pinpricks. Shutting the door, I slid down the back of it and fell to the floor, sobbing. Fred crawled out from under the couch where he'd been hiding and licked my toes. I scooped him into my arms and cradled him like a baby as I cried into his soft fur.

What had I done?

Chapter 26
Brett

I lay in bed, staring at the ceiling, still trying to figure out what the fuck happened last night. It was past ten in the morning, and I had zero motivation to do anything. I should have gone for a run or checked work emails, or looked at the potential properties for the mall. None of those things held any appeal.

All I could do was think about Penny and the shit show that happened last night. I understood she was hurt by the secret that Trent and Gia kept from her. If I wasn't secure in my friendship with Trent, I would have been hurt too, but I saw that train coming a mile away.

I should have never said anything to Penny about secrets, especially since Trent, Gia, and I were hiding a whopper from her. If she ever found out we had a threesome, she'd lose her ever-loving mind.

Trent regretted it.

Gia wanted to forget it ever happened.

To me, it was just sex.

No different than any other tryst Trent and I had been involved in over the years. I knew that night it was different for Trent. He'd been possessive, not as eager to share as normal. Damn… he'd lain in bed with Gia and cuddled her at the end of the night. Trent wasn't a cuddler.

When Trent and I picked her up that night at the bar, we assumed she was a tourist. How the fuck were we to know she'd show up in his office the next Monday as an employee?

And if Penny ever found out I had sex with Gia… she'd be devastated. It was bad enough the *Las Vegas Not So Confidential* flashed other women in her face.

The three of us made a pact to keep the secret, and I intended to honor it. I meant what I said… the past was the past. There was no sense dredging shit up you couldn't change.

What bothered me more than the secret were the words that came out of my mouth. I was wrong to shove the women I'd slept with in Penny's face. But the last bit was the worst.

"FYI… I don't need hookers to get laid."

"Of course you don't! You're Brett fucking Kingston. Women fall at your feet wherever you go."

"You sure did."

That was the nail in the coffin.

The words I couldn't take back.

Was I the asshole?

Yep.

I deserved the slap that flew into my face. I couldn't even be mad about it.

Chapter 27
Penny

Bea helped me get into the dress and zipped up the back. I held my breath, hoping it wouldn't get stuck.

Fifteen pounds.

That's how much I'd lost since I last tried the dress on.

"It fits," Bea declared.

I turned in the mirror and examined myself. The dress did fit. Barely.

"Come out so we can see," my mother spoke through the dressing room curtain.

I hesitantly pushed the curtain aside and stepped out. My mom held her hands up in front of her mouth. "Oh, Penny, it looks good."

Loretta looked down at me from where she stood on the pedestal as the seamstress stuck pins in her dress to take the waist *in* another inch. "Turn around." She motioned with her finger. Sucking in my gut as much as I could, I turned in my heels. "Myra, do you have that dress in the next size up?" she asked the seamstress.

The heat started in my belly and traveled all the way up my chest to my cheeks. "Loretta, please," I begged.

"Please what? It doesn't fit, Penny. As I suspected, you look like a stuffed sausage. Myra, do you have the dress or not?"

The poor seamstress scrambled away from Loretta. "We'd have to order it, Miss Loretta. That's the largest size we have."

"Order it," she demanded. "I won't have my wedding photos looking like we put twenty pounds of flour in a ten-pound sack."

Myra scurried into the back room upon Loretta's demand.

"Stop being mean, Loretta," Bea scolded. "It looks good."

"I don't want good. I want great. I'm only getting married once and I won't have anything tarnish the pictures."

I stepped back toward the dressing room to take the hideous thing off my body. At one time, I wanted to make my sister happy. Now, I wanted to hide in the nearest closet and never come out.

"Loretta, stop!" my mother yelled. "This is totally uncalled for. She's your sister, for God's sake. Try a little sympathy."

Sympathy? My mother wanted people to feel sorry for me? I ripped the straps from my shoulders and pushed the dress down my body. "Screw you, Loretta! I don't want to be in your fucking wedding!" I tried to keep the tears out of my eyes, but this, compounded with what happened with Brett last night, nearly pushed me over the edge. I left the dress on the floor and ran for the changing room. I pulled my sweats over my generous hips and the T-shirt over my head, then grabbed my purse and fled the store, running to my car as fast as I could.

Fuck them. Fuck them all!

Red. Green. Orange. Red. Brown. Green.

I sorted the M&M's on my kitchen table. In my weakened state, I'd stopped on the way home and bought a sixteen-ounce bag. One fucking pound of the candy I'd deprived myself of for the last several weeks. What did it matter? No matter how hard I tried, I'd never be good enough.

Not for my mother.

Not for Loretta.

And definitely not for Brett.

I dipped a red M&M in the bowl of peanut butter and popped it in my mouth. So fucking good. Another red one. A green one. An orange one. One by one, I ate every single candy laid out on the table.

After eating rabbit food for the last several weeks, my stomach revolted. I ran to the bathroom and threw up a mess of chocolate and peanut butter. When my stomach was empty, I leaned against the toilet and wiped my mouth. Going back to the kitchen, I picked up the bag and tossed it in the garbage. I threw the peanut butter away too, bowl and all.

Was I not allowed to have a single thing that brought me happiness?

I resented them all.

My mother.

Loretta.

And most of all, Brett.

The only one faithful to me was Fred. "They can all go to hell," I said, squeezing him tightly.

My phone pinged with an incoming text.

Loretta: You can't not be in my wedding. We have six guys. I need six girls. Everything will be lopsided. I need you to honor your commitment.

No *I'm sorry*, no apology whatsoever. It was so like my sister to not give a crap about how I was feeling. It was all about her, as usual.

Me: Should have thought about that when you were being a bitch.

Loretta: I'm not being a bitch! It's the most important day of my life and you're being oversensitive. If you ever get married, you'll understand.

If I ever got married? I had pictured my wedding since I was a little girl. I understood, but I'd never treat anyone the way Loretta treated me.

I was pissed but didn't want to mess up her special day. I couldn't disappoint my family like that.

Me: Fine. I'll be there.

At this point, I didn't even have a date for the wedding, though I didn't plan on sharing that tidbit with my sister or anyone else. She'd throw my failure in my face and chastise me. I didn't need to hear it.

Going to the cabinet, I poured three pills into my hand and washed them down my throat with a glass of detox tea. Come hell or high water, I was going to fit in that dress.

Chapter 28
Brett

It'd been three days since I talked to Penny. I'd thought about calling her a hundred different times, but I honestly didn't know what to say. For the first time in my life, I felt like a shit human being.

Instead of dealing with Penny like I should have, I buried myself in work. I met with the board and updated them on the Vegas Vista mall. They were elated Kingston Enterprises was leading the project. *Taking us to the next level* was the exact wording. There was always the pressure to do something bigger. Better. Weren't we already bigger and better than our competition? The constant need to grow exhausted me. Was the acquisition of a new tech company not enough? Apparently not.

After my meeting with the board, I met with Frank, the Vegas Vista developer, to discuss location and properties. We'd narrowed it down from five to three, finally selecting the perfect plot of land for the development. It was already zoned for commercial use and had a couple of older strip malls on it. It was far enough off the main drag to escape the hustle and bustle yet close enough to be within a short drive. Perfect for both locals and tourists. I already had someone researching the property value and what it would take to make it ours. Everything had a price, and we were more than equipped to meet it.

With that done, I decided to stop over at Mystique to let Trent know about the tickets I promised Karla Blitzer. I could have done it over the phone, but he wasn't going to be happy about it and I figured an in-person meeting was best. If I happened to run into Penny, so be it. Maybe we'd be able to sort out the shit between us.

After a quick drive across town, I took the elevator to the second floor, saying hello to Teresa, the receptionist. I'd been here often enough that she buzzed me through without a second thought.

As I walked toward Trent's office, I saw Gia in the hallway. "Hey, Gia."

"Hey. How's Penny feeling?"

I stared at her blankly.

Her head tilted to the side. "She called in sick today. You didn't know?"

I shoved my hands in my pockets. "I… um… I haven't talked to her."

"Oh." Gia tapped a finger to her lips. "Did you two have a fight?"

"That's not your business." Great. Now I was being an asshole to Gia too. "I'm sorry, that wasn't necessary."

"No, it wasn't. I'm assuming you're here to see Trent. Hunter's back, so he's grumpy as fuck too. Go be grumpy with him." She tossed her hair over her shoulder and walked away.

Seemed that pissing off women was my specialty. *When did that happen?*

I passed Tom's desk on my way to Trent's office. The kid was wound so tight, I was afraid he'd have a stroke before he was thirty, although working for my best friend probably didn't help matters. "Hi, Tom."

He sat up straight, adjusting his glasses. "Hello, Mr. Kingston. Is Mr. Dorsey expecting you?"

I resisted the urge to roll my eyes. "No. It's an impromptu visit."

He picked up the phone. "Hold on. Let me see if he's available." I waited patiently while Tom did his due diligence. Even if Trent was busy, he'd make time for me. That's how we worked. "Alright, sir." Tom hung up the phone and glared at me. "Mr. Dorsey said you can go on in."

Not sure where the attitude was coming from, but I had bigger fish to fry other than worrying why Trent's PA was giving me the cold shoulder. When I entered his office, Trent was pacing in front of the window that looked down over the gaming floor, hands fisted and a scowl on his face. "Rough day?"

"Fucking Hunter. He's back one day and already making my life a nightmare. He keeps trying to put the moves on Gia and it makes me want to punch him in the face again. I swear if he sees one bit of impropriety between the two of us, he'll run to my father like a tattling three-year-old."

"Why don't you tell your father about you and Gia? Then you won't have to hide it anymore."

He ran a hand through his already tussled hair. "I want to... it's... what if it doesn't last and I've risked both our jobs for nothing?" He plopped down in his leather chair and let out a deep sigh.

I sat across the desk from him. "What makes you think it won't work out? You two are great together. She's a keeper."

"Yeah, she is, but am I good enough for her? I haven't had a relationship in forever. What if I fuck it up?"

"You're asking the wrong person right now. Penny is pissed at me, and I can't say I blame her. I basically shoved all the women I've slept with in her face."

Trent picked up a pad of sticky notes and tossed them at my head. "You're a dumbass."

They hit me in the chest and fell into my lap. I picked them up and flipped the pages between my fingers. "I know. I didn't think not seeing her over the last few days would bother me, but it has. She's all I can think about."

"She didn't show up for work today."

"I know."

"I can't remember the last time she called in sick, so she's probably as miserable as you are. You should fix it."

"How?"

Trent laughed. "You run a billion-dollar company. Surely you can figure out a way to tell her she's different than all the other women you've slept with."

"I suppose." Remembering my initial reason for my visit, I cringed. "I'm going to need two more tickets for the fundraiser. I'll pay for them, of course."

Trent lifted a brow. "For who?"

I held my hands up. "Don't kill me, but they're for Karla Blitzer."

His eyes bulged. "Why the fuck would you invite a gossip columnist after the things she's written about you?"

"It's basically hush money. I exchanged the tickets to get her to quit writing rude stuff about Penny. Figured she'd find someone else to write about."

"At my event?"

I nodded.

"You really are a dumbass. I assume you're taking Penny. You're putting her right in the line of fire."

"I promised Penny a new dress. All Karla will be able to write about Penny is how amazing she looks."

Trent steepled his fingers and tapped the tips together. "I see your strategy and it might just work. I should buy a dress for Gia too. There's no way she can afford a formal gown. Actually, we should send the girls together to shop for dresses. I think they'd like that."

"Perfect. I'll make an appointment for them at the salon too. Hair, nails, makeup... the works."

"For two guys who suck at relationships, we're killing this shit." Trent laughed.

"We always did make a good team." I checked my phone for any messages from Penny, but there weren't any. A new dress and a trip to the salon would be worthless if I didn't get her to forgive me first.

How could I prove she was different than all the other women I'd been with?

"Where are we going?"

"There's someone I want you to meet."

I stopped at Penny's condo after work, only to find her and Fred cuddled together on the couch watching a sappy romance movie. She looked as miserable as I felt.

After apologizing profusely and both of us agreeing to leave the past in the past, I talked her into this little field trip.

I had to do something to show her I was totally committed. Not flowers. Not a gift. And definitely not sex. It needed to be meaningful.

We pulled up to the gated community and I put the code in to allow us access.

Penny's gaze flitted around at the large homes as we drove down the winding road. "Are you sure I'm dressed for this? These houses are huge!"

I picked up her hand over the console and gave it a squeeze. "You're perfect."

She smoothed out the black cropped pants she was wearing and checked the buttons on her sleeveless blouse. "I don't think I'm dressed properly." She flipped down the visor to check herself in the mirror. I'd given her fifteen minutes to change, throw her hair in a ponytail, and put on some makeup. I didn't want her making a bigger deal out of this than it was. Although truthfully, it was a pretty big deal and the only way I knew how to prove that our relationship was more than just sex.

"You're worrying too much." I pulled into the circular drive at the end of the cul-de-sac and shut off the engine, then jumped out and ran around to the passenger side to open Penny's door.

Making no move to get out of the car, she sat there staring up at the sprawling ranch-style home made of beige brick and glass. It had the largest portico in the neighborhood, making the already huge house look bigger. My father hadn't spared any expenses when he had it built. "Who lives here?"

I took her hand and helped her out of the car. "My mom."

"Holy fuck," she whispered. "This is where you grew up?"

"Yep." Seeing the astonishment in her eyes, I added, "It's simply a house, Penny."

"It's more than a house. It's a mansion," she said, taking everything in. "Wait! I'm meeting your mother?" She slapped me on the arm. "You should have told me that before we left. I would have worn a sundress." She pulled her blouse down to cover her ass. "I'm totally unprepared for this, Brett." She pulled back her lips and showed me her teeth. "Do I have anything stuck in there?" Too impatient and nervous to wait for my answer, she leaned over and looked in the side-view mirror, scrubbing her finger back and forth across her teeth. She pushed a few stray curls back into her ponytail and straightened to her full height, which wasn't much. "How do I look?"

I pulled her in for a hug and kissed the top of her head. "You look beautiful. My mom's a sweetheart. You'll love her and I'm pretty sure she's going to love you." My throat got dry with all this talk about love. I'd only told one woman I loved her, besides my mom, and that was a very long time ago. Since then, I'd never said the words to another female.

I might have said I loved their dress or their body or the way they sucked me off, but never *I love you*. Those words were reserved for one woman, and I wouldn't cheapen them by throwing them around so casually. If I ever said them again, they would mean something.

We walked under the portico hand in hand, and I opened the front door like I still lived there. My mother was notorious for forgetting to lock it, even though I constantly reminded her. It was a safe neighborhood, but you could never be too careful. Once Penny was in, I locked the door behind me. "Mom, we're here!"

Penny's head swiveled from side to side as she took in my childhood home, with its tall ceilings and modern design. Not much had changed about it over the years. It was too big for the three of us when I lived here, and it was certainly too big for my mother to live alone. She talked about moving to a smaller condo, but this was her home. The place that held all the memories of my father. I couldn't blame her for not giving it up.

My mom rushed down the hallway from her bedroom, hopping on one foot and trying to shove a sandal onto the other one. "Already?" She came to a skidding halt in front of us. "Next time, give me a bit more notice."

"You look great," I said, leaning into her outstretched arms for a hug. "I told you not to make a fuss."

"I'm your mother. I'm going to make a fuss if I want to," she said, pinching my cheek like I was still eight years old. Then she turned to Penny and gave her a hug too. "It's so nice to meet you."

"It's nice to meet you too, Mrs. Kingston."

My mom waved her off. "That's so formal. Sara is fine." She led us through the house and out to the back patio that overlooked the mountains.

"This is absolutely gorgeous!" Penny exclaimed as she sat in a chair at the table. I took my tie and jacket off and sat next to her, resting a hand on her thigh.

"The view is what led us to build here. When the sun sets, it's stunning. I'm sorry I didn't plan dinner. Brett called an hour ago and I was elbow deep in dirt from working in the garden. I do have a veggie tray, fruit, and a pitcher of peach margaritas though."

"No worries. He only gave me fifteen minutes to pull myself together, so I can relate. He didn't even tell me where we were going."

My mother scowled at me. "Brett, you can't spring something like this on a woman. We like to be prepared."

"I told you not to go to any trouble, Mom. It's a casual visit."

She harrumphed. "That doesn't mean I can't be a good hostess. Would you like a margarita, Penny?"

"I would love one. Thank you, Sara."

My mother scurried into the house to get our drinks. When she started drinking, my mom was a Chatty Cathy. That, combined with Penny's tendency to ramble, would make for an interesting evening. I squeezed Penny's leg. "Are you okay?"

"I'm fine. I wish you had told me we were coming here. I feel like we barged in on her."

"Trust me, she doesn't mind. My mom has been waiting years for me to bring someone home."

Penny cocked her head to the side. "What do you mean?"

I ran my hand along my scruffy chin. "Well... you're the first woman I've brought to meet her since high school."

"Are you serious?"

"Yes. I wanted you to see how important you are to me. Whatever this is between us isn't just sex. It's more than that. I really missed not talking to you or seeing you over the past few days. I know I don't have the best reputation..."

She grabbed my face between her hands and pulled me in for a kiss. "This means a lot to me. Thank you."

I smoothed back the stray curl that kept escaping her ponytail. "No. Thank you for giving me another chance. I don't deserve it."

"We were both wrong. I'm sorry I poked the bear. I should have left well enough alone."

"You two are adorable together," my mom said as she emerged from the house carrying a tray with snacks and drinks. "This makes me so happy."

"Here, let me help you." I rushed to her, took the tray, and brought it to the table, passing the glasses around.

Penny took a sip and licked her lips. "Oh, my goodness! This tastes like heaven. I'm going to need the recipe."

"The secret is peach puree and a little orange juice. Gives it the perfect amount of sweetness."

"It's divine," Penny said, taking another sip.

My mom's margaritas were a little heavy on the tequila, but with the sweetness, you barely noticed it. I hoped I wouldn't have to carry Penny home at the end of the night. "Easy. These things are dangerous," I said, taking her glass and pushing the veggie tray in front of her. I had no idea if she'd even eaten today. "Maybe I should order us some dinner."

"You do that, and we'll keep drinking." Mom pushed Penny's drink back in front of her. "So, Penny, tell me about you."

"What do you want to know?"

"Everything. Start with your job. You work with Trent at Mystique, right?"

Penny wavered her head back and forth. "Sort of. He's my boss's boss. I wouldn't say I work *with* him, more like I work *for* him. I'm the personal assistant for the director of entertainment and events. Mostly I make a ton of phone calls and keep everyone organized."

My mom patted Penny's hand. "Don't undervalue yourself, sweetie. Brett's PA, Maryanne, used to work for my late husband. He'd have been lost without her. She works her ass off."

"Maryanne is a godsend," I agreed. "Although, I bet I'm easier to work for than Trent."

"You're both intense and hardheaded, so it's probably a close race. You should have seen those two when they were kids, all long legs and gangly arms."

I pointed at my chest. "I was never gangly. That was all Trent."

"You were gangly too, in your early teens. Most boys are. It's nothing to be embarrassed about."

"I'm not embarrassed, but I do think your memory might be going."

Penny's head ping-ponged between us as we bickered back and forth. She held a hand over her lips to keep from laughing. I liked seeing her smile and regretted taking that from her over the past few days.

"I'm sharp as a tack." My mom tapped her temple. "You were both gangly, but you were good-looking boys. We practically had to beat the girls off with a stick." Then she turned to Penny. "Those two were thick as thieves, always getting into trouble. This one time…"

"And that's my cue to place our dinner order. Don't believe everything she says." I kissed Penny on the head and went inside. Standing at the sliding glass door, I watched them talk and laugh together. It felt good seeing the two most important women in my life getting along. Not that I doubted they would; it'd just been a really long time since I had *two* important women in my life.

Chapter 29
Penny

"I've never been to a dress shop this fancy," Gia whispered in my ear.

"Me neither." I pulled the price tag from inside a sequined dress. "Oh my god! I think I'm going to faint. This dress is over two thousand dollars." That was more than my house payment.

Gia tucked it back into the dress and smoothed her hands down the front of it. "We're not supposed to be looking at price tags, remember? We're supposed to be enjoying the experience," she finger quoted. That's what Brett and Trent said when they sent us on this shopping trip.

"That's such a rich person thing to say." Don't get me wrong, it was extremely generous but also a bit intimidating. What if we snagged a dress or some other snafu happened? I felt like I should bleach my hands before even daring to touch the expensive fabrics.

"I guess when you grow up as millionaires, you barely look at prices anymore. We don't have stores like this in Waukegan. We have Target and Meijer. But even when I lived in Chicago, I never had an occasion to wear anything this elegant."

"I've lived my whole life in Vegas, but seriously, who has money for these types of dresses?" We looked at each other at the same time and started laughing as we both said, "Rich people."

An attractive blond approached us. "Good afternoon, ladies. You must be Gia and Penny."

Gia touched her chest. "I'm Gia and this is Penny," she said, pointing her finger at me.

"I'm Vivian and it'll be my pleasure to help you both find fabulous dresses for the fundraiser. Mr. Kingston and Mr. Dorsey have assured me that price is not a consideration, so let's have some fun, shall we?" She clapped her hands together excitedly. "I've already pulled some dresses aside that I think you're going to love."

We followed her to the back of the store. The dresses on the mannequins were so long they nearly touched the ground. "I doubt anything here is going to fit me. I'll be dragging it all over the floor," I whispered. Gia was at least five foot seven, with the shape of a Barbie doll. These gowns would look gorgeous on her.

"We have an in-house seamstress, Miss Quinn. Don't you worry, we're going to have you looking fabulous." I was a bit embarrassed Vivian heard me, but I'd rather scrub toilets than shop for a dress.

I was down over fifteen pounds but still had more to go. "You must be a miracle worker."

Gia bumped me with her hip. "Don't be so hard on yourself. I've noticed the weight you've lost." Suddenly, she stopped and spun me around. "Wait. You didn't go on a diet to lose weight for Brett, did you?" she whispered.

My lips pressed together in a thin line. I hated talking about my size, especially with someone built as perfectly as Gia. She didn't even trust me enough to tell me about her relationship with Trent. I wasn't sure where that put us on the friend meter, but I didn't want to lie either. "Yes and no. Of course, I want to slim down for Brett because he sees me naked and I'm body insecure, but that's not the only reason. My sister's wedding is coming up and I want to fit into the dress without ordering a bigger size. She doesn't think I can, so it makes me want to try harder to prove her wrong."

"Competitive, are we?"

"Damn right I am. Nothing would make me happier than shoving it in her face." Admitting that felt good. Loretta teased me about my "baby fat" my entire life and I was sick of it.

"Yoo-hoo! Ladies! Back here," Vivian called from the dressing area. Gia and I quickstepped to the back of the boutique. "Gia, the dresses on this rack are for you." She tapped the rolling rack on the right and then the one on the left. "And these are for you, Penny. Now that I've seen you both in person"—her eyes roamed our bodies—"I have some other ideas too. Why don't you get started and I'll go see what else I can find."

I sifted through the rack, pushing aside one designer gown after another. "What color do you think would look good on me?"

"Something dark to go with your hair." I heard what she wasn't saying, *a dark color will make you look skinnier.*

I pushed the baby-blue, pink, and cream-colored dresses to the side. Grabbing the navy, cranberry, and black dresses, I headed to the dressing room. Trying on dresses was my personal hell. Every dress either pulled too tight across my boobs, buckled at my hips, or highlighted my soft middle. If it fit great in one area, it didn't in another. Not one of these dresses was made for someone with my body type. And that didn't even take into account that they were all designed for someone much taller. Even with heels on, I felt like I was drowning in them.

"How are we doing?" Vivian called through the curtain.

I was ready to bolt and tell Brett I couldn't go to the masquerade ball. Maybe I could come up with some excuse about a family emergency or having to leave the country. Surely, I wouldn't mind missing the event if I was sipping a mai tai on a beach somewhere. "Not that great," I answered.

"Come out so we can see," Gia said. "I want to get your opinion on this red gown I've got on."

Hesitantly, I hiked up the dress so I could walk and pushed the curtain aside. The looks on both Gia's and Vivian's faces told me everything I already knew. "It's awful. I don't have the body for these dresses."

"Now, now," Vivian said, placating me. "It's not you It's the dress. Don't get discouraged. I won't let you walk out of here without the perfect dress. How about champagne while I find it?"

The woman was a saint. I'd asked the impossible of her, yet she wasn't dissuaded from her mission. "Champagne would be lovely."

"Me too," Gia piped in.

"Of course. Champagne for both of you."

While Vivian went to find me the "perfect" dress, another attractive woman brought us our bubbly. Being beautiful must have been a requirement for working in this high-end boutique. Gia and I were both extremely careful not to spill anything on the dresses. God forbid a cleaning charge was added to the tab.

Holding her glass away from her body, Gia turned in a tight circle. "What do you think?"

"It looks amazing on you, but I'm not sure of the color." The red sequins were doing nothing for her red hair.

"Yeah, red's not usually my color, but I love the dress."

"Are you wearing your hair up or down?"

"I was thinking down." She gathered the strands with her free hand and held them on top of her head. "What do you think?"

"Down. Maybe they have it in an emerald green. That would look good with your red hair."

Gia sifted through the rack again and pulled out a gorgeous sequined gown. "I'm going to try this one." She took her champagne into the dressing room, leaving me alone and awkward in a dress that made me look like a little girl playing dress-up.

Tossing back my glass, I swallowed down the rest of the sweet alcohol and set my glass on a nearby stool. Bless Vivian, but she was on a wild-goose chase. I couldn't wait to get home and throw on a pair of comfy pajamas.

"I found it!" Vivian practically burst with excitement as she brought over another dress.

One. If this didn't fit, I was ready to book that trip to the Caribbean. The dress was black satin with a beaded bodice and skirt. I took the gown from her and held it up. It was pretty, but I lost my shit when I saw the price tag of almost five thousand dollars. "Oh my god! No!" I tried pushing it back at Vivian, but she was having none of it.

"Mr. Kingston said not to spare any expense. His exact words were, 'I want Miss Quinn to look stunning. I don't care how much it costs. Make it happen.' He'll be very disappointed if he finds out I found you the perfect dress and you refused to try it on."

I groaned. "This is emotional blackmail."

"Take these too." She shoved lingerie and a pair of black open-toe, jewel-covered stilettos into my hands. I set everything in the dressing room and held up the lingerie. It wasn't lacy or sexy. It was Spanx.

I handed them back to Vivian. "I'm already wearing Spanx, but thank you." It was depressing that she didn't realize I already had them on, but it was cute that she thought they might help.

Vivian took my hand and plopped the undergarment back into my palm. "Not like this, you're not. You don't actually think those women who walk the red carpet all have perfect figures, do you? Nope. They all wear those. Trust me." She turned me by the shoulders and gave me a little shove forward. "Now, shoo."

Actually, I did think those women had perfect figures. They had personal chefs and personal trainers and money for liposuction.

I shucked off the abomination I was wearing and hung it back on the hanger. Holding up the undergarment Vivian had insisted I try, doubt set in. It looked like it was made for a twig and I was more of a hearty tree branch. Blowing out a breath, I removed the one I was wearing and squeezed myself into the torturous contraption. Once everything was in place, it was actually quite comfortable. I examined myself in the mirror. My waist looked slim, which was amazing. My belly didn't stick out at all. Maybe there was hope.

Stepping into the beaded gown, it slid effortlessly over my hips and up my body. I zipped it as far as I could and looked in the mirror. The deep *V* in the front made my boobs look amazing without being too scandalous. It was hard to tell the exact fit with the zipper half-down, but I was encouraged.

I sat on the bench and pulled the dress up to bare my feet. The shoes were Jimmy Choo and probably cost another thousand dollars. It was too late to worry about the money. With a five-thousand-dollar dress, what was another thousand? I slipped the fancy shoes on my feet and buckled the straps. The question was, would I even be able to walk in these shoes?

"I'm dying out here! Let us see," Gia said.

Holding the dress up so I wouldn't trip over it, I pushed the curtain aside and stepped out. "Could someone please zip me?"

Gia, wearing the emerald-green sequined gown, quickly zipped up the back of my dress. She and Vivian stared at me. I thought this one looked pretty good, but maybe I was wrong.

"I knew it. I knew it!" Vivian exclaimed. "I haven't failed a client yet. It's a perfect fit. We just need to take the hem up and maybe make this slit a little bigger," she said, pulling at the long skirt. "Let me get Vessa. She'll have you fixed up in no time."

Vivian disappeared, and I turned to Gia. "What do you think?"

She pressed a hand to her chest. "It's absolutely perfect. Like the dress was made for you."

I couldn't help the smile that took over my face. "I like it too. Let me see the back of yours." Gia turned in a tight circle. The dress dipped low in the back, showing off her flawless skin. "I think we've found our dresses." I held up the bottom of my dress so she could see my feet. "Better go get yourself some Jimmy Choos."

She hopped up and down. "I want some. Ooooh, or Manolo Blahniks." Gia loved shoes as much as kids loved candy, and like me, she couldn't afford designer ones. We should have felt guilty for taking advantage of the guys' wallets, but this was a once-in-a-lifetime opportunity.

Gia ran off to find some shoes as Vivian returned with the seamstress. Vessa must have been at least seventy with the lines on her face to prove it. "Step up," she said in a heavy accent as she pointed to the raised platform. I lifted the dress and cautiously stepped on the pedestal, careful not to break my ankle in the high-heeled shoes. The last thing I wanted was to go to the ball with a cast on my foot.

Vessa quickly pinned up the bottom of my dress. Then, to my horror, she ripped the slit farther up my leg to the middle of my thigh, put a few pins in it, and motioned for me to get down. "That's it. You done. Take it off and I'll fix while you wait."

I was stunned by how quickly she measured and pinned everything. Once the dress was off and my regular clothes were on, Vivian led me and Gia—who'd already found a pair of shoes she was in love with—over to the purses. "Go ahead and pick out your purses and I'll start bagging up your purchases. Penny, you'll need to try your dress on one more time."

Gia held up her shoes to the purses, checking to make sure the shades of silver matched. "Can you even believe this day? When Trent said he was sending us shopping for dresses, I never imagined we'd be here. And a personal shopping assistant? It's over the top."

"Is it weird that I'm excited for Brett to see me in my dress? I mean, it's not juvenile, is it?" The age difference between us hadn't been that much of an issue, but I worried about looking immature in front of a man who'd been with dozens of women in fancy dresses.

"Penny, you've earned every bit of that excitement. Brett is going to come in his pants when he sees you." She laughed. "Okay, that sounded gross, but I'm serious. All he's going to be able to think about is getting you out of it."

Sexy wasn't my forte, but the dress did make me feel sexy. "God, I hope so."

Gia and I spent the entire day at the salon—massages, mani-pedis, hair, and makeup. By the time we left, I felt like a queen. Now, after giving Fred a ton of love, I was on my way to Brett's to get dressed because even though I loved the little furball, I didn't want to worry about getting cat hair on my dress or having one of his razor-sharp claws putting a snag in it.

When I pulled up in front of Brett's apartment building, Stanley, the doorman, opened my door for me and took my keys. I doubted I'd ever get used to this type of service. "Thank you so much, Stanley." He always refused the tip I tried to give him, so instead, I handed him the bag of pastries

I picked up on the way. "I hope you like chocolate." It barely cost me anything, but it was better than nothing.

"It's my favorite, Miss Quinn." He peeked in the bag and licked his lips. "Thank you." I opened my trunk and pulled out the garment bag while Stanley got my small suitcase and rolled it into the lobby for me. "Planning to stay a while?"

Dare to dream, Penny. But the thought of staying more than a night or two gave me mixed feelings. On the one hand, I could see myself sitting by the pool, drinking my morning coffee and being wrapped up in the sheets with Brett every night. On the other hand, I had Fred, and a penthouse suite was not equipped for a frisky cat who liked to sharpen his nails on pretty much everything. I'd made a commitment when I adopted him, and I didn't intend to break it. "No, Brett and I have an event tonight." I didn't want to shove everything in a duffel bag and risk ruining my shoes or mask. The small suitcase made sense.

"Well, if I don't see you, have fun." When the elevator arrived, Stanley rolled my bag in and used his key card to send me to the top floor.

The whole way up, my stomach filled with butterflies. I'd barely seen Brett over the last few days. I'd been busy helping Gia with the last-minute preparations for the fundraiser tonight, and Brett was knee-deep in the Vegas Vista project. I was excited for him to see me all dolled up for the evening. The women at the salon were serious miracle workers. My skin looked flawless and there wasn't a bit of frizz in my hair. It was smooth and sleek with big bouncy curls. Of course, they used half a can of hairspray to keep it in place, but I didn't really care.

The elevator doors opened on the top floor, and I stepped out without looking, nearly walking right into Amanda. "Oh, I'm sorry." I'd only seen her that one morning but from the look she gave me, I already knew everything I needed to know about her. She clearly had a thing for Brett, and I was standing in her way. She hated me.

I tried to step around her, but she blocked me. "You're still around, huh? I know you're his shiny new toy, but I feel like you should know the truth up front. Brett Kingston doesn't do relationships. I've watched dozens of women come and go. The only constant in his life for the last three years has been me. It may be fun now, but eventually, he'll tire of you and move on."

All the good feelings I had drained away. I was caught so off guard by Amanda that all I could say was, "I'm sorry?"

"Not yet, but you will be when he realizes you're not good enough for him. You're obviously total opposites. He needs someone with the right breeding. Someone who knows how to navigate this life. And when he *is* ready to settle down, I'll be waiting. I'm a patient woman, so don't think I'm going anywhere." She stepped into the waiting elevator and gave me a wave of her fingers. "Buh-bye."

I flipped her the bird before the doors closed. "What the fuck?" Her words shouldn't have bothered me, but they did because deep down, I knew she was telling the truth. I didn't belong in this lifestyle. My time with Brett was a brief interlude from my average, boring life.

Women like me didn't get to have men like him.

Chapter 30
Brett

The way Penny looked tonight was worth every dime I spent. When she stepped out of the bathroom after getting dressed, my jaw nearly hit the floor. I wanted to fuck her right then and there, but she refused, too afraid of messing up her hair and makeup or, god forbid, the gown she was wearing. Let it be known I had absolutely no issue with ripping the dress from her body and staying home.

With both our masks—mine plain black and hers embellished with black feathers—firmly in place, we entered the ballroom at Mystique. It'd been successfully transformed into the French Quarter. The jazz band played a sultry tune while the photographer snapped pictures of couples dressed to the nines against the New Orleans background. Everyone was having a great time, laughing and drinking.

I wondered if Karla Blitzer was here. With everyone wearing masks, it was hard to tell who was who, though I was sure she'd recognize me with no effort at all. She could take all the pictures she wanted because there wasn't one negative thing she could possibly say about Penny. I'd made sure of it.

Penny tugged on my arm. "Gia's over by the silent auction. Let's go say hi."

I'd seen Trent talking with the bigwigs when we came in. He and Gia were still pretending they weren't together, both afraid of losing their jobs. He needed to talk to his father and make it official. Sneaking around always had a way of biting you in the ass. Just my two cents.

"Everything looks amazing!" Penny squealed as she grabbed Gia's arm. "You really pulled this off."

Gia hugged Penny tightly. "*We* did. I couldn't have done any of this without you."

"You both worked hard and should be proud of yourselves," I chimed in. They'd worked *damn* hard on this event and Trent pushed against them every step of the way.

"Thank you, Brett." Gia gazed over my shoulder, clearly looking for Trent.

"He's mingling with the board members. You're seated at our table, so you'll see him at dinner," I said. "I know this is hard, but Trent is loyal. He'll make things right."

She sighed. "I wish it were already out in the open so we could enjoy the night together."

"Maybe it'll happen tonight. Who knows?" Penny said optimistically. That was her, all rose-colored glasses. Wishing something to be true didn't make it so. I'd learned that lesson a long time ago.

"Doubtful," Gia said. "I'm going to check to make sure all our vendors are set. I'll talk to you two at dinner." Then she was off in a flurry, talking to people and shaking hands.

After Penny and I got drinks at the bar, she insisted we get our picture taken in front of the backdrop. Then, she dragged me over to the fortune-teller she'd hired for the event. I didn't believe in that shit, but it made her happy, so I went without complaint.

"Let me see your hand, dear," the old lady said.

Penny held out her palm and giggled. "This is so much fun."

The fortune-teller ran her finger over Penny's palm, tracing the lines. "You have an open heart. Stay true to yourself and love will always find you. Sometimes you have to crawl through the darkness to find the light. That's very important to remember." She closed Penny's palm and gave it a squeeze.

"Oooh, cryptic. I love it!" Everything the woman told her sounded like it came from a Chinese fortune cookie. Some vague shit that could apply to anything if you wanted it to. Penny took my hand and pushed it in front of the old woman. "Now, your turn."

I humored Penny by opening my palm. It was all a bunch of mumbo jumbo. Someone preying off innocent people who wanted to believe this shit was real.

The old woman stared at my large palm, then swirled her finger around and tapped the middle of it. "Life is short. But you know this. Don't make the same mistake twice."

My breath hitched and I snapped my hand closed. I stared at the old woman who couldn't possibly know. Her eerie words hit a little too close to home.

"You know what I'm talking about," she said with finality.

I dragged Penny away from the booth and she almost stumbled in her heels. "What was she talking about?"

"How would I know? She's just a crazy old lady rambling. It doesn't mean a thing."

"Then why are you upset?"

My palm burned where she'd touched it, so I shoved my hand in my pocket and rubbed it on my thigh. "I'm not upset."

"Hmmm. You seem like it. What do you think she meant by me having to crawl through the darkness to find the light?"

I sighed. "It's not specific to anything. It means things aren't always easy, that's all."

Her face fell. "Oh."

"I'm sorry if you were looking for some deeper meaning, but there isn't any." Penny was smart. I couldn't believe she was falling for that woman's scam. "Why don't we get another drink and head over to our table?"

Still sounding disappointed, she acquiesced. "Good idea. My feet need a rest."

I needed a bourbon or two to quell the thoughts in my head.

The liquor worked.

Besides having Hunter sitting at our table with a smug look on his face, dinner was enjoyable. I felt bad for the blond fawning all over him. Hunter had no interest in her. She was more of a decoration than anything. He could have at least pretended to care about his date instead of staring at Gia's cleavage all night. It was fucking annoying, especially since Trent couldn't say anything without outing himself.

Once Gia's speech was over, we were able to remove our masks and the dancing began. I'd been waiting all night to have Penny in my arms. I figured we'd spin around the dance floor for a while and then head back to my place, where I'd have to use all my self-control to resist ripping her dress off. "Would you like to dance, Miss Quinn?" I held my hand out for her to take.

Putting her hand in mine, she stood from the table. "I'd love to, Mr. Kingston."

I led her to the dance floor and wrapped an arm around her waist, clasping her hand against my chest. "Have I told you how beautiful you look tonight?"

"You mentioned it. You look very handsome in your tuxedo too."

Her green eyes captivated me, and I couldn't look away. "Fair warning... I'm going to ravish you tonight. I'm going to fuck your pussy and your ass. My cock is going to be buried so deep inside you, you'll forget your own name."

Penny wobbled in her heels and my arm tightened around her waist to keep her from falling. "You can't just say stuff like that," she scolded.

I smirked. "Why? Does it make you wet?"

213

She nodded.

"Good." I pressed my hips forward so she could feel exactly how much I wanted her.

A beautiful shade of red crept up her neck and into her cheeks. "Behave, Mr. Kingston."

"Make me," I challenged her. "I'm a man who knows what I want, and right now, that's you. I won't let anything stand in my way when I want it."

"How much longer do you think we should stay?" she asked coyly.

"We've done our due diligence." I'd been to hundreds of these events, but I didn't want to pull Penny away if she was having fun. "Are you ready?"

She nodded again. "More than ready."

I couldn't keep my hands off her in the back of the limo, but I was foiled again by the bodysuit under her dress. Once back at my penthouse, I caged her against the door. "You have two minutes to get out of that dress, or I'm tearing it off your body."

Her lips formed an *O*. "Not the dress!"

"Ticktock, sweetheart."

She slipped out from under my arms and took off down the hallway, only to run back. "Unzip me."

I slid the zipper down her back, and she took off running again, stumbling in the heels. "Leave the shoes on!" I yelled after her.

Heading to the bedroom, I stripped my jacket and tie off along the way. I set my cuff links on the dresser and started to unbutton my shirt. When the bathroom door opened, Penny leaned one arm against the doorjamb and propped the other on her hip. She had on a lace and silk negligee that hit her midthigh and those sexy-as-fuck shoes. Her confidence since we'd first met had skyrocketed. She still had her moments, but right now, she was all sex kitten, and it made my dick swell with lust. I loved her full breasts and her wide hips. They gave her the shape of a real woman, something I could sink my hands into.

"You like?"

"Very much so." I stalked toward her with one mission in mind—to ravage the fuck out of her. Grabbing her face between my palms, I pressed my lips to hers, stroking them with my tongue. Her hands slid inside my open shirt, rubbing along my pecs and over my shoulders, pushing the fabric down my arms. I shook the shirt off and threw it to the floor, then cupped her ass and lifted her up. Penny's legs wrapped around my waist as her arms clung to my neck. Her head fell back, exposing the slender column of her neck and inviting me to nip along the skin.

I carried her to the bed and laid her down. She propped herself on her elbows, one leg stretched out and the other bent at the knee. "Are you just going to look at me?"

"Among other things." Pulling my belt through the loops of my pants, I nodded to the headboard. "Scoot up." Without hesitation, she moved back. I thought about binding her hands with my belt but given everything I had planned, it would be too constricting. Instead, I grabbed a silk tie from my dresser drawer. "Hands over your head."

She gulped but did as I asked, crossing her wrists on the pillow. "Are you going to tie me up?"

"Yes. Are you okay with that?"

"I think so."

I leaned over her body, tracing my finger along her jaw. "I would never do anything to hurt you. Do you trust me?"

"I do. I'm… nervous."

"That's because you think too much. All I want you to do is feel. Let me take control and surrender yourself to the pleasure." I placed the silk over her eyes and tied it behind her head. Then took another tie and wrapped her wrists, securing them to the headboard. Tight, but not too tight. I gave her some wiggle room, but not much. She wasn't going anywhere. "Do you know how fucking sexy you look like this?"

She shook her head back and forth. "No. I feel… vulnerable."

"And I like you like that. Mine to do with as I please. Mine to suck and lick and fuck. Mine to take as I like." She whimpered as I took the rest of my clothes off. "I'm going to fuck every hole you have, starting with that sassy mouth of yours." Straddling her shoulders, I fisted my cock and nudged it against her lips. "Open."

As anxious as me, Penny opened her mouth and her tongue darted out, licking the drop of precum from the head. She licked her lips and opened wider. I eased into her mouth with the intent of being gentle, but her lips locked around my dick as her tongue lapped at the underside. Fuck, her mouth felt like heaven, warm and wet. Holding on to the headboard with one hand and gripping my cock in the other, I pushed in farther. Not many women could take all of me, but I was determined to try. "Tilt your head back and breathe through your nose."

She followed my directions beautifully. There was something very erotic about watching your dick disappear down the throat of a woman. When I hit the muscles at the back of her throat, I pushed a bit more, short thrusts that strangled my cock. I should have stopped when she let out another whimper, but I couldn't. It felt too damn good. "I'm gonna come down your throat. Swallow."

Her throat began to pulse around my cock and there was no way I wasn't coming. My balls pulled tight, and the pressure built as I continued thrusting into her mouth. "Fuck!" I exploded, releasing everything down her throat. I slowly pulled out and a bit of cum dribbled down the side of her mouth. Wiping it with my thumb, I held it to her mouth. "Lick."

She sucked my thumb into her mouth and released it with a pop. "Good girl. You sucked my cock so beautifully that I think you deserve a reward." I'd been a bit rough, but she didn't complain. Sometimes I forgot about her lack of experience because she handled everything like a pro.

"I like rewards," she said, breathless. "Please."

The plea from her lips stirred my cock, which should have been impossible since I'd just come down her throat, but he was greedy. I kissed her pouty mouth, letting our tongues tangle together in a slow dance, the salty taste of my cum on her lips.

Now was the time to be gentle. Peppering kisses down her throat and cleavage, I pulled one breast free of the silky negligee, then the other. She looked so gorgeous like this—blindfolded, with her large tits on display. I grabbed one, running my tongue over the tip and sucking it into my mouth while my other hand ran down her body and played with her pussy. She was so fucking wet, and my fingers glided over her clit, rubbing it in small circles with light pressure.

Her body arched. "More."

I lavished her other breast and sank my fingers deep inside her. So wet. So warm. So soft. Not able to wait another minute, I lay between her thighs, putting her legs over my shoulders. Lifting her ass off the mattress, I rubbed my beard on the insides of her thighs and feasted on her pussy. My god, she was addicting. Lapping at her pussy, I couldn't resist coating my thumb in her wetness and rubbing it over her ass. With a gentle push on her puckered hole, I slowly moved it in and out, letting her get used to the feeling.

She immediately tensed up. "Let me in and stop thinking. Trust me to make you feel good. Breathe." When her muscles relaxed, I attacked her pussy again, flicking her clit with the tip of my tongue while still fucking her back hole with my thumb.

"Oh, god, yes, yes, yes!" Her hips thrust toward my face. "Don't stop!"

I had no intention of stopping until she came all over my lips. When her body clamped down on my thumb and her back went rigid, I knew she was close. Sucking her clit long and hard, her body detonated, going off like a bundle of dynamite. She rode my face through the orgasm then went boneless as a jellyfish.

I gave her exactly thirty seconds to get her bearings because I wasn't even close to being done with her.

Chapter 31
Penny

My body was wrung out from the intense orgasm. Although the blindfold was supposed to help me stop thinking, all I could do was think. I mean… what was a woman supposed to do when a man said, *I'm going to fuck every hole you have, starting with that sassy mouth of yours*?

One down. Two to go.

I was only worried about one of the two that were left.

Would it hurt?

Would it be messy?

Would I like it?

So many questions I needed answers to.

I had no doubt Brett's words were promises and he had every intention of following through. I didn't want to disappoint him. Or for him to decide I was too inexperienced to engage in the type of sex he desired.

"You're thinking again." A finger rubbed across my forehead to smooth out the lines that betrayed my confidence.

"I can't help it. I'm sorry."

"Don't be sorry. I'll take care of you and make sure you're ready."

The sound of a drawer opening and closing forced my body to clench. What was in that drawer? What was he doing? "How will you know I'm ready?"

"I'll know. Do you want the blindfold off?"

Did I? Maybe it would be better if I couldn't see what was coming. "No. I'm good." Brett cupped my face and kissed me slowly while he played with my nipples. They were so sensitive, and I needed more. "Suck on my tits."

He chuckled. "There's my girl. I'll appease you, but don't think for a minute that you're in charge."

Yeah, I got that when he tied my hands to the headboard. Also, when he stuck his cock down my throat. I was completely at his mercy and even though it scared me a little, it also thrilled me. His mouth latched on to one of my breasts, laving and nipping and sucking. Then he gave the other the same attention as his fingers pulled the negligee up to expose my stomach. I'd specifically worn this so that all the important parts of my body were accessible without having to be totally exposed, but Brett was intent on exposing all of me anyway. Even my imperfect, slightly rounded, and very soft belly.

With featherlight touches, his fingers ran down the length of my body, tracing around my belly button and heading for my pussy. I'd never been touched so much by a man as I had by Brett. No one had ever shown any interest in making sure my needs were met. They were more interested in the final act. With Brett, the foreplay was as good as the fucking, maybe even better. Well, probably not better, but it was an existential experience all on its own. The way he touched me, caressed me, made my body sing ... it was everything I'd read about in my romance novels but never experienced for myself.

"You're so wet and needy. You want my cock inside you?"

"Please, do it. I need your cock inside me. I want you to fuck me until I can't remember my name."

In one fell swoop, he flipped me over. I let out a gasp as I hit the mattress and the restraints pulled tighter on my wrists. Brett's arm wrapped around my waist as he pulled me to my knees. It wasn't my favorite position because my ass was on display, but it did allow him to get impossibly deep. And *that* I loved. He rubbed something cool and wet on my back hole. I tried not to tighten up, but it was useless. "Relax. It's only a bit bigger than my finger—nowhere close to the size of my cock, but I need to get you ready."

I took a deep breath and tried to relax, but it wasn't easy. There was a bit of pressure as what I assumed was a butt plug slipped inside me. It wasn't totally uncomfortable. It felt weird, but it didn't hurt. Then Brett's cock slowly pushed inside my pussy. It was a whole other feeling. I felt full. "That's it, sweetheart. Take my cock like a good girl."

I forgot about the plug and relished the feeling of him deep inside me. Sex with Brett was always amazing, but this was next level. And when he hit the magic spot, my hips moved of their own accord, pushing back into him. My orgasm was right there, just out of reach. My core tightened and tingles burst along my skin. My head swam with endorphins, then a sharp smack to my ass lit me on fire.

Brett gripped my hips so hard I swore I'd have bruises. He pulled out and my body wept at the empty feeling. I was so close. Another sharp sting to my other cheek. "You naughty girl, trying to steal an orgasm without my permission. Don't you dare come."

My head dropped between my elbows resting on the bed. Tears welled in my eyes as the tingles dissipated. *Damn him!*

The hair was lifted from my neck and soft kisses trailed down my spine. Then a soft buzzing filled the room. He ran a vibrator from the inside of my knee to the apex of my thighs, skipping the place between, and moved it down the other leg. "Stop teasing me and let me come."

He ran the vibrator over my pussy lips and clit. "You want this?"

"Yes! Goddammit, yes!"

He held it on my clit and the tingles began again. My mind drifted away. The pleasure was all-consuming, taking me to a place I'd never been before. My body was like a rubber band, ready to snap.

And then it was gone again. He'd never edged me before and I found it both frustrating and intoxicating. If I could get my hands free, I'd either slap him or hop on his dick. It was fifty-fifty. "Brett! Let me come!"

"I like you like this. So damn impatient." He pulled the plug halfway from my ass and swirled it inside me. It felt... good. Then it was gone, and two fingers slipped inside me, scissoring and stretching my butt. "You're almost ready."

I let out a frustrated sigh. I wanted to come. Was that too much to ask? Cool liquid dripped between my butt cheeks, and he rubbed it in and out of my hole. Next was a gentle nudge of something much, much bigger than the plug or his fingers. I tried not to clench, but another swift smack to my ass told me I'd failed. I took a deep breath and let my body go lax. This time the nudge came with the addition of the vibrator on my clit. It didn't take long until my head was swimming again. I barely noticed my body stretching to accommodate his cock, and when his hips hit the back of my thighs, I knew he was all the way in.

"How do you feel?"

"Full, but I'm good. Please fuck me," I gasped.

Slowly he moved in and out of me. It didn't hurt a bit. As a matter of fact, it wasn't enough. I began moving with him, trying to increase the speed. Next thing I knew, the vibrator was inside my pussy, vibrating me from the inside out. His hand rubbed circles on my clit as he fucked my ass with the toy pulsing inside me.

It was too much. A complete and utter sensory overload. I surrendered all control and let my body take everything he was giving me.

My pulse quickened. My breathing shallowed. The tingles before were nothing compared to the fire racing through my veins. Every pulse, every thrust, pushed me closer and closer to the edge of a cliff I'd never climbed before. And just when I thought I couldn't take any more, my orgasm detonated like a bomb. White spots danced behind my eyelids and the sound of blood rushing in my ears blocked out everything. I couldn't move. I couldn't speak. I couldn't think. All I could do was feel. The shock waves started at my core and traveled to my fingers and toes. My head swam and I drifted in and out of consciousness. My body convulsed uncontrollably.

It was glorious and all I wanted was for it to last forever. If this was a dream, I never wanted to wake up.

I was warm and safe.

That's all I could think as my eyes fluttered open. My head lolled to the side and the world came back into focus. I leaned back against Brett's hard body in his Jacuzzi tub, bubbles up to my chest.

"Welcome back." He lifted my chin and pressed his lips to mine. "You scared me."

"I'm sorry." He must have carried me to the tub because I didn't remember a thing.

"Don't be sorry, sweetheart. I put you through a lot."

I remembered the feeling of sparklers under my skin and my head floating away. The complete euphoria. "I'll do better next time," I whispered.

He chuckled. "You were perfect. Everything about you was more than I could have asked for. How do you feel?" He picked up a sponge and dripped warm water down my neck.

"Tired."

"Are you sore?"

I shook my head. "Not really, but this feels nice."

He lifted my arm and ran the sponge over it, then the other. "You'll feel it tomorrow." He held up my wrist and kissed the faint red marks from pulling on the tie. Then he did the same to the other wrist. "Thank you."

"For what?"

"Trusting me with your body and letting me push you beyond your comfort zone. I don't take that for granted."

"I liked it. I've never orgasmed like that before."

"It's been a while for me too."

I didn't like to think of him with someone else, but like he'd said… the past was the past. I was the one he'd fucked tonight. I was the one cradled against his body in a warm bubble bath. I was the one who'd be sleeping in his bed tonight.

Brett finished wiping down my body with the sponge, taking care of me. He peppered kisses along my neck and shoulders. "Let's get you into bed." He helped me out of the tub and dried me with a fluffy towel. Then he carried me to the bed and set me down on the soft sheets. Handing me two aspirin and a glass of water, he asked, "Do you need anything?"

I swallowed down the pills. "You." I patted the empty place beside me. "That's a given." He lay down next to me.

I rolled toward him, put my head on his chest, and draped my leg over his. "Thank you for tonight. I had a really good time at the ball."

He kissed the top of my head and wrapped his arms around me. "You're very welcome."

With my body tangled around his, I was the most content I'd ever been. I wished the feeling could last forever.

By Sunday night, I was back in my own bed with Fred sleeping next to me. I tossed and turned all night, missing the warmth of Brett's body. As much as I wanted us to spend every night together, it wasn't realistic. We'd only been together five weeks, depending on when you started counting. Even I knew that wasn't much time.

One thing was for sure though... I was irrevocably in love with Brett Kingston. It wasn't just emophilia. I'd been in unrequited love a dozen different times, but none of them felt like this. This was bone-deep love. A feeling so consuming that I was sure a swarm of butterflies had taken up permanent residence in my body.

When I woke up each morning, I thought about him. I wanted to see him, talk to him, be with him. When I was with him, there was no other place I'd rather be. When he kissed me, nothing else existed. And when he made love to me, I floated away to another place.

I hadn't said the words yet. They'd been on the tip of my tongue several times, but if he didn't say them back, I'd be crushed. So, I kept those three little words to myself because not having them reciprocated would make things weird between us.

I mean… obviously he cared about me, but I doubted he loved me. To him, we were having fun together. To me, we were building a future. There was a big difference between the two.

Rolling to the side, I rubbed Fred's belly. "What do you think? Think Brett could ever fall in love with me?" He rolled on his back and licked my hand. Not sure what that meant, but it was more positive than a hiss or a scratch.

After dozing off for a few hours, my phone pinged from its place on the nightstand. I rolled over again and looked at the clock. It was barely five o'clock. On the off chance it was Brett, I reached for my phone and glasses.

It wasn't a text. It was an email from Trent. My head spun as to what could be so important to deserve an early morning email. Since I was already awake, I clicked on it. There was a video attached, so I clicked on that too.

What I saw had me bolting upright. There was no way! But there was. The evidence was on my screen.

Why the hell would Trent send me an email with a video of him and Gia having sex in his office? I checked to see who else received the email. "Oh my god!"

Everyone! Everyone in our office received the email, including Trent's dad, *the* Mr. Dorsey. Holy Shit!

I quickly texted Gia. When she didn't respond, I sent another. And another.

Fuck it! This was worth waking her up for. I called her.

"It's too early," she answered with a yawn.

"Sorry. Did you see my messages?"

"Not yet. What is it?"

"You need to look right now. I'll wait." I waited while she watched the video. This had to be the most mortifying thing I'd ever experienced, and it wasn't even of me.

"Oh my god!" she screamed.

"Gia? Gia? Talk to me!"

"How?"

I gulped, hating to have to tell her more bad news. "It came through my email a few minutes ago. It was sent to everyone in our office."

"Who? How?" She was in shock.

Now I had to deliver the worst part. I cringed. "It came from Trent."

"But...but I've been with him all night."

It didn't make sense to me either. Something was not right. "I don't know, girl."

"How quick can you pick me up from Trent's?"

"I can be there in ten minutes," I said as I pulled on a pair of shorts.

"I'll meet you out front."

I raced around the apartment, grabbing my shoes, keys, and purse. This was a clusterfuck. Gia had no one in Vegas to turn to. No family. No friends. I was the only person who could help her.

When I pulled up in front of Trent's apartment building, Gia stood at the curb in a pair of cotton shorts, a baggy T-shirt, and no shoes. I wasn't used to seeing her so casual, but I wasn't looking like a beauty queen myself.

She jumped in the car and threw her bag in the back seat. "I can't tell you how much I appreciate this."

"No worries. What's the plan?"

"Take me back to the hotel. I've got to pack. There's a plane leaving for Chicago in two hours, and I need to be on it. Can you take me to the airport?"

I started driving to Mystique, where Gia stayed since moving here. "You're leaving?"

She threw her hands in the air. "What else am I going to do? Everyone in the office is going to see that video. They're going to think I got my job by sleeping with Trent. I'm going to be a joke."

"But you've worked your ass off."

"It won't matter. Why would Trent do this to me? I trusted him. I fucking trusted him!"

I'd been asking myself the same question. "What if it wasn't Trent? What if someone else sent it from his email?" I already had a suspect, but I kept it to myself.

"The damage is done. I can't show my face at work anymore."

She was determined to leave and honestly, I would have probably felt the same. I thought about what Brett and I had done in his pool. He assured me it was safe, but now I wasn't so sure. One word... drones. Any reporter that really wanted a story about him wouldn't hesitate to use a drone. God, I hoped a picture never showed up of us in a compromising position. I. Would. Die.

I parked in front of Mystique, telling the valet we were employees and would be back within twenty minutes. We raced to Gia's room, and I helped her pack her essentials. I agreed to box up the rest of her stuff, including everything in her office, and ship it to her.

Next thing I knew, we were in the drop-off lane at the airport. I gave her a tight hug. "I know we haven't known each other long, but I'm really going to miss you."

"I'm going to miss you too," she said as she hugged me back.

We were both in tears as I watched my friend and boss walk into the airport and out of my life.

Chapter 32
Brett

"The next available flight doesn't leave until three."

Through the phone, I could practically hear Trent running his hand through his hair. Hunter leaking that video sent Gia into a tizzy—not that I blamed her—and onto the first flight she could get to Chicago. By the time Trent found out, it was too late. She was gone.

Now he was at the airport waiting for the next flight out and chasing her across the country. The guy was head over ass for that woman. Guess he didn't have to worry about telling his dad about their relationship. The entire office had seen the video. "I'm sorry. That sucks. I can have the company jet fueled up and ready within an hour or two."

"Nah. I appreciate the offer, but the time will give me an opportunity to figure out what I'm going to say. Plus, I have no idea how long I'll be gone. I hate that she ran. I hate that she thinks I would betray her. And most of all, I hate that we're fifteen-hundred miles apart. I'm not sure she's gonna want to come back."

"Then use the ole Trent Dorsey charm on her. Remind her why the two of you are great together. It could have been way worse. At least her tits and pussy weren't in the video."

Trent growled on the other end of the phone. "Don't talk about her tits and pussy."

"Just sayin' it could have been worse. It was more like soft porn."

He sighed. "I know. It's still embarrassing though. And now everyone in the office knows we're fucking. I didn't get to tell my dad about us on my own terms."

"Hunter's a fucktard." He'd been a shit when we were growing up, running around and tattling on us every chance he got, but this time he'd gone too far. "What are you going to do about him?"

"I don't know. I haven't gotten that far yet. My first priority is Gia."

"You'll get her back," I said, not knowing if it was the truth. "Whatever you need, let me know. And if you decide Hunter needs a good beatdown, you know where to find me."

"Thanks, man. I'll keep you updated."

After hanging up with Trent, I leaned back in my leather chair and stared out my office window. I didn't sleep for shit last night. Two nights with Penny wrapped in my arms and I missed having her by my side, her back pulled to my chest. The smell of her strawberry shampoo was like an aphrodisiac and her warm, soft skin pressed against mine was addicting.

It hadn't even been twenty-four hours and I missed her. Thinking back over our time together, I couldn't remember another time in my life when I'd been more content.

Floyd, Kingston Enterprise's CFO, knocked on my open door, pulling me out of my daze. I waved him in, and he took a seat across from me. "We have a problem."

My CFO was a problem solver. He rarely came to me with issues, so my curiosity was piqued. I mentally ran through our companies that were in transition. Leaning forward on my desk, I steepled my fingers. "What's going on?"

"It's the Vegas Vista property. I made a fair-market-value offer and the owner declined."

That was disappointing. I tapped my fingers together, determined not to get worked up before knowing the details. "Interesting. Did he say why?"

"He's owned the property for thirty years and said the strip malls on them add value to the community. That the businesses there are mostly family owned and he wasn't willing to terminate their leases."

It was ridiculous. There were a dozen strip malls around town that sat half-empty. Plenty of space to relocate. It'd be an inconvenience, but that's what progress entailed. Vegas Vista would bring more traffic to that part of town. It would be good for everyone, including small businesses. The location was the perfect place. We'd gone over all the demographics and financials.

I tapped on my desk with my index finger. "I want that property. Sweeten the pot and make him an offer he can't refuse. Everyone has a price."

Floyd was as shrewd of a businessman as I was. "That's what I thought you'd say. I'll dig into his personal financials to see if there's anything we can use as leverage."

"Dig deep." We had to make this deal. I'd already sold the board on our plan. My reputation and their faith in me to continue as CEO counted on it. I wouldn't give them a reason to second-guess that decision.

"On the off chance he's clean as a whistle, how high do you want me to go?"

We needed that piece of land. "Double it if you have to."

He stood and tucked his papers under his arm. "Understood."

I had faith in Floyd. That property would be ours by the end of the week and then we could move forward on Vegas Vista. It was nonnegotiable.

Once the closing was final, we'd give the current tenants notice that their leases were going to be terminated in ninety days. It gave them time to secure new storefronts and relocate. That would put us right on schedule to demolish the current strip malls standing on the property. I'd been hesitant to get involved with the Vegas Vista project, but as the pieces started to come together, my hesitancy turned to excitement.

An alert came through my phone and when I clicked on the story from the *Las Vegas Not So Confidential*, I couldn't help but smile when I read it. My investment in Karla Blitzer paid off.

Vegas Billionaire Off the Market

Listen up, ladies! I've seen it with my own eyes and the rumors are true. Seems our Vegas billionaire, Brett Kingston, is smitten. He was seen at Mystique's Unmask Domestic Violence fundraiser this past weekend with the same mystery woman we've caught him with over the past few weeks.

So, who is she?

Sources tell me her name is Penelope Quinn and she's a marketing executive for Mystique. Can you say power couple?

Miss Quinn and Mr. Kingston both looked radiant, decked out in their formal wear and despite my former cynicism, I can see why the billionaire has fallen for the petite brunette. Her designer dress was to DIE for and showed off her curvy figure magnificently. Miss Quinn was the picture of elegance and sophistication. As she mingled with the guests, her enthusiasm and smile were difficult to match.

And let me tell you, the way Brett Kingston looked at her...swoon. Although the business mogul usually shies away from public displays of affection, the kiss he shared with Miss Quinn on the dance floor was hot enough to set your panties on fire.

The tiger is definitely circling his mate.

We'll be keeping an eye on this situation and, as always, giving you the scoop on everything not so confidential.

230

The article practically had me down on one knee proposing, but I didn't care about that. What I cared about was that when Penny read the column, she'd feel confident about herself. That was worth ten grand.

Chapter 33
Penny

"I'm so glad you came back." I gave Gia a hug. She'd locked herself in her office as soon as she arrived.

She hugged me back. "I wasn't sure about it, but Trent assured me Hunter was gone. Was everyone talking about me?"

"There was some talk, but it was more about Hunter. The entire staff took offense to what he did to you. I don't think they were very sad to see him fired." Gia and Trent were gone for a week and returned last night. "How was your visit home?"

"Weird." She tapped on her lip. "When Trent met my family, I felt like I was sixteen again. It was a nonstop game of twenty questions, and I kept waiting for them to find something wrong with him. I guess seeking your parents' approval never really goes away." She sighed. "I can't believe he flew to Chicago without a suitcase and then drove another hour to Waukegan. Can you imagine him shopping at Walmart for jeans and sweatshirts? It was a sight; I'll tell you that."

I tried to imagine Brett shopping at a discount store and the thought made me giggle. "Yeah, the guys are definitely used to an experience that's a bit more sophisticated." My lips twisted to the side. "I wonder if Brett even shops for himself. I can't see him standing in front of a rack of underwear, picking out boxer briefs. I bet he has a personal shopper."

She nodded. "Rich people lead totally different lives than us. Are we crazy for thinking we can fit into them?"

It was a question I'd been asking myself for weeks. As much as I wanted to think the money didn't matter, it did. "I think you and Trent will be fine. The man flew halfway across the country for you. If that doesn't say love, then I don't know what does."

She giggled. "Trent showed up to the dive bar I was sitting in looking like a wet dog in a five-thousand-dollar suit. I suppose if he was willing to drive through a Waukegan snowstorm and drink shit whiskey, we've got a chance."

I smiled because, from where I sat, they had more than a chance. "Has he told you he loves you yet?"

"Yes. Actually, he said it before the video was released, so I know it wasn't reactionary. Has Brett said it to you?"

I shook my head. "No. I've been trying to be patient, but it's so hard. I'm afraid I'm going to blurt out *I love you* and he's going to look at me like I grew another head."

Gia's lips turned down. "It'll happen. According to Trent, Brett had a girlfriend back in high school. He bought a ring and everything. I don't know what happened, but since then, he's never had anyone serious in his life. It's all been work, work, work. So, the fact that you two have been together for this long is a good sign."

There was a lot of information packed in those few sentences and since Brett and I agreed not to discuss the past, it was information I wouldn't have gotten from him. *High school?* Jeez. That was almost fifteen years ago. What could have happened that made him so closed off? Clearly, he never got over it. That put me in a precarious situation. "It's not enough though. I don't want to wake up six months from now and realize he's never going to love me. What if I'm just a convenient... distraction?"

233

"I hate to tell you this, but because I'm your friend, I feel I need to." Gia paused. Tapping her manicured nails on her desk.

My heart was already fragile. It couldn't take another hit. "Tell me what?"

She sighed. "Brett doesn't have any problem finding distractions. He's been with a lot of women, Penny."

"I'm aware." It was one thing for his dating history to be printed in a gossip column. It was quite another for it to be thrown in my face. Again. All I wanted was to forget about the random two hundred women that came before me. Every rule had its exception. Why couldn't I be his?

"What I'm saying is maybe you need to prod him a little bit. Show him what a future would look like between the two of you. Show him there's more to life than work. Do something unexpected for him."

I rolled my eyes. "That's great advice. Now if you could point me in the right direction, I might be able to do something with it. In case you haven't noticed, I'm not great at this whole dating thing. As a matter of fact, I might be terrible at it."

"You're not terrible at it. Think about what Brett likes."

"He likes sex. Dirty, filthy sex, to be exact."

She waved her hand dismissively in the air. "Well, there you go."

Gia acted as if the answer was clear. However, her words were like hieroglyphics I couldn't decipher. "What do you mean, *there you go*?"

"He likes work and sex," she said, counting them off on her fingers.

Still confused, I added, "He also likes Mexican food."

"Even better. This is what you're going to do." Gia laid out the rest of the plan for me in graphic detail.

It was a good plan.

An hour later, dressed in a pencil skirt, a button-up blouse, and the sexy heels I wore to the fundraiser, I knocked on Brett's office door. I'd called

Maryanne to make sure he was in the office and I wouldn't be interrupting a meeting.

"Come in," he barked gruffly.

I opened the door and poked my head in. "Hey, you."

His face morphed from grumpy to surprised. "Well, this is unexpected." He pushed back from his desk and stood.

Locking the door behind me, I held up the bag in my hand. "I brought lunch."

He devoured me with his eyes from head to toe, licking his lips. "That's perfect because I'm starving."

Putting a little sway in my hips, I strolled toward him and set the bag on the corner of his desk. "It's your favorite."

He curled one hand in the hair at the nape of my neck and wrapped the other around my waist, pulling me flush to his body. "It certainly is." With me locked in his grasp, he attacked my lips with a fierceness I'd come to expect from him. The kiss consumed me and set my blood on fire. Hot, molten lava coursed through my veins as I melted into him. Pulling my skirt up my hips, he scooped me up and set me on the edge of his desk.

I traced the outline of his hard erection that was clearly visible through his suit pants and stared up at him innocently. "Mr. Kingston, this is inappropriate work behavior."

He chuckled as he unbuttoned my blouse and pulled it off my shoulders. "What's inappropriate, Miss Quinn, is you showing up here like a naughty secretary and tempting me to fuck you."

"Me? I just brought tacos from Tico's. Don't you want a taco?"

"I'll have a taco, alright." His fingers ran along the seam of my pussy through my silky panties. "I hope you're not too attached to these."

Before I realized what he meant, he ripped the underwear at both sides, pulled them off, and shoved them in his pocket. Wetness pooled between my legs and my pussy clenched. I felt like the heroine of a romance novel, and it gave me goose bumps. "I did like those." I pouted playfully.

He squeezed my cheeks and lifted my chin. "I'll buy you more." Picking up the phone with his free hand, he barked, "I'm not to be interrupted until Miss Quinn leaves," and slammed the phone back into its cradle, all the while giving me a predatory gaze. "Spread your legs for me, naughty girl." Before I had a chance to react, he pushed my thighs so far apart it was obscene.

I gasped. This is what I loved. He commanded my body without permission. Zero fucks given about propriety. When the man wanted to fuck you, he would and have you begging for more.

"I'm going to eat your pussy until you come all over my face, then I'm going to bend you over this desk and fuck the sass right out of you."

My eyes widened at his bluntness. I should have been used to it by now, but I doubted I'd ever get used to the way Brett dirty-talked me.

"Don't act like you didn't know what would happen when you showed up at my office in that skirt and those fuck-me shoes. You knew exactly what you were doing, didn't you?"

"Yes. Now get to making good on those promises." I put my hand on his shoulder and pushed him down between my legs.

He sank to his knees, never breaking eye contact. "I'm going to spank your ass for that."

"Another promise." I lifted my hips toward his face.

"Yes, it is." Then without any further ado, he buried his face in my pussy, wrecking me for any other man. He feasted and feasted like I was his actual lunch, and he was indeed starving.

I frantically pushed aside the things on his desk so I could lean back. He wasn't messing around, and within minutes, every muscle in my body began to tighten like the *click, click, click* of a roller coaster ascending. My body wound tighter and tighter, taking me higher and higher. I teetered at the top and pressed a hand to my mouth to silence the scream I knew was coming. My body snapped and the free fall began, tumbling me into an abyss of erotic pleasure where I lost space and time.

I'd barely recovered before Brett flipped me onto my stomach and pressed my breasts against the cool top of his desk. My toes skimmed the floor as he pushed between my legs and buried his cock in me.

A swift smack to my ass caused my pussy to flood until it dripped down the insides of my thighs. "That's what you get for being a naughty girl." Then a smack to my other cheek. "And that's for your sassy mouth." His

236

fingers dug into my hips as he pounded into me fast and hard, his balls slapping my already sensitive clit. He hit that spot deep inside me that sent me spiraling. My pussy began to clench around his cock. "Don't you dare. Not yet," he growled.

With my cheek pressed against his desk, I panted, "I can't... stop... it."

"Wait, goddammit." After a few more furious thrusts, he roared, "Now!"

Fireworks exploded and sent electrical pulses through every inch of my body. I was completely spent. Brett lay over my back, as exhausted as I was.

"Are you okay," he mumbled.

"Uh-huh."

He brushed my hair aside and gently kissed my neck and bare shoulders. "That was amazing, baby. I haven't had such a delicious lunch in forever."

Still squished against the desk, I pointed to the bag. "There're still tacos."

Brett laughed. Letting his dick slip out of me, he pulled me to my feet and smoothed my skirt down over my ass. With a soft kiss to my lips, he nodded to the other side of his office. "There's a bathroom. Go clean yourself up."

I pulled my blouse over my shoulders and stumbled into the attached bathroom. One look in the mirror confirmed that coming to his office wasn't a mistake. My pupils were blown, my cheeks glowed, and I had a smear of lipstick on my chin. Strands of hair stuck out at odd angles. When people said someone looked *just fucked,* this is what they meant.

My lips curled up. If someone had told me two months ago that I'd be standing in Brett Kingston's office after being thoroughly fucked, I would have never believed them.

Gia was right. Brett might not have said the words yet, but what we had together was more than a casual fling.

Us.

This relationship.

It meant something to him.

Chapter 34
Brett

Penny never ceased to surprise me. Her showing up to my office in those fuck-me heels and sexy skirt was not what I was expecting. I'd never had sex in my office before, it was unprofessional and irresponsible, but she had me breaking all the rules.

"Thank you for bringing me lunch," I said as I stuffed the last of a crispy taco into my mouth.

She quirked an eyebrow. "Just lunch?"

I took her chin between my fingers. "Tacos are my absolute favorite, especially yours."

She pushed my hand away with a laugh. "Eww, gross."

"You didn't have a problem with it when my head was between your thighs." I laughed.

"That was different," she said, wiping her mouth with a napkin. "Sex talk is the exception. I'm pretty sure you could say anything to me in the heat of the moment and I'd melt into a puddle of goo."

"Noted. You like my filthy mouth."

"Oh, I'm your biggest fan." She smiled mischievously. "I like your mouth, your fingers, and your cock."

"Now, who's the dirty talker?" I took it slow with Penny in the beginning, but over time she'd proved to be a minxy little vixen in the bedroom. Being with her was the most fulfillment I'd ever gotten from a woman. And it wasn't just the sex. Yes, the sex was great, but so were the intelligent conversations and witty humor.

Penny was a diamond in the rough and for the first time since Katy, I had the feeling I'd found my person. The one I didn't want to be away from. The one I could be open and honest with. The one who could be my forever.

She twined her fingers together and rested her chin on them. "So, how's your day going?"

Her cuteness made the organ in my chest thump harder. "It's going well. We closed on the Vegas Vista property today."

"That's exciting. Where is it being built?"

I gathered our trash from the table and pointed to the stack of papers I'd pushed aside. "The aerial view is right there. It's a great piece of property. Lots of traffic and space to build."

Penny pulled her glasses from her purse and reached for the papers while I threw the taco wrappers away. She inspected the photo and looked up at me with her big cat-eye glasses. "You're building here?"

I stood over her shoulder and gazed at what would become Vegas's newest and most extravagant mall. "Yes. We researched the hell out of it, and it's prime real estate."

She bit her lip and let out a breath through her nose. "And what about the strip malls that are already there?"

I knew this would be an issue, but the decision had been made. "They'll be demolished, and we'll start fresh."

She stood up and put her hands on her hips. "You can't be serious."

"Listen, I know you're against gentrification, but you need to look at the bigger picture."

She picked up the aerial photo and held it in front of my face. "Oh, I see the picture just fine. This"—she pointed to one of the buildings—"is Between the Covers Café, my family's bookstore."

Fuck! How did I not know this?

She pointed to another spot. "And this is Mr. Polanski's deli." And another spot. "This is Mrs. Chen's nail salon. And right over here," she said, moving her finger, "is the antique store owned by the Bethel sisters. They've been there for thirty years!"

I took the photo from her hand and set it back on the table. "I'm sorry. I didn't know that was where Between the Covers Café was. It was an oversight I should have been aware of."

Penny blinked up at me. "So, you're not going to build there?"

She was kidding, right? "The deal is already done. There's nothing I can do about it."

"Bullshit!" She stomped her foot. "Cancel the deal!"

I laughed at the absurdity. "I can't cancel the deal. Do you know how much it cost us to secure that property? The wheels are already in motion."

Her forehead creased and her eyes narrowed. "And what about the existing businesses?"

"They'll be given a ninety-day notice of lease termination. Plenty of time to relocate." It was standard business procedure.

She let out a maniacal laugh and looked up at the ceiling. "Oh my god! That's such a rich-person thing to say. Like it's so easy to relocate. The rent will double, plus the cost of moving into and renovating a new space. Those businesses, including the bookstore, will go bankrupt."

I took her by the shoulders and steadied her. "You're being dramatic."

She twisted away from me. "I'm not being dramatic. I'm being realistic. I'm begging you to find somewhere else to build. If you care about me at all, you'll do it!"

"That's not fair! You're being immature, selfish, and unreasonable."

"I'm being selfish?" She pointed to herself. "I'm being selfish? Take a good look in the mirror, bucko. You're willing to destroy a dozen small businesses for the sake of your precious mall. That's selfish!"

"It's a billion-dollar deal! What do you want me to do? You act as if it's personal. It's not. It's business."

Penny sucked in a breath and clasped her hands in front of her. "Excuse me for taking it *personally* that you're single-handedly destroying the business *my family* spent the last twenty years building. For a fucking mall! I guess that's the difference between us. Where I see people, all you see is money. You flaunt it around and think you can get whatever you want by throwing cash at it. Newsflash… my family's livelihood is not for sale!"

"That's fucking insulting and hypocritical! You didn't have a problem when I was wining and dining you! A five-thousand-dollar dress? A drop in the bucket, right? Those thousand-dollar shoes on your feet? Chump change, right? Oh, and what about the ten grand I paid Karla Blitzer to be nice to you in her column? You didn't have a problem when I was throwing around my money then!" I was so fucking mad words spewed from my mouth without thought or care. I never intended to tell her about the reporter, but it was too late now.

She gasped and clutched her chest as if I'd stuck a knife into it. "I never asked for any of that," she whispered. "I've loved you since day one and I worked so hard to be what you wanted me to be, but I can see now it was all a waste." A tear dripped down her cheek. "We were never going to work. If you felt like you had to pay off a reporter so you wouldn't be embarrassed, clearly, we have bigger issues." More tears spilled down her cheeks as she picked up her purse and headed for the door.

I should have felt bad for making her cry, but rage blinded me. She blamed *me* for this falling apart? Well, fuck that! "You're no different than the others, using me to get something for yourself!"

She stopped at the door and turned toward me with mascara running down her face. "I never cared about your money. All I wanted was for you to love me."

"You would have been better off asking for the money."

Penny unbuckled the Jimmy Choos from her ankles and slipped out of them. "I hear these go for big bucks on eBay. Have a nice fucking life." Then she left my office on bare feet.

I stood there and stared at the open door.

What the fuck just happened?

Chapter 35
Penny

My feet burned from walking on the hot asphalt. I yanked open my car door and fell into the seat, letting my head hit the steering wheel. Every fiber of my being was decimated.

Not only did I lose Brett, but my family was going to lose Between the Covers Café.

Why did I have to fall in love with him?

A huge sob stuck in my throat and worked its way up. The tears fell at a rapid pace as the reality of the situation hit with the force of a Category 5 hurricane. The sobs racked my body until I was nothing but a blubbering mess.

I don't know how long I sat in the parking lot, but at some point, I drove home, not that I remembered how I got there. Inside my condo, I poured myself a glass of boxed wine and slid down the cabinets until my butt hit the floor. The tears kept falling. I'd never been so embarrassed or humiliated in my life.

The article from the *Las Vegas Not So Confidential* was a complete sham. She'd been paid to give me compliments. He was so worried I wouldn't live up to society's expectations that he actually paid someone to be nice to me. That information killed what little was left of my self-confidence.

He was never going to love me. It was foolish to think he would. I was another good-time girl to him. A temporary reprieve from the revolving door of beautiful women in his life.

For once, I wanted someone to pick me above anything else. *Why couldn't I have a storybook kind of love?* Because it was simply that… a story. Fiction. A figment of someone's sexy imagination.

In what reality did the nerdy girl get the sexy billionaire?

Not mine.

The kind of love I wanted didn't exist for me.

Fred cautiously approached me and rubbed against my bare legs. I picked him up and hugged him to my chest. "It's you and me, buddy. Just you and me."

I finished the box of wine and passed out on the couch in a puddle of my own tears.

Then I called in to work on Tuesday.

And Wednesday.

And Thursday.

And Friday.

Brett broke my heart.

Chapter 36
Brett

The lease termination letters sat on my desk untouched for the last week. I didn't have the heart to sign them yet. I kept thinking about Between the Covers Café, Mr. Polanski's deli, Mrs. Chen's nail salon, and the Bethel sisters.

It made zero sense, but Penny's words echoed in my head. Did I care more about money than people? I didn't want to think that was true. I was more than generous. I donated hundreds of thousands of dollars to worthy causes all over the country. My tax returns proved it.

But business was business. Emotions were irrelevant. If you wanted to be successful, there was no room for warm, fuzzy feelings.

The board was counting on me to follow through with Vegas Vista and I intended to do it. Setbacks and failure were not options.

So why was I dragging my feet on signing those letters?

I hadn't heard a word from Penny in a week. Not a phone call. Not a text. Not anything.

I reached for the phone several times, but I never followed through. This couldn't be solved with an *I'm sorry*. We had opposing interests and neither one of us was willing to budge.

I missed the fuck out of her.

Every day I woke up, ran five miles, came to work, then went to bed. Rinse and repeat. I was grumpy as hell, barked orders at my employees, and I'm pretty sure I tap danced on Maryanne's last nerve.

My chest ached. My mind was foggy. The vein in my temple threatened to burst. There was nothing physically wrong with me. It was all in my fucking head. Psychosomatic symptoms from watching a petite, quirky brunette walk out of my office with tears running down her face.

And I wanted them to go away.

Trent picked up a chip from his plate and shoved it in his mouth. "So, what's going on?"

I hadn't told him about the blowout I had with Penny, but there was no doubt he knew there was trouble in paradise. I took a bite of my sandwich. "Nothing."

"Riiiight. Everything's great, right?" More chips and obnoxious chewing followed.

I glared at him. "You got something to say, then say it." This was none of his business and I didn't need a guilt trip from my best friend.

"Penny took all last week off. Did you guys go somewhere?" he asked as he casually ate his lunch.

"You know we didn't. What did Penny tell Gia?"

"Nothing. She hasn't said one word about what's going on. All I know is she took a week off and showed up today looking like someone ran over her cat."

"No one ran over her cat." At least, I didn't think anyone had. Maybe if I'd picked up the goddamn phone and called her, I'd know. "We broke up."

245

Trent nodded his head repeatedly. "By *we,* do you mean you broke up with her?"

"It was mutual. We came to an impasse."

"About?" he prodded.

I didn't appreciate the inquisition, although it shocked me it had taken this long to happen. I was ninety percent positive that when Penny left my office, she would run to Gia with all the gory details. That's what women did… gossip. I thought she would be champing at the bit to make me look like the bad guy. *Why didn't she?* "The Vegas Vista project."

"Keep talking," he said, shoving more food in his mouth.

I rolled my eyes. "Kingston Enterprises bought a prime piece of real estate. The location is perfect. The traffic volume is perfect. The size is perfect. Everything is perfect. The investors and the board both signed off on it. There're a couple of strip malls that need to be demolished, but other than that, everything is a go."

"That sounds fantastic."

"It is, except for one tiny, little issue."

He raised a brow at me.

Having completely lost my appetite, I pushed my plate aside. "Penny's parents' bookstore is in the strip mall."

"Fuuuuck."

I snapped my fingers and pointed at him. "Exactly. She said they can't afford to relocate, and it will bankrupt them, along with the other businesses. She wants me to find somewhere else to build."

"So, why don't you?"

I threw my hands in the air. "It's a done deal. The property is already purchased, and the wheels are in motion. I can't stop them."

"You could, but you won't."

"That property cost a fortune. I can't change directions now. The board and investors would flip their shit. I'd look incompetent and they'd rethink their confidence in me to run the company. I have to move forward."

"That's bullshit and you know it," Trent spat at me. "No one is more competent than you. I've seen you renegotiate and work deals since you were sixteen. You're a fucking pro. You could change this if you wanted to."

I folded my arms angrily across my chest. "Maybe I don't want to. Maybe it's better this way."

"Why?"

"Because she's in love with me."

Then *he* rolled his eyes. "Obviously. Everyone who saw you at the fundraiser could tell the two of you were in love."

I looked my best friend in the eyes and lied. "I don't do love."

Chapter 37
Penny

"Penny, come out and let us see," my mother called through the curtain.

Today was the final fitting for Loretta's wedding, which was only a week away. The bridezilla herself was waiting with bated breath to see if I'd be able to pull magic out of my ass and fit into the dress.

"One minute." I slipped the black bridesmaid dress off the hanger and stepped into it, then contorted my arm to pull the zipper up. Looking in the mirror, my heart sank.

Impatiently, Bea pushed the curtain open and tugged me out of the dressing room. Loretta stood on her pedestal and looked down at me, her brows furrowed. "Turn," she said, motioning with her finger.

I made a slow turn while Loretta scowled at me. "Is that the right dress? Check in the back room," she ordered Myra, the seamstress. "There's got to be a mistake."

"It's the right dress," Myra assured her.

Loretta waved her arm around. "How? She's swimming in the damn thing."

Turned out that a broken heart worked better than any diet pill ever could. If I could bottle the feeling of your heart being ripped from your chest, I'd be a millionaire.

Bea pointed a finger at my older sister. "You wanted her to lose weight. She lost it and now you're still not happy. Do you have any idea how hard Penny worked to lose weight? For you!"

My mother pushed between my sisters. "Now, girls, calm down. I think Penny looks wonderful. Nothing a little tuck or two can't fix." She glanced at the seamstress and pleaded.

"I can have it fixed in less than an hour," Myra acquiesced.

"See," my mom said. "Easy-peasy. Nothing to worry about. Everything is going to be perfect, Loretta."

"Brett and I broke up," I blurted. My eyes filled with tears as Myra stuck pins in my dress.

Bea rushed into my arms, nearly knocking me and the seamstress to the ground. "I'm so sorry. Are you okay? Why didn't you call me?"

I simply shrugged. I couldn't tell them why we broke up. I was still hoping the lease termination papers wouldn't come until after the wedding. My parents didn't need one more thing to worry about. This wedding was stressful enough.

"Oh, for fuck's sake!"

"Loretta!" my mother scolded.

My sister pointed to her chest. "This is supposed to be about me. I'm the bride, and as usual, Penny's trying to steal all the attention."

My blood boiled. My entire life, I'd lived in her shadow. "I'm sorry my broken heart is such an inconvenience to you. Don't worry, I'll find a date so you're not embarrassed by your loser sister."

She put her hands on her hips. "I didn't say you were a loser."

"You've implied it my whole life because I wasn't as popular or pretty or skinny as you. I'm over it. As a matter of fact, I'm over you."

"Fine."

Then my mother cried, Bea silently pumped her fist, and Myra looked as if she couldn't wait for us to leave.

The feeling was mutual.

"What's up, Penny?"

I stood in front of Tom's desk, wringing my hands nervously. "I have a favor to ask you."

"Okay. What can I do for you?"

I let out a big sigh because this was harder than I thought it would be. "Let me preface this by saying you're free to say *no*. There'll be zero hard feelings. Actually, I kind of expect you to say no because I've been a shitty friend when you've been nothing but nice to me."

Tom pushed his glasses up with a finger. "You haven't been a shitty friend."

"Yes, I have." I'd done the same thing to Tom that people did to me my whole life. I judged him without giving him a chance or getting to know him. "My sister's wedding is this weekend and I need a date. I was wondering if you'd be willing to go with me. As a friend." I didn't need him thinking the ask was anything more than what it was—a desperate plea.

His lips twisted to the side. "You and Brett aren't getting back together?"

I never told Tom or anyone else that we broke up, but I guessed that's what happened when you flaked out and didn't show up to work for a week. People talked and I gave them a lot to talk about. "Not anytime in the foreseeable future. We should have never dated in the first place. I was living in la-la-land thinking someone like him would stay with someone like me."

Tom stood and pulled me into the conference room, shutting the door behind us. "What do you mean *someone like you*? There's nothing wrong with you."

I took his hand and held it in mine. "I know what I am. I'm the weird, nerdy girl who enjoyed dessert too much and vegetables not enough. I've been that way my whole life."

"You're not weird or nerdy. You're perfect the way you are, except you've lost too much weight. Are you okay?"

I shook my head. "Not yet, but I will be." Tom was so sweet. I wished my heart would thump harder for him, but it didn't. I was destined to fall in love with men who were unattainable. "So, about the wedding? I know it's last minute, but…"

"I'd be honored to go with you."

"Thank you." My eyes welled again. I should have been out of tears, but the goddamn things kept coming at the most inconvenient times. I was a mess.

Tom pulled me to his chest and cradled the back of my head. I wrapped my arms around his waist and cried into his chest like an idiot. "You're more than welcome. Brett Kingston's a fool. He doesn't deserve you."

If only that were true.

Chapter 38
Brett

"What's the holdup?" Frank asked. "I haven't got a solid date for demolition yet."

Considering he was the architect of Vegas Vista, I understood his excitement to get started. I should have been excited too, but I couldn't muster it. The lease termination letters were still in a file folder, awaiting my signature. I steepled my fingers and rested my elbows on my desk. "I was wondering…"

Frank held up a hand. "Please tell me you're not backing out. It took you forever to get on board and now we're at a standstill."

"Let me finish. I was wondering if one of the other locations would be better suited."

He blew out a frustrated breath. "We've been over this. We looked at all the properties. This is the one!"

"But what if it isn't? What if there's someplace we haven't considered yet?"

"You already purchased it. What the fuck is the problem?"

The problem was a five-foot, green-eyed brunette. All I could think was, *WWPD?*

What would Penny do?

She'd sacrifice herself for others. No questions asked because that's the kind of woman she was. Her selfless spirit was part of what I loved about her.

Then I thought about my father. Would he be proud of me for destroying a dozen family businesses purely for financial gain? I highly doubted it; family was everything to him. I'd gotten so absorbed in proving myself that I forgot what Kingston Enterprises stood for.

"The problem is I'm not convinced this is the best move for Kingston Enterprises. Whatever we do, I want to be proud our name is on it. I'm putting the project on hold until I do further research on alternative building sites."

"This is fucking bullshit! I'm filing a complaint with your board." The steam practically billowed from Frank's ears as he threatened me.

Nothing pissed me off more than being backed into a corner. I bit and when I did, I struck hard. "Do what you have to do. But if you do, I'll pull out of the project completely; consequences be damned. You need me a hell of a lot more than I need you. If you had the capital to do this on your own, you'd have never come to me with it. Give me the time I'm requesting, or find another investor to finance you."

"I'll sue you!"

That made me laugh. I loved the negotiating. I was a master who'd learned from the best—my dad. He was ruthless but had strict morals that never wavered. "Go ahead and try, I guarantee you'll lose, and your mall will be nothing more than dust in the wind. I'll destroy your reputation and you'll be hard-pressed to find anyone willing to collaborate with you," I said with a smirk. My morals were a little looser than my father's.

His hands clenched and unclenched. "You've got me over a goddamn barrel. What the fuck am I supposed to do?"

I leaned back and clasped my hands over my stomach. "It's your call."

He pounded his fist on my desk. "A week!"

"Longer if I deem it necessary. It's nonnegotiable."

"You're a prick, Kingston!" Frank stomped out of my office and slammed the door behind him.

God, that felt good.

There was only one thing left to do.

Get my girl back.

Chapter 39
Penny

The wedding was everything Loretta could have hoped for. The gorgeous venue was decorated with fairy lights and overflowing flower arrangements. Everything went off without a hitch, including my dress, which fit like a glove.

I got to sit with Tom during dinner because, of course, Loretta and Beau sat up on a riser alone and looked down at their guests like we were mere peasants. He was the perfect gentleman, complimenting me, pulling out my chair, and even laughing at my dad's horrible jokes.

It was too bad that when I looked at Tom, I didn't feel a single spark. Not a zip, not a tingle, nothing. Although logically, we would have made a good couple, he felt more like a brother than a lover.

Seemed like my inconvenient ability to quickly and completely fall in love only applied to men who would never love me back. But Tom was a good guy, and I was determined to smile and enjoy the evening despite the hole in my chest. As much as I tried to accept the reality that Brett and I were over, my heart hurt. Or the place where my heart used to be.

The toasts were made, the cake was cut, and the bride and groom finished their first dance. When the floor began to fill with guests, Tom picked up my hand. "Would you like to dance?"

I plastered a smile on my face even though dancing was the last thing I wanted to do. "I'd love to."

Tom led me to the dance floor and wrapped an arm around my waist. "Are you okay with this?"

I put a hand on his shoulder. "Absolutely."

Bea twirled around the floor with her date, a guy she'd met at the gym, looking radiant. She always had a man on her arm, although they changed frequently. Bea insisted she was holding out for "the one," and until then, she was content playing the field and having fun. It must have been nice to have men lining up and falling at your feet. Somehow, I'd missed the gene both my sisters possessed. I wasn't quite the ugly duckling, but the feeling was the same.

My carefree sister caught my eye and mouthed, *he's cute*. I smiled at her. Tom *was* cute, but even wrapped in his arms, I felt nothing. All I thought about was the last time I danced wrapped in another man's arms. The man that set me on fire from the top of my head to the tips of my toes. The man who chose money over me. Walking out of his office that day was the hardest thing I'd ever done, but it was the right thing. Looking back would only cause more heartache.

Tom squeezed my hand, bringing me back to the here and now. "In case I haven't told you, you look beautiful tonight."

I blushed. "You mentioned it."

"I know I'm not who you wanted to be here with, but I'm glad you asked me anyway."

He was so sweet… it crushed me. "I'm glad I did too, even if I haven't shown it. You've been a really great friend to me, and I don't deserve it."

His face fell. "A friend?"

I gazed at his handsome face and said the only thing I could. "I'm sorry. I didn't mean to lead you on."

"You didn't. I was hoping for more, but being friends is a start."

"You're a good guy, Tom." I kissed him on the cheek. "I'm not ready for anything else, but I want you to know how much I appreciate you."

He squeezed me tighter, and I laid my head against his chest. We swayed to the music, and although I was still broken, I knew one day I'd be okay again. It would take time, but I'd get there.

"Oh shit," Tom whispered as the song ended.

I looked up at him. "What?"

He turned me toward the DJ. Taking the mic was the man who shredded my heart and left me to bleed for the last three weeks.

"Do you want me to get you out of here?"

I folded my arms over my chest. "No. I want to hear what he has to say." *How dare he show up here looking edible in his fancy tux?* As he tapped the mic, everyone in the room turned his way.

"Good evening. My name is Brett and I have something very important to say." He tugged on his collar, looking less than the cool, calm, and collected man he usually was.

"We know who you are!" Bea shouted as she moved closer to my side. My mom and dad sidled up next to me and even Loretta and Beau appeared out of thin air. Surrounded by Tom and my family, I felt loved and protected.

Brett chuckled into the mic. "I'm sure you do. I didn't mean to interrupt this lovely wedding, but this couldn't wait." He nervously ran his hand along his beard. "A couple months ago, I met this really great girl. She was adorable and funny and a tad bit quirky. The first time we had lunch together, she asked me, 'Are you happy?' And my answer was, 'Happy enough.' I had plenty of money, a thriving business, and good friends. What more could a guy ask for, right?"

"Love!" someone shouted from the crowd.

He chuckled again. "I'm getting there. See, when I was in high school, I fell in love with a girl. She was my whole world, and I couldn't see a future without her. I wanted to propose to her, but I kept putting it off because we were so young. When I finally bought a ring, I planned a romantic picnic for us, but she never showed up. She was in a car accident and was killed instantly on her way to meet me." His voice hitched and I saw the pain in his eyes. "I never got to say the things to her I wanted to say. I never got a goodbye. It broke me so bad that I promised myself I'd never fall in love again. Nothing was worth that amount of pain. So, I philandered through life, never committing to another woman. I thought it was the safe thing to do."

Hanging on his every word, the crowd tsked and sighed. But not me. My eyes welled with tears as the pieces fell into place.

"Anyway," he said, clearing his throat. "Then I met Penny. She made me laugh more than I'd laughed in years. She was brutally honest and called me out on my bullshit. She had me texting and calling at all hours of the night. When I wasn't with her, all I could do was think about her. Make no mistake, she never chased me. I chased her. And that was a first for me."

Loretta grabbed my hand and twined her fingers with mine. "Is this for real?" she whispered.

I nodded, waiting for him to continue.

"I fell hard for her... and then I messed up. I won't bore you with the details, but I was so mad that I said things I shouldn't have. She broke up with me, and I let her walk out of my life."

Someone in the crowd groaned, a bunch of people shook their heads, and the flower girl shouted, "Boys are stupid!" Everyone laughed.

Everyone but me.

"It was the biggest mistake I've ever made. I've been miserable without her. I don't know how she managed to crawl under my skin, but I do know I'm not the same man without her. She always thought she wasn't good enough for me, but the truth is, I wasn't good enough for her. She's perfect the way she is."

Then he looked away from the crowd, and we locked eyes. Everything else disappeared. It was just him and me. "Penny, I've been a fool and I hope you'll forgive me. I should have told you this a long time ago... I'm in love with you. Hopelessly, irrevocably in love with you. My life is empty without you by my side. I want to dip M&M's in peanut butter with you, I want to eat tacos with you, and I want my clothes to be covered in hair from your grumpy cat."

I put a hand to my mouth and giggled as a tear ran down my cheek.

"But most importantly, I don't want to go another day without you. Let me make things right. You asked me if I was happy. The answer is I didn't know what happiness was until I met you. I love you, Penelope Quinn." He dropped the mic to his side. When I didn't move, he picked it up again. "That's it."

Tom gave me a little shove and whispered in my ear, "You should go to him. Put the poor guy out of his misery."

I started walking and the crowd parted, cheering and clapping. Without realizing it, my feet flew across the floor. He met me halfway and I jumped into his arms, my legs wrapping around his waist. Our mouths fused together in a kiss that was totally inappropriate. "I love you too, Brett."

"Don't ever leave me again, Penny. I'm nothing without you."

Epilogue
Brett

I stood in front of Between the Covers Café and smiled.

Penny wrapped an arm around my waist. "You did good, tiger."

The whole strip mall had a face-lift, with a new roof, a covered walkway, new signs, and fresh landscaping. I also lowered the rent for the tenants and gave each business a stipend for inside renovations. The changes brought in more traffic, and the businesses thrived.

I was blessed beyond what I deserved, and it was past time I gave back to the community in a meaningful way, seeing the effects instead of simply writing a check. Mr. Polanski offered me free sub sandwiches for life, Mrs. Chen insisted on giving me a pedicure, and the Bethel sisters gave me the ugliest painting I'd ever seen but hung proudly in my office.

Penny's parents gave me the greatest gift I could have ever asked for... their daughter. They accepted me into their family without hesitation, even after the hell I put Penny through.

I couldn't stand spending even one night away from her, so I convinced Penny to move into my penthouse a month ago. Coincidently, Amanda moved out of the building a week later. Neither one of us was sad to see her go.

Penny transformed the penthouse from a bachelor pad into a home. She was mostly worried about Fred, but I solved that problem. We got Fred a friend, another rescue cat Penny named Ethel. I bought them the most elaborate playscape any cat could ask for, full of tunnels and towers. They even had a deluxe catio so they could spend time outside. The frisky felines were as happy as two cats in a field full of catnip.

As for Vegas Vista, we found a piece of property that overlooked the mountains. It was completely bare, no one had to be evicted or any buildings demolished. Even Frank begrudgingly agreed it was a better location. The scenery alone would bring tourists and locals alike. And with the plans Frank had, there was no doubt the mall would become Vegas's newest hot attraction.

My father would have been proud of the man I'd become. Of all the lessons he tried to teach me, it was Penny who taught me the biggest one. Money didn't make your life full.

Love did.

Another Epilogue
Penny

I fell to my back after our second round of sex. The ocean breeze fluttered the gauzy material attached to the top of the bed and the scent of hibiscus filled the air. "That was phenomenal."

Brett hovered over the top of me. "I love you, Penny."

I ran my hand along the side of his face. "I love you too, Brett."

"You've made me so happy, but there's a way you could make me happier." He reached into the nightstand drawer and pulled out a black box. Sitting back on his knees, he flipped it open and took out the most gorgeous diamond ring I'd ever seen. "Marry me."

I pushed up to sit. "Are you serious?"

"Completely. Nothing would make me happier than calling you my wife. Marry me, Penny."

My eyes filled with tears, and I nodded. "Yes! A hundred times yes."

He slipped the ring on my finger and kissed it. "One more thing."

"Anything." I gazed at the sparkling rock on my hand.

"I don't want to wait. Let's do it tonight. Right here on the beach in Maui."

My eyes bulged. "Are you insane?"

"No. This might be the most sane thing I've ever done."

Of course, I wanted to marry him, but this was crazy. "I don't have a dress, and what about our parents?"

He peppered kisses along my neck. "Our parents arrived last night, and your mom has your dress."

It seemed impossible, but that was Brett—always one step ahead. "How did you know I'd say yes?"

He winked at me. "I took a chance."

"Oh my god! Are you sure about this? It seems really fast. What if you change your mind? What if you realize this isn't what you want? We should give it more time…"

Brett pressed a finger against my lips. "This is what I want and I'm not changing my mind. Marry me tonight, Penny."

I wrapped my arms around his neck. "Yes!"

That night we stood on the beach, barefoot at sunset, and said our vows. It was the happiest moment of my life.

I had a man who loved me.

A man who cherished and respected me.

A man who supported me in whatever crazy ideas I had.

A man who accepted me, quirks and all.

A man who thought I was beautiful just as I was.

Turned out some fairy tales did come true.